Th

Book Two in

The Magical Therossa Trilogy

A Fantasy Story

by

Kathleen B. Wilson

Also by Kathleen B Wilson

The Secret of Tamsworth Forest

Published in Great Britain 2017 by Brighton NightWriters

Cover artwork and design Kathleen B Wilson

Printed by Create Space

ISBN: 978-1978019041

CHARACTERS IN THE THEROSSA NOVELS

In This World

Sue Dawson	Sister to Priscilla and Barry
Barry Dawson	Sue's younger brother
Priscilla Dawson	Sue's older sister
Aunt Moira	Aunt to Sue, Barry and Priscilla
Mrs Denton	Grandmother to Sue, Barry and Priscilla
Professor Harding	Searching for the other world
Cyril Grant	The Professor's assistant

In the Other World

Sonja	Sue's other identity
Raithe	Prince of the realm and Sonja's twin brother
Ruth	Queen of Therossa and mother of Sonja and Raithe
Thane	Hunter and tracker
White Hawk	Thane's wolf
Saturn	Thane's horse
Shaman	A gifted healer
Neela	The Shaman's assistant
Annalee	Thane's sister
Tansy	Tracker and friend of Annalee
Amos	Tracker, leader of his people and horse expert
Lex Ansell	Renegade leader

Zeno	Lex's stepbrother
Nenti	Renegade guard
Miccha	Renegade guard
Roddo	Renegade guard
Deena	Snake queen
Tam	King of Therossa
Vance	Tam's boyood friend, also Thane's father
Oran	The evil priest, also the king's distant cousin
The Druzuzi	A tribe of people living underground with great magic
Sheeka	Red dragon
Silver	White dragon, daughter of Sheeka
Jacques	A gypsy
Cailli	A tracker
Zuboarra	Chief of the gypsies
Elina	Servant to the gypsies
Tug	Servant to the gypsies
The Cloaked Man	

CONTENTS

PROLOGUE – The Story So Far

Most people walking through Tamsworth Forest needed a guide, but seventeen-year-old Sue Dawson knew enough about the forest not to get lost. When she realised Professor Graham Harding and Cyril Grant, two unsavoury men living at the hotel, were following her she decided to teach them a lesson, but to her dismay ended up by getting herself lost. Luckily, Thane was there to rescue her. He knew everything about the forest, including the secret it held. So it was easy for him to lead her, unsuspecting, into a world where magic was widespread. At first, Sue was unaware of where she was and met the inhabitants of Therossa. Here the people dressed differently, but were friendly and welcomed her like a long-lost friend. But she became alarmed when they referred to her as being 'Sonja', the Queen's daughter. Now Thane was compelled to tell her exactly where she was and why he had brought her there. She demanded to be returned to her own world. Thane promised to take her back after she met the Queen, for it had been the Queen who had ordered him to fetch her.

Thane was her best friend, a few years older than her and always dressed like a Gypsy; but he wasn't a Gypsy in this strange land. Sue trusted him and saw no harm in agreeing to his request. This was an adventure she could share with her older sister, Pricilla, and younger brother, Barry. She soon found out that not everyone accepted her, and fell foul of Raithe, the Queen's son. His hostility towards her was dangerous. With help from Annalee, Thane's sister, he succeeded in betraying her to the Gypsies of Therossa.

The Gypsies hated anyone not of their blood and she was kept a prisoner of this barbaric, brutal tribe for a long time, eventually escaping with help from Elina, and a strange boy named Tug. These two were not Gypsies but seemed to be privileged prisoners. Elina was old and died at the same time as Sue escaped. Sue's imprisonment did not leave her unscathed. Her body bore the marks of ill treatment for months to come. Her mind became confused. Especially when Zuboarra, the Gypsy chief, insisted that she was the Princess Sonja, worth a lot of money to them when they sold her, and that it was Raithe who had set up the trap to get rid of her. He was her twin brother.

Back in Tamsworth Forest, Barry was using up his holiday by searching for the entrance to this magical world; the same as the Professor. After hearing Sue was missing, his search intensified. He knew he was being watched carefully by the Professor. It was a hopeless task on his own, but Barry had help from White Hawk, Thane's wolf, who showed him a way to break through the barriers to Therossa.

Here he met up with Annalee and Tansy, two trackers, also searching for Sue by following any tracks left by the Gypsies. They were joined eventually by Thane, with his wolf, and this band of friends found her just in time to save her life. She was very ill. The Shaman healed her. That was all part of the magic in this land. Tug, who had also had been beaten senseless for aiding her escape, was kept in the shaman's care. A selected group of people led her across the mountains to meet the Queen. Sue was sceptical. She knew this person wasn't her mother.

The countryside enthralled her. She was in awe of the forest of Redwoods. She had never seen anything so beautiful and majestic in all her life. The massive trees held a city, including the Queen's retreat built in one of the largest Sequoias ever seen. As she climbed up the massive trunk, dreading meeting the woman who thought she was her daughter, Sue came face to face with her mother. There could be no mistake. The Queen looked exactly like her Aunt Moira who ran the hotel in Tamsworth Forest. All the secrets that had been kept from Sue were suddenly made clear. This woman, who called herself a Queen, was Raithe's mother, and her own as well. To a selected gathering of people, the Queen told her touching story of how the twins had been parted at birth because her father banished her from her home. She married the man she loved, King Tam, and he brought her to this world with just one of her babies. Now she had met her daughter, she pleaded with Sue to stay. But Barry insisted adamantly that she lived with him in the hotel on the edge of Tamsworth Forest and that they had to return home.

Distraught, Sue was pulled two ways. She didn't want to be parted from Thane, but she gave in to Barry's demands. When the time came to part from her mother, her twin brother Raithe gave her a magic ring, a ring that would always keep them in touch. Originally it came from Tam, and she was sad not to have met her father. He was away fighting for the country.

The two worlds were on the verge of parting. The crossing back was accomplished just in time, but Thane and his wolf were now trapped in her world. Sue was not happy to be back. Everything had changed. No one had expected her to return. All her grandmother wanted was for Sue to stay and not wander off again. Even Barry became disillusioned when he heard his parents had gone to America.

Sue was standing in the sitting room with Barry and Priscilla, when she heard the sound of a hunting horn. She knew beyond doubt that Thane had found a way back and was returning to Therossa. He had called to her, and she made up her mind.

"I'm going with him. Say goodbye to everyone for me," she said, and she fled out of the room towards the forest.

NOW READ ON . . .

CHAPTER 1
THE MIST

With the sound of the hunting horn ringing in her ears, Sue ran across the hotel grounds and in amongst the bordering trees. Twilight had fallen. Already deep shadows covered the great forest. Behind her, cheerful lights blazed from the hotel windows. This was the time of day when guests returned home after a strenuous day out, rambling. The forest was deserted because it was hard to discern the paths directly it got dark. A brooding silence reigned everywhere. There was no wind and the leafy boughs of the trees were immobilised. Their branches reached to the heavens in suspended animation as though they were waiting for something to happen. There was a feeling in the air that doom was about to descend upon the unwary.

Sue had no such feelings as she ran, seeking Thane. He was calling to her in his own unique way and her blood tingled with anticipation. She knew that the sound of the horn was especially for her when she saw White Hawk streak ahead into the forest. As she followed the wolf, her expectations were high. Soon she would be reunited with her friends, Annalee, Tansy, her mother and Raithe.

Reaching the cover of the trees she paused and took one last look back at the hotel. She waved, feeling sure Priscilla would be watching from a window. Once in the trees, her pace became slower. She couldn't keep up with

White Hawk. The thick foliage increased the depth of the shadows, to the extent of blotting out light. For some reason, she had not expected it to be so dark, even though it was natural at this time of night. Tree limbs reached out, touching her shoulders like spooky fingers. Roots became unforeseen hazards. Sue hurried as best she could. Above the sound of her panting, she became aware of someone following her. She felt a sudden irrational fear. Why couldn't she have waited until the morning, when it was light? Whatever was following, was gaining on her.

"Sue…Wait…Not so fast. I'm coming with you."

The voice stopped her. Astonished, she spun round and waited for her brother to catch up. A feeling of relief swept over her.

"What do you mean?" she asked, "You can't be coming with me. You were the one who wanted to come home. Haven't you forgotten you're going to America? I've made up my mind. I'm returning to my mother."

Barry drew alongside. He took a few deep ragged breaths before saying, "I'm not going to America." His tone was adamant. "Priscilla knows it's not for me and she will explain to the parents, so don't argue with me, Sue. I intend to come with you to Therossa."

"But I shan't be coming back."

"I know." The rest of his words were blotted out by the harsh sound of a horn. Sue immediately made a move in its direction. Barry was forgotten, but he was more alert than she. He stopped her as soon as she made the first step. "You're going in the wrong direction. The sound came from over there," he said as he pointed to his left. She pulled away. "You're wrong. It's straight ahead. The trees have deflected the sound."

"Sue, take my word for it. It's… "

"Look, I'm right," interrupted Sue, and she pointed ahead, "look, along that path. There's Thane – or rather there was Thane, but I can still see Tansy," and with that, she started to move forward.

Barry strained his eyes to pierce the darkness. Nothing could be seen except tree trunks. The shadows were denser. It was impossible to see anything.

"Sue! It's this way," he called, hoping she would follow him, but she didn't pause as she struggled on to see what was ahead. A thick mist started to seep through the trees. Its tendrils stealthily crept up to her and swirled round her body. The chilly touch of it made her gasp. She was reminded of ghostly hands attempting to ensnare her. Remembering Barry, Sue turned to look for him. No one was near her. He had been swallowed up in the darkness. She became afraid.

"Barry! Where are you! Come back before I lose you. We must keep together. You're going in the wrong direction."

"I'm not!" Barry contradicted. "It's this way. Follow me." His voice sounded muffled, but at least it reached her. She turned, and gasped. The mist had thickened. All sound around her was deadened. She was totally blanketed in a sea of cold, swirling cloud. Barry's voice could no longer be heard. If Thane blew the horn again she would never hear it. She was hopelessly lost. The mist showed no signs of lifting. If anything, it was thickening and the sensation of suffocating was strong. To move forward, she was compelled to put her hands out and feel the way. This phenomenon was impossible. She felt blind.

"Thane, where are you!" she called. Her voice sounded muffled to her own ears, in which case, how on earth did she expect anyone else to hear her? She stumbled on to keep moving. No good would come from standing still; she would only get colder.

"Thane, Barry!" she sobbed. A hand suddenly clutched her arm. It was so cold it was like ice on her skin. Whoever it was obviously realised speaking was pointless. By the firmness of the grip it had to be Thane, although he looked only like a shadow. He didn't ask, he started to guide her with fluid movements. The mist was so thick she could almost taste it. It cloyed her mouth, which caused her to feel disorientated. She started to choke, her legs buckled beneath her and she fell. Only the grip on her arm remained firm.

* * *

Barry stumbled along the path instinctively knowing he was going in the correct direction. His nocturnal vision was usually good. He wondered why Sue had stopped calling, and looked over his shoulder. Then he saw the great wall of mist building up. Even as he watched with startled eyes, it loomed threateningly over his head and curled swiftly downwards to engulf his body. In sudden terror he shrieked out. "Sue! Where are you?"

Barry could not see or hear a thing. He had no idea where he was. Through panic, he had lost all sense of direction. It was like being in a huge bag of fog with no visible way out. All that mattered to him at this moment was Sue's welfare. She must be terrified on her own, especially if the way he felt was anything to go by. This phenomenon was unnatural. Never in all his life had he seen a mist like this covering Tamsworth Forest. Enclosed in his cocoon of white cloud, he started feeling sick. Automatically his hand went to his mouth as he lurched onward, totally confused. His glasses were useless. Droplets of water misted the lenses making them worse to see through than frosted glass.

An arm shot out through the cloud and grabbed his shoulders. For one split second Barry thought it was Sue, until something was pulled over his head and smothered him. With frenzied fingers he clutched the covering with the intention of pulling it away. Then Thane's voice came to his ears. He recognised it even though it was fragmented. "Leave it alone, son. Your face needs to be covered."

Barry found the order difficult to obey. Being dragged along in a sack caused claustrophobia. He started to question himself. Was he being gullible obeying orders? It had sounded like Thane, but that didn't mean to say it was him. Why on earth should he have to cover his face against mist? Maybe it was someone else. He had heard about the Gypsies from Sue. While reflecting, he started to struggle and was rewarded by an oath from his captor, who said, "Pack it in, Barry, or I'll leave you to a fate you won't like."

Barry succumbed, allowing himself to be dragged along. His face was getting hot. He wondered how much longer he was expected to endure this suffocation. It came as a relief when they halted and the covering was dragged away. The light hurt his eyes after total darkness. He was compelled to remove his glasses and wipe the condensation from the lenses. It was not until he replaced them that he surveyed the scene from where he stood. Barry decided it was an underground passage. From the glow of several torches could be seen rocky walls and a low roof overhead from which hung several stalactites. Just a little way from him were Tansy and Annalee, sitting on a flat rocky ledge which did not appear to be very comfortable. Tansy stared at him quizzically; she was the first to break the silence his unexpected arrival had caused.

"I must say you're the last person I ever expected to see again. Didn't home come up to scratch?"

Barry shook his head as though to clear it. "Where am I?"

"Back in Therossa," replied Tansy. "The place you were so keen to get away from." There was censure in her voice and Barry flinched. His mind reeled. It was not possible to be back in Therossa. The journey had been too easy. He remembered the difficulties he had experienced the first time and took another look around him. He felt the friction in the air. Animosity oozed from Thane. He looked furious. Barry wondered what he had done to deserve this, and met Thane's hostile stare with braced shoulders.

"Why are you following me?"

"Following you," echoed Barry in a stupor. "Why on earth should I follow you? You dragged me here if you remember."

Thane should have remembered Barry was rarely lost for words and endeavoured to smother his annoyance. "You were calling out my name, so I could hardly ignore you. What the hell were you doing out there if you weren't following me? Looking for rabbits?" The last word came out sarcastically. He saw the dull flush of indignation colour Barry's cheeks, and admired him for not cowering away.

"For your information I was following Sue," Barry retorted. "And it was not your name I was calling out – but hers." He took another breath before adding, "Do you think the mist out there affects one's hearing?"

A muscle twitched in Thane's jaw while he resisted the temptation to hit Barry. But Annalee gasped and distracted them all.

"Why would Sue be in the forest when it's dark? That is plain stupidity."

"So is blowing your horn in the dark," Barry snapped. "Sue was coming to find you and I was unable to stop her."

Thane's eyes glinted dangerously. Conflicting emotions chased across his face. Suddenly he seemed a much older man. "What are you on about, Barry? What horn?"

A sensation of fear touched Barry. He suspected something was wrong. He glanced at them all, wondering if he had been hallucinating – but no. Sue had heard it as well. He looked at them all.

"You blew your horn," he blurted out accusingly, "and White Hawk raced away to obey its call."

Thane's eyes did not leave the boy's face. "I have not blown my horn today."

"Well someone did. We both heard it and it was all Sue needed. She was desperate to find you, having made up her mind to return to Therossa. She wants to be with her mother and," he paused, because he was going to say 'you' but changed it to, "and I wanted to come with her. Then the mist came and spoilt everything. We had an argument because she thought she saw you and started in the wrong direction. I told her she was wrong and I went a different way." He paused, seeing the horror on the girls' faces, and added quickly, "I would never have left her but the mist swallowed us both up and I lost her. You found me, but – but she is still out there."

"No! No!" Annalee clutched her throat. "Thane, we've got to do something."

Thane's face was grim. Out of the corner of his eye he saw Tansy slide up to Barry in case he reacted badly. "It's too late for her, now," he said. "I knew I should have stayed with her." He clenched his fists in despair. "The mist will have done its worst by now and they will have her in their power, the Drazuzi are not good hosts." Then noticing Barry's puzzled expression, he tried to explain. "They use the mist to ensnare people when they want slaves. I have never had contact with them so I'm not sure how they work."

"But they don't usually come out to accost people unless …" Tansy's voice trailed off. Thane finished for her. "Unless, there is someone else who's made it worth their while?"

Barry glared at them. "Will you tell me what you're all on about? Who are these people you call Drazuzi, who you think have got Sue?"

Annalee reluctantly said, "The Drazuzi live underground. I think they would die in the sunlight. They are a race of people who live in this land but we know very little about them. If they've found Sue, it's anyone's guess as to what they will do. To us they are an unknown species."

"Then let's go and find them." To Barry it was a simple, straightforward matter.

"How does one find a person in the thick mist?" queried Thane.

"Easy. Let them find me. I'll wander around as bait and when they capture me, you three can follow and see where they take me."

"That's rather a good idea." Thane grinned, but then his voice turned serious. "Nice try, Barry, but it's not that easy. The very fact that you said Sue thought she saw me shows that the real enemy are the rebels of the state. They have deliberately lured her away – though how the devil they knew where she was beats me. We shall wait until the mist clears before we move."

Barry's anger rose. "You can wait as long as you like, but I'm going to look for my sister." He had not taken three steps along the passage before Thane yanked him back.

"You will stay here even if I have to tie you up. Do you think I want to wait?" His voice hissed through clenched teeth and his expression dared Barry to move. "That is no ordinary mist out there, boy. That mist eats away your memory if you breathe enough in."

"But Sue needs me..."

"She doesn't need anyone," Thane growled, and he flung Barry towards the girls. "Right now Sue wouldn't know you if she met you – so save your breath."

CHAPTER 2
THE DRAZUZI

The atmosphere was bitter. The raw cold ate into her flesh and goose pimples rose on her skin. Sue was aware of being in a cave, but was unable to recall how she got there, or figure out how or when she arrived. Did she walk in here of her own accord or did someone put her there? The place was completely alien. Looking around the gloomy cave made her feel lonely and afraid. What possible reason could she have had for coming here, completely cut off from civilization? It held several people and a wintry wind caressed all the rocks and crannies. There was no opening to the outside world. The people around meant nothing to her, and she took them all as part of the environment. Their presence did not spark off any curiosity and failed to hold her attention. She flicked her eyes over the pitted walls, her mind a blank. She didn't know why she was sitting there.

So she rose to her feet. The sensation of blood coursing through her numb limbs was agonising and then she wondered, why had she moved? Where was she planning to go? She must be going somewhere? A dull ache throbbed at the back of her eyes and she shook her head to get rid of the woolly sensation that filled it. This was like hitting her head against a brick wall.

Sitting down again on the cold rock, she drew her knees up to her chest and hugged them, trying to hold on to a little warmth. She closed her eyes to blot out everything. Where was she half an hour ago? What was her name? This blankness was scary and the emptiness within her hurt. She must have a name, mustn't she? Nausea overwhelmed her as she realised she had no memory. Someone, somewhere, must be missing her – or was she just a person on her own?

A grotesque figure loomed in her vision. She gave it a cursory glance. It meant nothing to her. She couldn't decide if it was a man or a woman. The face looking down was sunken like a skull. The only thing alive about it were the eyes, overlarge, dark and expressive. Lips were drawn back showing extra-large yellowish teeth. If the figure had any hair it was covered, and a mantle of brown material swathed its body down to its bony knees, below which were two spindly legs that ended in over-large bare feet. The thin arms terminated with malformed hands. Then several other figures like this one appeared, wandering over the cold rock floor. It made Sue shiver and suddenly the Arctic-like environment intensified. She stared impassively from one figure to the other, neither frightened nor pleased to see them. In her present state, she accepted them as part of her surroundings. At least they were not feeling the cold like she was and there was not a fire in sight to provide warmth.

The figure before Sue did not speak, but once it had her attention, it beckoned, and started to walk away. Everyone was on the move; there was a mass exodus towards an interior cave. Sue hesitated. Why didn't they speak? She wondered if they were dumb. Her hesitation was her downfall. Several had gathered, waiting to escort her, but her reluctance to move allowed their impatience to take over. A hand stretched out and touched her arm.

Sue could not prevent her gasp of agony as she felt a spear of ice cut through her body. The coldness where they touched nearly paralysed her. She sprang to her feet and stumbled after them without another sound. A luminous light came from the walls, but the glacial atmosphere made the place feel frigid. She hugged her arms tightly about her body. No one seemed to notice her discomfort. Maybe further in there would be some sort of fire that would make her feel warm and so stimulate her imagination. No one could live in this temperature for long, but all too soon, disappointment engulfed her.

Sue ended up in a huge cavern. Standing perilously near to the edge of a sheer drop, as she discovered when she looked down into the fathomless depths. Darkness obscured everything below and a freezing breeze rose and stung her skin. Darkness also soared high above into infinity, blanking out everything up there. Sue dragged her eyes away from the precipice to stare at her surroundings. Light glowed round the edge of the cavern, fading into the distance. It seemed the cavity opening was extensive and spread far beyond her vision. Away from the walls, the darkness was intense, a solid mass of shadows. She heard a noise vibrating on the air, but could see no reason for it.

The inhabitants of this place were constantly moving, either to the left or right as they went about their business, all the time ignoring her, so why was she here? Did she know these people? Did they know her? Why couldn't she remember? She stood on the edge of the chasm, trying to focus her eyes because nothing made any sense. She was taken by surprise when something bumped against her legs. Instinctively she moved and saw a miniature version of one of these people lose its balance and fall backwards. It could have only been a child and as it fell over the void, about to vanish, a peculiar wheezing shriek which echoed, round the cave left its mouth. Sue's reflexes acted immediately. She stretched out and caught at a flailing arm. The child was no weight. As her hand made contact, she gripped hard and managed to swing it back to the safety of the ground. The people gathered round, zooming in on the incident. They took the child away. On the face of one, was something that resembled a smile – then Sue found herself on her own again as though nothing had happened.

Her ears picked up another peculiar noise. Sue could have sworn she heard the trot of horses coming from the passageway. Then the blast of a horn reverberated round the cavern walls and echoed in her ears. She raised her hands to cover them. The sound had an unsettling effect on the people, making them scuttle to the walls. Three, however, stayed behind and threw a cover over Sue's head and then dragged her with them. She struggled to free her face but one of them pulled her hair angrily and replaced the cloth. Once they had her pressed against the rocky wall, they all stood in front and surrounded her like a barrier.

Through a convenient gapin the material of her cover, Sue saw six horsemen canter into the cavern. Four men followed on foot, holding flaring torches aloft. They separated, two going off in either direction. All were soldiers wearing shiny helmets with visors covering their faces. Only the horsemen held swords. The man in charge removed his helmet showing a hard face and piercing eyes, which swept the area around him. His gaze settled on the strange people and they cowered; although nothing was said, Sue sensed the hostility of these strange people towards the newcomers. The man in charge had a dark pointed beard, clipped and smart. It gave him a certain debonair look but his thin mouth showed how ruthless his character was. He spoke to the skeletal people in a harsh unrelenting voice. She realised they could understand every word he said by the strange stillness about them. The soldiers holding the torches walked past them. The flares were thrust into their faces as they passed. She wondered what they were looking for, but at that point she was pulled down and hidden in the dense shadows made by their bodies.

* * *

A makeshift camp erected in the tunnel was adequate accommodation for Thane and his companions while they waited for the destructive mist to lift. They only had at their disposal a couple of blankets, which Annalee rolled into the shape of a sausage to act as headrests. One she kept for herself to share with Thane, and the other she gave to Tansy to share with Barry.

He declined the blanket and rested his head against the wall. Tansy squinted at him but refrained from making any comment. Conversation between the four of them became desultory and Barry kept himself detached. All he wanted was to find Sue. He respected Thane's wishes, even though he didn't believe the nonsense that Sue would not recognise him. It was Thane's subtle way of keeping him there. Sooner or later they would go to sleep, and then he would put his plan into action. He intended to leave.

Tansy already had her eyes closed and before long Annalee's head slipped and rested on her brother's shoulder. The torches were spluttering but a lot of life still remained in them. Thane emitted a few soft snores. Barry bided his time. He studied the rock formation while he waited. When at last he thought his companions were fast asleep, he rose stealthily to his feet. The tunnel loomed dark and uninviting. It daunted him for a moment, but he was determined to go on. He edged himself carefully away from Tansy, taking care not to waken her and started down the tunnel. Once he passed the light shed by the torches, he was in darkness and compelled to slow down. He stumbled a lot and grazed his knuckles. He swore softly under his breath, while he sucked at the wounds.

"Suppose I lead. Would that help?"

Abruptly Barry stopped, swung round and saw Tansy. "Are you following me?"

"Of course I am. Didn't you expect me to?"

"Then you weren't asleep?"

"Correct. I had the feeling you were going to do this." Tansy came alongside, and realising how hurt he was to be thwarted, gave him a little push. "Don't take it to heart, Barry. You have no idea what it's like out there. Here, put on one of these masks and cover your mouth and nose, Thane was not exaggerating when he told you about the mist."

She put something soft in Barry's hand. He lifted it awkwardly to his face and made such a hash of the job that in the end Tansy put it into the right position. Then without another word she passed by him and led the way. Barry was gratified to realise he was no longer on his own. Directly they reached the tunnel entrance, a cool breeze fanned their faces and the mist swirled aggressively about them. It appeared to be thicker than ever, but the blackness wasn't as intense as it was in the tunnel. There were outlines. Barry looked towards Tansy and saw that her face was covered as well. Although it was his plan to search for Sue, he now had no choice in the matter but to follow Tansy since she was in the lead. She was after all a tracker, though what she could see in such foul conditions, he did not know. They pushed their way through the fog, bending back foliage drenched with water droplets. Before long their clothing was soaked. To Barry, they didn't seem to be making any progress. For the first time he wondered about his own stupidity for coming out. He blamed himself for dragging Tansy on a fool's venture. Visibility was bad. They could have done with White Hawk's help. He would have found his way by smell, but the wolf was nowhere to be seen. In fact, Barry had not seen him at all recently.

Eventually, they stumbled across a wide path and followed it. The fog stung their faces where the masks left them exposed to the elements. Even Tansy had to admit tracking was useless in such conditions. Barry was about to suggest they turn back when without warning she caught hold of his arm and pulled him off the path. As a branch slapped across his face, she said urgently, "Don't make a sound."

Barry wiped his face and glared. As far as he was concerned, sound was already muffled, but even he registered surprise on hearing the reverberating beat of horses' hooves. Through the mist came flaring torches which cast an eerie subdued light as they pierced the fog. The horses galloped by, completely unaware of their presence. Six soldiers with covered faces rode the horses, and four men were running, all fully armed. Tansy's quick intake of breath was almost a hiss and she said, "That's Captain Ansell. What bad luck. He mustn't see us."

"Who's he?"

"He's a very dangerous man. Quick, Barry, let's follow them while we can see their light."

They trailed behind the band of men, moving at a steady pace. There was no need to fear discovery. The men were not expecting to be followed. Barry wondered uneasily if Tansy knew her way back because everything they passed was indistinct, and he already felt lost. The lights suddenly stopped moving. Above the snorting of horses came the murmur of men's voices. Then the lights vanished as if they had been swallowed up, leaving behind intense darkness. Tansy crept as near as she could to the entrance of a cave. The luminous walls showed where the men had gone. She stopped Barry from entering the interior.

"It will be dangerous. They could come back at any time," she warned.

The two of them crouched behind the bushes near at hand. Barry wanted to ask questions while they waited but one look at Tansy's face kept him silent. He knew she would snap at him. Inactivity made him feel the cold. She must have felt him shiver, and pressed his hand reassuringly. "They will soon be out," she murmured.

"How do you know? This might be their headquarters."

Tansy's laugh was muffled. "I don't know what's in that cave," she said, "but it's certainly not their headquarters. It might lead to the Drazuzi though." As her voice died away, the sound of returning horses reach their ears. The soldiers cantered out and lined up. The one in charge seemed to act aggressively towards them. His voice was indistinct behind the covering visor.

"Divide into pairs," he ordered, "and keep searching the forest. We must not fail this time. She has to be out here, still."

The soldiers dispersed without a word, going off in four different directions. Each group took one torchbearer. Only the man Tansy had referred to as Captain Ansell sat motionless on his horse. It was obvious he referred to Sue. They exchanged dismayed glances. Until he moved off, they were trapped.

* * *

To Sue, it seemed a long time before the skeletal people allowed her to move. She scrambled stiffly to her feet. No one else approached her, but they all converged in a group some distance away. She was forgotten again. The chill of her surroundings seeped into her bones. Her hands trembled and with an effort she stopped her teeth chattering. It was like being housed in a refrigerator. A noise whispered about her ears. She thought it was the murmur of the wind. Then it struck her that what she could hear was the people speaking to each other. She edged nearer to listen, but they withdrew further away.

Dejectedly she moved back to the edge of the drop and stared into the darkness, wondering what she would see if light were suddenly to flood this enormous cavern. From where she stood, if she were to turn around, she would have had a perfect vision of her surroundings on either side. The skeletal people, she noticed, were leaving the region by means of travelling along a wide ledge, and the luminous wall gave off just enough light to make moving safe. Sue realised that before long, everyone would be gone and she would be left all alone. She was becoming lethargic. Her limbs were stiffening with the cold. The last one of the grotesque figures was just about to leave, when it timidly approached her. Another followed it. Their faces all looked alike. Sue had no means of distinguishing one from the other. One tentatively touched her. Once again it was like an icy sword entering her flesh and she almost imagined her arm turning blue and falling off. She flinched and the hand was withdrawn immediately, but the person pointed to the ledge. After a while Sue comprehended. They wanted her to follow them. She stumbled along obediently. It was hard to walk; she thought her blood must be congealing. The ledge looked daunting. One false move and she would fall into the pit. The people kept at a respectful distance while she shrank back against the wall for support and moved along by shuffling sideways.

The nightmarish journey ended when another cavern was reached. This one was well lit, but there was no warmth. Sue gazed at the steps ascending before her to another ledge, where a second cave, its ceiling supported by many pillars. Coming from somewhere in the back regions, a blue luminous glow could be seen. The grotesque figures did not mount the steps but pointed, indicating that it was the way for Sue to go. She knew a moment of panic. The steps started to break up and dance in her vision. Her head was reeling and she closed her eyes for a moment, then everything became still. Her strength rapidly evaporated. Her knees gave way and she sank to the ground. No one came forward to help her. Stifling a sob she started to crawl up the steps on her hands and knees while the people watched her indifferently. Halfway up she came to the end of her endurance and collapsed completely. The cold air danced over her skin. An apparition at the top of the steps held out its arms. A blue luminous glow radiated out like an aura. A deep voice said, "Stand up and come forward."

Sue shook her head and looked up. The light hurt her eyes and she wondered who this was; the shimmering outline could be anyone, man or woman, and since she could not see any face, she gave up. The spoken words resounded in her head but she did not see anyone speaking. From her crouched position she carefully studied the person standing above. A feeling of well-being flowed through her body. Warmth started to seep into her limbs. The ice in her blood melted – but who was this person? Did she know them? Had she got the strength to climb?

"Yes, my child – you do," said a voice in reply to her unspoken words. Sue was startled. She knew she had not voiced her thoughts out loud, yet they had been answered. This was like telepathy. The person before her knew what she was thinking. Was this the way one communicated here? Was there a communication of minds? Sue struggled to her feet but before she continued to ascend the steps she looked back to see the skull-like people. The place where they had been was now deserted. Keeping herself steady, she made her way to the top. The glowing figure was already moving away and she was none the wiser as to whether it was a man or woman. Sue tried to hurry and catch up, but suddenly everything blurred and she fell. Several more luminous forms gathered about her and they threw a warm cloak over her shoulders. They did not have faces either. Then the world spun alarmingly and she felt herself picked up and borne away. She did not resist.

* * *

At first glance the spacious room where Sue found herself looked clinical and austere. Coldness vibrated off the marble floor, and the tall pillars that arched around it. The highly polished surfaces reflected light from a score of wall sconces. Silken curtains were draped around the walls but there were no visible openings of doors or windows. The whole thing must be an illusion. Several people stood in small groups and they had nothing better to do than gawk in her direction. They appraised the newcomer, but remained detached. Sue studied them unobtrusively, noting immediately that their long flowing cloaks and gorgeous gowns contrasted greatly with her rather scruffy green tracksuit. She could differentiate now between men and women, but she wondered uneasily if she belonged here. There was no spontaneous friendship being offered to her by them. Sue felt as though she were an object on display. Then the luminous figure she had first seen came up to her. His face appeared ageless and his hair, which fell to his shoulders, was white. He stood within touching distance, and as before, he never spoke, but his voice sounded in her head, saying,

"It is good that you have returned home safely. Tonight we shall rejoice. Have you spoken to your friends? They have been so very worried about your absence."

Sue stared at the assembled people in bewilderment. Why did she not feel any sense of friendship? There was nothing about this place that triggered off any memories of her past. There must be something seriously wrong with her, she thought, and then she heard the words, "You are still confused, child, but do not worry. A fall like the one you had can erase the memory for months."

"Who are you?" The words escaped from her mouth before she could prevent them.

The white-haired man smiled benevolently. "I forgive you this time for not remembering me. I am the Priest. There will be plenty of time before I remind you of your vows."

"What vows – where am I?" asked Sue, her eyes roving around the room, and a hint of fear crept into her voice. Why could she not remember anything? She heard in her head the Priest calling for his entourage and, coming from different corners of the room, six white-shrouded women surrounded her.

"Take our returned novice to the banquet. She will feel stronger after some food," said the Priest.

CHAPTER 3
THE PRIEST

Barry had the misfortune to get cramp at an inopportune moment. Muscular spasms shot through his leg, almost doubling him up. Using both hands he rubbed his calf, hopefully trying to improve the blood circulation. Tansy nudged him warningly, and jerked her head in Captain Ansell's direction. The man was still there, staring carefully into the darkening mist and showing no sign of impatience while he waited for his soldiers to return. He had not moved for the last half-hour, which was bad luck for the two in hiding. The mist was lifting. Before long, they would be exposed, as the foliage around them was not dense enough to hide them.

Barry hated inactivity at any time. Now he grimaced in pain as he found his hands were proving useless. An involuntary gasp escaped his lips as his leg knotted for the second time. Captain Ansell turned his head a fraction in his direction.

"You would be much better out here in the open, lad, where you can move easily," he said. "It must be quite cramped in those bushes."

His voice sounded bored as though Barry's presence was of no consequence, but over the visor, his dark eyes were sharp and he stared at the boy suspiciously. Taking in his youth and the way he was dressed, he said, "Just what are you doing there?"

Realising he had been seen, Barry stumbled out of the bushes into view, barely able to keep his balance. Tansy followed behind him, and not giving Barry the chance to reply, said stiffly, "We are lost."

Captain Ansell laughed humourlessly. "You... lost." His eyes appraised Tansy contemptuously. "You're the first tracker I've ever met who's come up with that excuse. What is the real reason for you being here? Skulking in the bushes with a minor?"

Tansy ignored the insult but it made Barry grow hot under the collar at being called a minor. "The same as you I expect," she returned ambiguously, "although I must hand it to you, Lex, ten out of ten for not letting us know you knew we were there. You could have saved me from spending an uncomfortable half hour. But then, you're not known for being considerate, are you?"

The Captain's lips tightened. He had never seen eye to eye with Tansy. She was arrogant and aloof because she mixed in high circles. "I was more interested in what you were up to."

"Spying more likely, but then you always were a sly old fox."

He would have cut her down to size, but at that moment his men started to reappear from different directions. Their approach was heralded by the torchbearers. Barry eyed them curiously. At first glance, they gave the impression of being well-turned-out soldiers, but a closer inspection showed a certain slovenliness of dress. They assembled before their leader, their horses pawed the ground, steam rising from their nostrils. The men leered at Tansy and Barry, but Tansy ignored them. They were outcasts loosely connected with the Therossian army and normally up to no good. One of them was eager to be on his way and said in a servile voice,

"There's nothing in the forest. Place is deserted like the cave was. They've either lied to us or she…"

"That's enough, soldier," cut in Captain Ansell swiftly. "We've wasted our time here. Get back to base at once."

The soldiers kicked their mounts and were off. The Captain twisted round in his saddle and said to Tansy, "You're wasting your time as well. On this occasion we are both losers."

"What did he mean by that?" asked Barry, frowning as he watched the horsemen disappear into the night. The mist was now so thin that the light from their torches could be seen from a great distance. When Tansy did not answer, he added, "Is it all right for me to remove my mask? It's stifling me."

"Wait until we get inside the cave." She preceded Barry to the jagged opening, which the soldiers had earlier passed through. A distinct chill hit them as they entered. To Barry it felt as though the air was frosty. The cave was empty from what they could perceive in the gloom, but further on, a soft glow came from a tunnel branching away into the distance. They removed their masks and stared round curiously. Barry hugged himself against the cold and stamped his feet.

"Why is it this temperature?" he asked and glanced longingly down the tunnel. "Are we going down there, it looks as though it could be warm further in?"

"It's an illusion," said Tansy picking her way towards the glow, but once in the tunnel the going was easier for them. Barry touched the glimmering walls and jerked his hand back as though stung. It felt like ice. He kept close to the middle after that, realising from where the coldness radiated. The next cave they reached was enormous. Darkness engulfed them. Except for the glow round the walls, nothing could be seen. It was sheer accident that they found the precipice before they fell over the edge. For a while they stood still, unnerved, trying to see the other side. Barry whistled through his teeth and the sound reverberated off unseen walls.

"What is this massive place?" Barry's voice echoed.

"I've never seen it before. I should think it is something to do with the Drazuzi. We are lucky to have found it. They keep their whereabouts well hidden. Keep alert, Barry. They deal in magic."

"Do they like us?"

Tansy shrugged. "I've never seen them. I don't know what to expect. I think we had better go back to Thane before we lose ourselves."

"But we've only just got here."

"We need torches if we're going to explore," Tansy answered firmly. "We nearly fell down there." She nodded to the precipice. "Anyway, I need extra warmth. Come on."

She turned back to the tunnel. Barry moved to follow her when a sound in the air made him look up. He drew in his breath sharply. "Sue," he breathed, and then much louder, almost like a shout, he called. "Sue – Sue – we're down here." He waved his arms wildly.

Tansy spun round. Seemingly moving through space, Sue was crossing the chasm. Impossible though it was, Sue was walking on air and surrounded by several glowing figures. She was oblivious of Barry and Tansy staring up from the ground. She hadn't heard her brother and never glanced in his direction. Barry's cries left her unmoved. But it was obvious that the people walking with her were filled with unease. Tansy received a premonition of danger. Alerted, she grabbed Barry roughly.

"We've got to get out of here quickly. Run, Barry," she ordered. The urgency in her voice reached him. He tore his eyes away from Sue and raced as quickly as he dared after Tansy. If nothing else, the exercise warmed him up. When they reached the empty cave they sensed something had changed, and pulled up. Dismay flooded over them. The opening to the outside world had vanished. They were trapped inside.

Tansy was incredulous. "It's got to be here, Barry. Start searching. An opening can't vanish. We mustn't be caught."

She frantically started touching all the walls, expecting Barry to be doing the same, but he watched her, bemused, wondering what she was talking about. Tansy saw him out of the corner of her eye. "Barry! Don't just stand there. Help me," she called again.

She continued to claw at the rough stone, berating herself for walking into a trap. Still Barry did not move. He had seen people approaching and shock had immobilised him. It was like a horror film coming to life. *These people are not human*, he thought, no one looking like that was human. Tansy then sensed their presence and came to stand by his side, watching with wide eyes as they were surrounded. The newcomers moved their hands forward and touched Barry and Tansy, who then knew no more. Their bodies fell to the ground.

* * *

Thane was in a foul mood and compressed his lips while he waited for Annalee to pack up their few belongings. He strode angrily towards the entrance of the tunnel and whistled sharply for White Hawk. With a red muzzle, the wolf came from the surrounding trees. He had been disturbed while eating a meal, but years of training made him obey the call.

Annalee knew better than to speak to her brother at that moment. His face looked like thunder. It was one thing to have Barry disobey orders. That was to be expected. But when it came to Tansy, she should have known better. What was she thinking of? Something must have happened to her. Surely she had enough sense not to let Barry talk her into doing something foolish.

Thane surveyed the cloudless blue sky through brooding eyes, worrying about Tansy now, as well as Sue. Besides being a friend, she was a valuable tracker. It was hard to believe that the debilitating fog of yesterday had completely vanished, but it had accomplished the job it had been sent to do.

Annalee touched his arm, making him jump. He immediately moved off, saying, "The only thing we can do is to track them. I'm sure Barry has left a trail a blind man could follow. Let White Hawk sniff the blanket that Tansy used last night."

Annalee held it to the wolf and he gave the blanket a cursory examination, but showed no sign of wanting to do any tracking. Annalee bit back a smile at the look on her brother's face. She decided to start tracking on her own. It was evident that Tansy and Barry had taken a roundabout route, but that was to be expected in such bad weather. When she eventually came to a halt, White Hawk's ears twitched and Thane looked at her with enquiring eyes.

"Well," he demanded. "Have you found something interesting to tell me?"

"Only that they stopped here."

"Why?" Thane was being difficult and his sister wanted to slap him.

"If I knew that, I could tell you where she is. Obviously they were hiding in those bushes. If you look, you can see from the tracks that several horses passed this way."

"Horses." Thane was suddenly interested. He bent to the ground and started to follow the tracks, his mind working out how many horses there were. White Hawk decided to join in and bounded around, erasing vital clues. Exasperated, Thane shouted at him. The wolf took himself away and sat by the rocky wall. Lifting his head, he howled. Thane was puzzled. The tracks ended where the wolf sat. Impossible though it was, they seemed to have vanished into the bank. The only way to go would be up, and horses didn't do rock climbing. He exchanged a baffled look with his sister, who bent to the ground further away and gave a shout of satisfaction. "The horses went this way," she explained, pointing further down the track, "but there is no sign of Tansy or Barry following them."

"So you're telling me they stopped here and vanished?" Thane asked sarcastically.

"Put like that – yes."

"I knew that silly bitch would go inside."

From the forest came a drawling voice. A horse and rider emerged from the trees. He was looking very sure of himself and a cynical smile touched his hard features. Brother and sister turned as one to eye him with dislike. Lex Ansell was no friend of theirs and normally they would have ignored him. Tension grew as he approached. His words could not be disregarded.

"What are you talking about, Ansell?" Thane demanded, "go inside where?"

The Captain moved closer, very much aware of their hostility. "I know you're looking for Tansy and that kid." His voice was full of mockery and Thane suppressed a desire to punch him on the nose. He had no time for rebels, especially Lex Ansell.

"So?" he asked.

Lex studied him thoughtfully. "The Drazuzi have got them if you haven't yet guessed."

"No one knows where the Drazuzi live," Annalee cut in scornfully and the Captain laughed with derision. "Some do – those who use their eyes, and I'm one of them."

Annalee felt her hackles rise. She was just about to flare up, when Thane pushed her to one side and caught hold of the horse's reins. He glared up at the man.

"If you know what is good for you, you will tell me where Tansy and Barry are."

"Ah – so you're worried." Lex was pleased to have the mighty Thane dancing at the end of a rope. "It's no good telling you where they are," he continued, "as the Drazuzi always make the first move. But I did see Tansy and the lad last night. Your silly tracker entered the cave before the Drazuzi resealed its entrance."

"How do you know?"

"It was obvious. She was heading that way when I left her. Trust a woman to poke her nose in where it's not wanted."

"So where's the entrance?"

"You're standing by it. I saw you from the trees and thought you would like to know." Captain Ansell laughed, whirled his horse around and galloped off, knowing full well they would never find it. He had the pleasure of knowing they were staring after him in baffled fury.

* * *

Other than soft music from invisible players, there was no other sound in the lofty room where Sue sat staring around the banqueting hall. She had a headache that just wouldn't go. She was surrounded by a host of white-shrouded people who never spoke to her, or smiled a friendly greeting. She felt unwanted. So why were they always by her side? If only they would leave her on her own. She wanted space.

The hall was even grander than the previous place where she first met the Priest. Arches curved criss-cross over the lofty dome-like ceiling. It was a work of art by some clever workmen. Beautiful embroidered tapestries covered the walls, which were intercepted every few yards by pedestals holding antique urns. These glowed dully in the light of a hundred candles. Even someone like Sue, who had little knowledge of such things, could see they were priceless.

The many tables running the full length of the room were covered in a shimmering material and were overflowing with an abundance of food. This was put there by some of the impassive skull-workers, whose hands and arms were encased in long gloves, but like the first room, there were no windows. This was disconcerting. Sue never even noticed how the workers came in or left the room. They were just there. Somehow, she could not accept this opulence. There was something wrong. Surely if this was where she came from then something would strike her as familiar. As it was, she could not remember anything. Even on her way here, surrounded by a bevy of the Priest's helpers, her brain felt dull, but the name Sue for some reason kept running through her head. Why? Where had she heard it? Her face must have expressed the perplexity she was feeling and someone nearby noticed. Before she knew it, the Priest stood beside her, his benign eyes full of understanding and love. He placed one of his thin hands fleetingly on her head and as if by magic, the headache vanished. She wondered how he knew how she felt.

"You still worry, my child," said the Priest.

As before, his words resounded in her head and she had difficulty in turning her thoughts into questions, so she said verbally. "What is my name?"

"Is that important to know?" enquired the Priest.

"Yes. It might help me regain my memory if I knew who I was," she replied.

The Priest waggled a finger at her playfully. "It comes to something when you forget your own name," he said, commiserating with her, "but of course you should know. You are Sister Jerrica, our youngest novice."

"Then it's not Sue," she replied, looking perplexed.

"Sue!" he snarled, and the change of expression on his face was instantaneous. It expressed a smouldering fury, which vanished in an instant when he became aware of her looking at him. He suddenly changed his expression to one full of love. "Of course it is not. Why did you think that?" he asked.

Sue looked down to her hand where the emerald ring flashed brightly, but the skin of the finger that it encircled was red and angry. "I don't know," she muttered wearily, "but it was in my mind."

The Priest waved her remark away carelessly as though it were of no importance and said with a throaty chuckle, "it is amazing what a blow to the head can do," but his eyes were riveted on the ring. He could feel its immense power pulsating around her. He wanted to touch it, but something inside him made him content just to look at it. "Where did you get that ring from, Jerrica?" he asked.

Sue withdrew her hands so that he could not see them as she sensed a difference in his attitude. "I don't know," she muttered.

"You know you may not wear it here," he rebuked her. "It is not allowed. Take it off. I will look after it for you."

His tone was friendly enough, but somewhere in its make-up there was a touch of authority. Sue heard the order above everything else and rebelled, immediately.

"No."

"Jerrica!" he exclaimed. "Your first vow, which you seem to have forgotten, is 'Obey your Priest at all times.' Give me the ring please."

Against her will, Sue's hand rose in the air and with a certain avaricious movement, the old man stretched out his hand to remove the ring. His greedy fingers were shaking with expectation and got within inches of his prize, when he sprang back with a sharp cry. The ring repelled him with a sudden shock. The fury in his eyes was not veiled this time and Sue shrank away from him. Realising what had just transpired, the Priest immediately controlled his features. With a gentle smile, he said, "My presence is needed elsewhere. The acolytes will look after you."

He suddenly vanished. She was relieved until the host of white-gowned ladies surrounded her. One came very close and almost stumbled. But as Sue jerked back, a warning filled her head. "Try not to anger the Priest. He makes a bad enemy."

In shocked surprise, Sue stared after her, but already the person was lost amongst the others. While she was trying to figure out the warning, it came again, telling her she was surrounded by illusion. Not to trust the love and friendship being offered, but she must sit and eat food with them. Bemused, she stared at the acolytes still ignoring her, and they showed no signs of having heard anything. So she helped herself to food. It was surprisingly good. As fast as she emptied her plate, it was refilled. She wondered where all this food came from. At this rate the feasting could go on forever. Beverages were drunk from golden goblets, with a liquid that was both cool and sweet. The skeletal people worked unstintingly at serving the assembled people, although they were constantly rebuffed. Sue's anger smouldered. What right had this well-dressed community got to treat them like slaves? Next time one of them came to refill her empty plate she smiled and tried to make eye contact. Huge dark eyes bore into hers, and although the mouth quivered, the person remained silent.

Time passed slowly. Eventually there was a movement and people began to stand and leave the room. Sue was forgotten, which did not come as a great surprise. She gazed around and saw a small door near one of the tapestries. An urge to be on her own was so great, she edged closer to it. "Go now, no one is looking." These words filled her mind. She had no idea who had spoken them. Sue looked towards the acolytes grouped together, and on sudden impulse, acted on the words. The door opened easily. A gust of cold air hit her. She slipped through and closed it silently behind her.

She stood still. It was pitch black. After her eyes became adjusted to the condition in which she found herself, she saw a spiral staircase – going both up and down. She chose to descend, thinking this way there was the possibility of finding a door leading to the fresh air. The wall was cold and there was no railing on the stair edge, so, to prevent a fall, she remained close to the wall and carefully made her way down. Her legs started to ache. She felt as though she had travelled a great distance. She didn't pass any doors. A strange noise began to filter up the stairs and more light dispelled the darkness. Then surprise engulfed her as she found herself on a balcony, unable to go any farther. She was looking into a pit of skeletal workers. They were in appalling condition. They slouched, giving off an aura of despondency. Their hands were tied with ropes, which in turn were attached to the bench they worked at, giving them just enough room to move. One of their legs was also shackled to their nearest neighbour, so no one could move very far without the help of someone else. Escape was impossible.

The atmosphere was hot. Many chose to work bare-chested, and these showed deep dark criss-crossing marks on their skin. Their situation was degrading; more so since the work they were engaged on was for enhancing the comfort of the Priest and his followers. Beautiful material flowed from unseen pegs. White gossamer drapes shimmered from overhead lines but the workers were in pitiful conditions and dressed in rags. This was slavery and someone had wanted Sue to see this. Her anger against the Priest built up. He lived above in luxury while he exploited these people. He was a devious man, who outwardly showed love and sympathy, while his heart was full of hate. Was this the reason why she had left here before? If it was – how did she get out? If only her memory came back, she would leave again.

Sue's eyes swept over the scene below. At the same time she was aware of sounds from above. She had been missed. There seemed to be trouble on the far side of the pit where two people were making a protest. They looked different from everyone else. One, a lad, raised his head and caught sight of her on the balcony. A sudden restriction in her throat caused her to gasp as a voice cried out,

"Sue! – Save us. We're prisoners. Sue! Don't turn away. Speak to us."

"You should not be here," hissed the Priest, who was suddenly by her side and pulling her away. "Tell me, how did you get this far?"

Sue tried to pull away from him but there were too many with the Priest. Suddenly she was back on the spiral stair and climbing up, but that voice from the pit still rang in her ears. It was not until she was put in the care of other acolytes, that the Priest left her side. She was led to a cell. It was a small room which had no window. She sat on the edge of the bed and buried her head in her hands. It had happened again. That name, Sue! It seemed to haunt her. Who was this Sue?

* * *

It was hard to differentiate between night and day. Sue accepted the fact there were no windows because she did not know any better. Her biggest unease came from the ring on her finger. She knew it attracted the interest of the Priest. The inflammation on her finger subsided each time she was on her own, but directly the Priest or certain acolytes came near, it flared up, almost as though it were warning her. On many occasions when she came face to face with the Priest, he never made the mistake of trying to remove the ring from her finger again. But in a fit of anger, he ordered that the white gown be put on her and the clothes she was wearing, burnt.

He also ordered that she was to be watched at all times, not that Sue had any inclination to wander. She hated the long flimsy white gown which in her eyes, revealed more than it covered.

The women kept their distance. Their haughty faces barely acknowledged her. She could sense their antagonism, but not the reason for it. It gnawed at her like a rat. She lay wearily on the bed. It was not a bad room. The cell had a degree of comfort, but nothing as opulent as it was everywhere else. Her head felt as though it were bursting, with so many thoughts whirling around. She tried to sleep. Through half-closed eyes she watched the two acolytes sitting by her door, engrossed in silent conversation. Somehow, they managed to veil their thoughts so that she could not pick up on them.

Her fingers began to tingle. The ring felt troublesome. Gingerly she rubbed her hand and pain flared through it. The cell door opened. A face appeared round the opening. Sue picked up the thoughts this time. The two acolytes who were with her had been ordered to step outside. To her relief they did not dispute the order.

Sue raised her hand and brought it level to her eyes. She studied the ring, and noticed the stone was extra bright. She touched the facets tentatively and her head started to throb. This had to be because she was missing something. Then she saw the face in the largest facet. Why did it look so familiar? What was it she couldn't remember? A voice suddenly came from the ring.

"Sue – Sue – where are you? Speak to me."

Bewildered, she looked at the stone, wondering if she was dreaming. Studying the face brought a lump to her throat. He had golden hair and expressive eyes that looked as though they were searching for something. Why did the person look so familiar? She closed her eyes waiting for the pain to subside. When she looked again, the face was still there.

"Who are you?" she whispered, and the face appeared blank, but then it changed to excitement. At the same time it also started to fade. Sue tried to will it back and the person in the ring spoke again.

"Sue...I'm so pleased I've made contact with you. There is something you must know at once. You are being drugged. You have to fight this condition before it vanquishes your will power and memory. You must listen to me. I am your brother."

Disappointment swamped Sue. "But my name's not Sue. You've made a mistake. I am Sister Jerrica and I haven't got a brother."

"You haven't got a memory either," returned the face urgently, "and you won't have until you escape into the fresh air."

"There are no windows," Sue was trying to explain, but the face in the ring cut her short. "That is because you are entombed underground. Go upwards to find an opening to the fresh air. Someone will be looking for you."

She immediately thought of the spiral stairway, to which access had mysteriously vanished since she had used it. What a pity she had gone the wrong way when the chance to escape from this place had fallen into her lap. It was then she realised the face was beginning to break up. Panic set in. She rubbed the ring. "Please don't go," she pleaded, "tell me... tell me... is my name really Sue?"

She waited breathlessly for an answer and it seemed ages before she heard a faint 'yes'. After that, everything became inaudible and the face vanished. She was left staring at a beautiful emerald – or could it have been a piece of cut glass? Her mind was in turmoil. Did she dream up the whole incident? Whoever heard of a talking ring! Was she going mad? She rubbed it vigorously again but nothing changed. This time her finger was normal and the tingling had gone.

The cell door opening interrupted her thoughts. Another head poked its way in. This was a totally different acolyte whose face was heavily veiled. She did not come in but her instruction was imperious.

"You are to follow me," she ordered. "The Priest desires an audience with you."

Sue reluctantly slipped off the bed. She would never get used to this thought-reading. Halfway across the cell she stumbled. In distaste, she grabbed up a handful of gown to free her feet. She would never get used to this long garment either. She was sure she had never worn one before. The way to the Priest's spacious apartments meant going upwards. Maybe she could find a way out but this was wishful thinking. They did not go the way she expected, instead, they traversed tunnel after tunnel. The air was growing distinctly colder and still the acolyte continued onwards. They met more and more of the skeletal people and the passageways became rougher. For the first time she felt alarm bells ringing. She was not going to the Priest's usual rooms. Was this a trap of some sort? Suddenly their course veered and the passageway descended steeply. The chill of the area penetrated the thin garment she wore. It reminded her of the chasm. She tried to catch up with the acolyte who seemingly floated along.

"Where are you taking me?" she cried out.

The acolyte stopped but did not turn. Her answer came loud and clear. “If you value your life, keep following me. Someone down here wishes to see you. I risk a lot bringing you here.”

CHAPTER 4
ESCAPE

Tansy and Barry lurched wearily over wet uneven ground and stumbled thankfully through the entrance to their dismal cave. For the next few hours they could rest, although not with any comfort. Barry deliberately splashed through a shallow depression so that their guard got wet. There was not even a flicker on the guard's face to show that he noticed. He turned away from them, lifted his arm and the manacles fell from their ankles. At the same time a grating lowered and blocked the entrance to their cave to stop them wandering out.

Barry slumped onto a narrow ledge and lifted his knees so that he could rub his feet. He was dejected and cold. His sunny disposition had vanished. The only light came from the walls, but its eerie glow made his depression worse. If it had not been for Tansy, he would have become violent.

Tansy prowled like a caged animal, always looking for a way out. There was not one part of their cell that she had not examined. She tried to keep up Barry's morale, but captivity underground was hard for her to bear as well. She was a free spirit of the forest and longed to feel the wind against her skin again. She lost count of how many times she had berated herself for putting Barry's life in danger. At the back of her mind, she had the suspicion that Lex Ansell had been waiting to see if she succumbed to temptation and entered the cave. Ever since their capture, she sent thought-waves to Thane and the Shaman. If anyone could save them, it was them, but she refrained from mentioning it in case it never happened.

Tansy discovered the way to speak to their fellow prisoners, but when Barry tried the same technique, he did not get any results. Everyone stared blankly at him and each other. That was a blow to his pride.

"I'm just thick," he muttered moodily, and continued his work of polishing copper vases until he could see his face reflected in the metal. If he did not work, he found out the hard way that someone had the means of causing him excruciating pain.

He peered at Tansy through the gloom, his face streaked with dirt and his shoulders aching from so much work.

"Sue ignored me when I called to her," he said. "She looked at me, Tansy, as though I was of no importance. She wasn't even interested I was there. I'm her brother for goodness sake." His voice was harsh in his throat. That incident had happened days ago but he still remembered it because it hurt him so much. He coughed to cover his emotion. Tansy came closer to him and sat down. Her arm stole round his shoulders to give him some kind of comfort, and she said kindly,

"The mist has taken away Sue's memory. She wouldn't even recognise Thane if she saw him – or anyone else she used to know. The people who live here are very clever."

Barry shifted slightly. "Will her memory ever return?"

"Not all the time she's here," replied Tansy. There was compassion in her voice. She hated seeing Barry this way. "I have no idea what these people want of her. In her present state she will believe anything they tell her. As I have said before, they are an enigma and we know very little about them. If the Captain had anything to do with her capture, then the chances are she was lured here to be got rid of."

"Her mother would have something to say about that," Barry answered. "Surely as she is the Queen, she has only got to request her release."

"Oh, Barry." Tansy hugged him. "I love your naivety. If they are enemies of the Queen, they are not ruled by her."

Barry hunched himself up into a ball. A piece of cloth enabled him to rest his head on the rocky wall without receiving an icy shock. The chill of the cave ate into their flesh and silence reigned supreme. Then someone came along and thrust two bowls through the grating. Only once had Barry pushed the bowls out again in temper and on that day they went without food. One bowl held food of a kind, the other liquid. Tansy collected them up, put the liquid to her mouth and sipped. A fiery potion slid down her throat, dispelling the cold. She made sure Barry drank the rest. The food was left. Neither of them was feeling hungry. Already Barry had started to slim down and, looking at him with critical eyes, Tansy realised that through this experience of their being prisoners, he had shed his boyhood. With a sigh she found her own piece of cloth and also rested her head against the cave wall. After a while, they unconsciously drifted together, using each other as a pillow and means of warmth.

Some time later the grating opened and a skeletal person entered the dingy dungeon and surveyed them both through huge dark eyes. They were vulnerable and fast asleep, exhaustion plainly visible on their faces. Anxiously looking over her shoulder to make sure no one was observing her actions, the skeletal person lightly touched Tansy on her arm and a shaft of pain brought her back to awareness at once. Her sudden movement also woke up Barry. They stared in confusion at the gaunt figure before them. A thought was transmitted to them. "Come with me."

Tansy picked up the thought immediately and knew her response of 'why' had been received. The visitor transmitted further communication. 'Golden hair' had saved her child, so she would save Golden hair's friends."

Tansy was stunned. Escape was not coming from Thane or the Shaman, but from an unknown source. Golden hair could only be one person, Sue. But Sue was unaware of where they were and she had no memory. These people they were amongst were more intelligent than she had thought. Barry stumbled to his feet and stood staring at them in bewilderment, not having picked up on anything. By the expression on Tansy's face, he knew something extraordinary must have happened. He touched Tansy's arm. "What's up?" he asked in an undertone.

Tansy shook her head in confusion. "I think we are going to get out of here. I must speak to this person and ask her some more questions."

"Her." Barry could not keep the disparagement out of his voice. "How do you know it's a her?"

Tansy pressed his hand warningly as she saw the visitor's eyes flicker. He might be dead to the skeletal person's thoughts, but she could pick up on his, if she wanted to. Tansy gazed back at the sunken face. "We can't go without Golden hair," she said.

The skull-woman did not answer. She turned to the grating, and once outside in the passage, looked back at them both. Then she said, "There is not much time. Please come."

Tansy nodded to Barry. "We must follow her."

"It might be a trap." Barry hung back, and in despair, Tansy yanked at his arm, saying. "For goodness sake, anything must be better than this place. You've got to learn to trust people, Barry."

"But..."

"But nothing! I trust her. Now come on." Tansy pulled him after her and Barry found himself in a tunnel and heard the grating drop back into place. Their guide needed no light. She could see her way without any. Very carefully they followed her, stumbling and feeling their way, and keeping in touch with the walls and each other. If they passed any more cells with a grating that kept prisoners in, they never noticed, it was too dark. Twice Tansy nearly fell and stubbed her toe, and Barry caught his head a glancing blow on a low hanging rock. The pathway was going upwards, and eventually, at a certain point, their guide stopped and asked them to stand in the shadows and remain silent until she came back for them.

"How come there can be shadows in the dark when... ow!" Barry yelled, but then fell silent as Tansy dug him in the ribs, and concentrated on picking up the rest of their guide's thoughts. Before departing she said, "You are at a place where three tunnels meet. If anyone comes near, do not make any sound and blank out your thoughts in case they are picked up."

"How long will you be gone?" Tansy asked, her face damp with perspiration.

"As long as it will take." The guide glided away and was swallowed up in the darkness. A terrible chill surrounded them and Barry shivered. Tansy moved closer to him for warmth. "I know what you're thinking," she said, "but I trust her." Her voice was full of confidence and Barry gave in.

* * *

Having seen lots of people at the start of their journey and then noticing they had suddenly become non-existent, disturbed Sue. She could only see by the glow which radiated from the gown of the acolyte in front of her, other than that the place was in total darkness, and all she could hear was dripping water. Her nerves were stretched to breaking point. She felt cold, but still managed to stay alert. So long as she didn't meet the Priest, she felt she could cope.

A blurred shape appeared in the darkness. Sue had no idea anyone was near until the indistinct shape of a body was caught in the glow. Conversation between the acolyte guiding her, and the newcomer, was deliberately obscured. But Sue caught the thought, "I shall be back for you in a little while," and the acolyte guiding her drifted away.

Something gripped Sue's arm. She was too slow to avoid contact with it. As it touched her skin, pain shot through her body. The icy coldness made everything go muzzy. Only her legs automatically followed the skeletal person. Sue didn't wonder why this was. She couldn't focus anymore. Neither could she speak coherently.

The skeletal person, covered from head to foot in dark material, reached the point where the three tunnels met and Sue learned that this person was pleased that two prisoners waiting there had heeded her warning. She picked up the thought that they were to move quickly. They must be away from here as time was short. Before long someone would miss them.

Tansy crept forward, eyes peering through the gloom, trying to adjust to the darkness and to make out who the other figure was standing beside their liberator. All she could define was something pale and ghostly. She felt Barry's breath on the back of her neck. Tansy spoke out loud for Barry's benefit, by saying,

"We've got to move quickly if we're going to escape."

"Who's that you've got with you?" Barry asked, and Tansy picked up the words of Golden hair.

Barry made a move forward and the thoughts from the skull-woman came sharply.

"I have drugged her for the purpose of your getting her away from here and the evil Priest. Awake, she would never go with you."

"I think she would," Tansy contradicted, but once again the other woman said, "She has no memory. She would not know who you were. By the time you could convince her, every entrance to this place would be sealed and you would never get out. Go now. Do not waste any more time."

"Which way?" asked Tansy.

The skull-woman pushed her into a tunnel. "Go down there. It is not very wide. A little way down there is an opening to a very narrow tunnel. This way you must take and keep going forward, no matter where it leads. Eventually you will find fresh air, then Golden hair's memory will return."

"Suppose someone follows us."

"You should have enough time to get away."

Tansy quickly related to Barry what had been said so that he was in the picture. He was trying desperately to look at the person he gathered they were taking along with them. Tansy had not told him it was Sue. She was endeavouring to get a grip on the girl to drag her along, but Sue, whose natural instinct was to be independent, tried hard to push her away. Barry brought Tansy to a halt by asking in consternation, "How the devil do we find an opening in the dark?"

Tansy swung round on their liberator, annoyed she had not thought of that herself, but the skeletal person had gone, leaving them to their own devices. Escaping was now in their hands.

"We've got to try," she muttered, "for Sue's sake. They're not going to let her get away easily."

"It would help if we could take Sue with us," Barry retorted. "Do you think we could look for her first?"

"Who do you think this is I've got my hands on? It is Sue! Come on, Barry, the skull lady said time was short."

Barry pushed his way in front and started to lead the way, elated his sister was beside him at last. Tansy moved slowly, feeling her way, finding it hard work to keep Sue walking. She might be drugged, but each step was hard work. Before long, they both thought that proceeding was going to be impossible. They might just as well be blindfolded. Their sense of direction was non-existent.

They were suffering from cuts and bruises because they couldn't see a thing in front of them. The skeletal person had good intentions, but she had eyes that could see in the dark. She had forgotten they needed light. Tansy had the feeling that someone was watching their puny attempts to escape from these subterranean passages, and laughing at them. Suddenly, Barry said incredulously,

"Do you know what, my eyes are becoming used to this environment. I can see my hand when I hold it up."

Tansy realised she could see Barry's outline which a moment ago had been impossible. Her first fear made her say, "Someone must be coming along with a light."

Barry snorted. "Don't be daft. Why would anyone expect us to want a light?"

Then her eyes fell on Sue's hand where the green light from her ring was pulsating. The glow from its facets became brighter even as she watched. Sue herself was completely unaware of the fact as she shuffled along like a zombie. Tansy's gasp made Barry spin round. He lifted his sister's hand. As he did so, the ring shone out like a torch. They could see the tunnel clear before them.

"What shall we do? Take the ring off her hand?"

"No!" replied Tansy vehemently. "Raithe gave it to her. It is a magic ring and will work only on her. Keep her between us and push on. Come on, Barry, we've wasted too much time as it is."

The light from the ring enabled them to avoid pitfalls, but once they found the narrow opening and squeezed through it, it became clear they could not all three walk abreast anymore. It was single file or nothing. Stalemate confronted them and while they were deciding what to do, they realised Sue had not waited, and was wandering off on her own, taking the light with her. The drug given by the Drazuzi woman was wearing off. Whether it was intended to or not, Sue would never know, but her head had cleared, and she was now wondering what she was doing in this cold claustrophobic tunnel. Where on earth had the acolyte gone? For a moment she did not realise that the people behind her were speaking out aloud, for the ring held her attention. The brilliant stone was pulsating in a way she had never seen before. Sue lifted it to her eyes and peered into its facets, hoping to see the face again.

"Speak to me," she breathed, and her sigh of disappointment when nothing happened, filled the tunnel. Tansy held Barry back because he was about to rush forward and speak. She shook her head, trying to warn him. But he threw off her restraining grip, and went straight up to his sister, causing her to jump. She stared at him vacantly and asked who he was.

Although she could not see much of him, she had a strange feeling she should know who he was. But Barry opened and shut his mouth like a landed fish and was lost for words. Tansy quickly intervened. With a forced smile on her face, she attempted to treat Sue like a stranger and said brightly, "We have been sent to show you the way out."

"But I'm not going out," Sue answered wistfully, "I'm going to see the Priest. He sent for me."

"That's right," Tansy agreed, missing the shadow that passed over Sue's face, and quickly changed her tactics by saying, "It's all on the way."

"Oh good." Sue said it but she did not look particularly happy. She didn't want to see the Priest. Maybe if she agreed to let these two people show her the way, she might be able to slip out by herself. The ring told her to reach the fresh air. So, uncomplaining, Sue went with Tansy and Barry, guided by the light from the ring.

*　　*　　*

The first thing they saw of the outside world was a patch of daylight on the tunnel floor. It was at the base of a twenty-foot shaft, impossible to climb up. The weary group stood below and stared up it in dismay. After their harrowing journey, with only the light from the ring to guide them, Tansy felt thwarted. To be so near to escape and then find it denied them, she felt like weeping. She thought back about the treacherous tunnel. They would have been captured long ago had it not been for Sue's ring. Sometimes the tunnel narrowed alarmingly, lots of the journey was scrambling over rock falls, and Sue's flimsy gown tore, exposing a lot of bare leg. After plunging through water and pockets of evil smelling air, what was left of the gown clung to her like a second skin. Barry blinked when they reached the dead end. He saw her clearly for the first time and wondered what had happened to his sister.

Air gusted down the shaft, circulating round the prisoners at the bottom. Sue, whose mind had been wrapped in a cocoon of indifference, suddenly felt her memory returning. Barry was chagrined that she didn't recognise him. Only Tansy kept herself alert for the dangers which now beset them. How could they escape up this smooth-sided chimney with no footholds?

Sue inhaled deeply, enjoying the fragrant scents that came from the big outdoors. With each breath she took her memory returned, until everything before her stood out in startling clarity. To see where she was stunned her. She remembered first the big house standing on the edge of Tamsworth Forest, and with it came the feeling of the rejection she had experienced on returning home. Then she remembered the fierce joy she had experienced on hearing Thane's call on the hunting horn, and knew where her heart really belonged. She had been on her way to meet him with Barry, who unexpectedly followed her, when fog had somehow separated them. All this flashed through her mind. Now she saw the expression on Barry's face and Tansy was studiously ignoring her.

This distressed Sue. They were scared she was going to rebuff them again if they spoke to her. Tears of remorse filled her eyes and Barry caught his breath. She looked human again. The veil of indifference had been stripped away.

"Barry," she whispered.

"Sue!" He forgot what he was thinking and hugged her. "Oh, Sue! It's great to have you back again with us," and because he was her brother he couldn't help adding, "I told you that you were going the wrong way. This is where it has landed you."

Sue ignored that, clasping Barry tightly with the feeling she never wanted to let him go. When Tansy turned to face her, she wriggled out of his grasp and hugged the tracker as well. "Tansy, I was on my way back to you. I can't believe I never recognised either of you."

Tansy returned the greeting with a feeling of embarrassment, and tried to laugh it off. “There was nothing you could do about it. For some reason, whoever got you here never intended you to leave. It’s thanks to a Drazuzi woman that their plans have gone wrong. She helped us escape.”

“Which is just as well you saved her child’s life,” Barry added. “What tough luck on this person who calls himself a Priest. We’re nearly out.”

Tansy pursed her lips and said, “don’t gloat too soon. Have you any idea of how we can climb up here?” She glanced up the shaft; “you might find we shall be staying here after all.”

Sue shivered at that prospect. Not only was her gown very thin and she felt cold, but she knew what powers the Priest had. Once he realised she had escaped his clutches, he would vent his wrath on them. She knew he could seal entrances. Like he had the spiral staircase she found. Turning to Tansy, she asked anxiously, “Do you still have your horn on you? If so, why don’t you blow it? I’m sure the sound would go up the chimney.”

“Always supposing there is someone out there to hear it,” replied Tansy. Seeing Sue’s crestfallen face, she added more kindly, “it’s more than likely we should attract the wrong attention, but yes. They never noticed this.” As she spoke, she withdrew the horn from her clothing and ran a finger gently along its side. “I think it’s worth trying. We’ll take the risk.”

Sue raised her hand and stared at the ring. “I spoke to Raithe with this, although I didn’t know who he was at the time. I’m sure the call will be heard because he said if ever I were stranded, someone would be waiting to find me outside in the fresh air. To my mind, that applies to all of us. Blow it, Tansy."

At that order, Tansy and Barry stared at each other. Sue did not realise how far-fetched it sounded. With a shrug, Tansy decided to give her the benefit of the doubt. She lifted the horn to her lips and blew three times for help. The sound blasted their ears in the confined space, and then echoed away up the shaft. The wind bore it away. Tansy looked towards Sue, her expression almost saying, "What do we do now?"

The sound had been louder than they expected. It died away and only the wind could be heard. They avoided looking at each other because they were all disappointed nothing spectacular had happened. Tansy replaced her horn and at the same time cocked her head and enquired, "Did you hear that?"

"What – someone up the shaft?" asked Sue.

"No – someone is coming along the tunnel after us."

Their blood ran cold. They looked in that direction. Nothing could be seen in the darkness although strange noises could be heard in the distance. Just as hopelessness was about to overcome them, a piece of stone caught Sue a glancing blow on her cheek. She looked up and saw the face of a white wolf peering down. "White Hawk," she cried out, incredulously.

He gave a small whine of greeting. Then he howled. Barry said dejectedly, and it dampened Sue's excitement, "I hate to say it, but a wolf up there is not going to save us down here."

"Then try this for size, lad," a deep voice shouted out. A very fine ladder which looked like rope slithered down the shaft. Barry leapt out of the way in alarm, but Tansy sprang forward and caught the end. She steadied it and turned to Sue, hissing urgently, "Start climbing."

Sue needed no prompting. The gown hampered her so she tore off some hanging tatters and started to ascend, Barry following close behind her. Then when Sue cleared the top, helped by many hands, she received lavish kisses from the long pink tongue of the wolf. Finally Tansy started to climb and pulled the ladder up behind her. At the top, she used her last ounce of energy to roll clear of the edge, just as a rumbling shook the ground. On hands and knees, surrounded by a group of soldiers, she glanced back over her shoulder. The shaft was no longer in existence. She smiled grimly. "Thank God we did it just in time."

"This time he was too late to keep hold of his prisoners."

* * *

A chill wind blew gently over the grassy plains and the sun played hide and seek with white clouds. There was little shelter. It was a bad place for making a communal fire, but the soldiers around them had managed to get one going and they were cooking a wild boar.

A few tents had been pitched at random, but the horses were trained enough to be allowed to wander free. Sue scorned the idea of sitting in a tent when one was offered her, so the soldiers left her alone and she now sat on a felled tree trunk, shivering violently in her inadequate clothing after refusing Tansy's jacket. She seemed unaware of the covetous glances directed her way by the soldiers. She watched them at work, and could not decide what they were supposed to be doing. They were not like any army she had ever seen before. Sitting stiffly beside her was White Hawk. She hadn't realised yet that he was the deterrent that kept the men away from her.

Tansy was nearby, relating to the officer in charge of this group what had happened to them. Barry didn't take to the soldiers, but he surreptitiously tried to edge up to his sister without the wolf noticing him. White Hawk would have none of it. He was a large adversary for anyone to take on and he would not leave Sue's side for a moment. No one could entice him away with food. He sat beside her, his eyes alert, and bared his teeth if anyone got within touching distance. Sue's arms crept round him for the warmth that radiated from his furry body.

The soldiers baited the animal, since there were no other wolves around, and tried to get a rise out of Barry, but they couldn't ruffle him, and only got threatening growls from White Hawk. Tansy eventually got the soldiers away by ordering them to make preparations for their departure. They didn't like receiving orders from a girl, but she pointed out they needed to reach Amos and Thane at the main camp. Only one young lad, not much older than Barry, came to help her, and received jeers from his companions. As Tansy strapped on a saddle, she asked the boy how it came about that the soldiers were in this vicinity at the right time. It was an unlikely place to find part of a regiment.

The soldier scratched his head. He looked confused. "As a matter of fact, this is the first time I've been out with them. To be truthful, I don't know. I think it was on account of that wolf meeting up with a certain renegade soldier."

"Renegade soldier?" Tansy stiffened and the boy flinched at her sharp tone, wondering what he had said wrong. "Does this renegade have a name?"

"Oh, he's still with us," replied the lad. "He's our Captain. Captain Ansell is his name. He got thrown when his horse took a stumble because that wolf got between his legs. The only words he said before he passed out were, 'Stop here, Drazuzi'."

Tansy's face was grim and she kept it averted from him. She already had her suspicions about this group of soldiers after her conversation with their officer. Now that she knew about Captain Ansell being incapacitated in one of the tents, she knew without a doubt they were in enemy hands. It explained White Hawk's attitude towards the men. They had escaped one prison for another. No way would these soldiers take them to Amos's camp, but to Ansell's headquarters, where once in his power there would be little chance of escaping. They had one thing in their favour. Ansell being out of commission was a stroke of good luck.

"Right," she said, forcing a grin to her face, "what's your name?"

"My name?" The young lad looked almost stupid.

"Yes. I can't keep calling you 'boy'," said Tansy. "You're a man, aren't you?"

"Zeno," he replied.

"Right, Zeno. Let's get busy. Take these horses over to the tents and I'll start on these three by the log. Barry will help me since he's not doing anything else. Are the water bottles filled?"

"Yes, ma'am." Zeno responded to her orders immediately. "These three have already got theirs. I'll see to the others, and then I think the food will be ready. It smells good."

An appetizing aroma was already filling the air, but Tansy turned her back on him and he scuttled away, pleased to be doing something useful. She deftly caught a white mare and hissed at Barry as she passed him. "Get those other two stallions over here and don't ask questions. We've got to get away from here as quickly as we can. They need saddling."

Barry jumped to his feet. Her tone of voice, and expression, told him something was wrong. He returned with the horses, and asked, "What's wrong?"

"We're with those renegades we met in the mist," Tansy whispered. "Captain Ansell."

"Then why did they save us?"

"He doesn't know we're here yet, but they also want us prisoners just as much as that Priest did."

The soldiers were busy getting the boar ready for serving and taking no notice of them. As far as they were concerned, the three people they rescued from the shaft were nothing to fear. Rex Ansell had not given any orders, and at the moment, he was in no condition to do so. Tansy and Barry harnessed up the horses, throwing blankets that had been lying on the ground over them. Amos would have gone spare at the soldiers' slovenly attitude. Without looking at her, Tansy said out of the corner of her mouth,

"Sue."

"Yes?" Sue looked up expectantly, trying not to shiver.

"How quickly can you mount this horse?"

"Well – I don't think the gown will hinder me – it's not so long now."

"Tear some more off the bottom and make sure," the tracker urged.

Sue looked startled. "What's wrong?"

"These are not soldiers of Therossa. They are the renegades who attempted to lure you into the forest before the Drazuzi captured you. We've got to escape while they are otherwise engaged, and find Amos."

Sue rose to her feet and proceeded to rip more of her gown away, right up to above her knees. The men noticed. There was a loud guffaw from them and a few cheers. One asked if she'd like some music. Trying to hide her embarrassment, she ripped the loose piece of material into two pieces and tied one round her head, giving the other to Tansy. With a knowing grin, Tansy did exactly the same with it and the men lost interest in what they thought was women's odd behaviour, but they liked the result. Barry sidled up to the two girls and passed a rein into each hand.

"Are we ready?" he asked grimly.

Tansy looked towards the milling men. They were in boisterous spirits. She nodded. "We go towards the trees." She vaulted easily onto the horse she was holding and Sue leapt up onto the black stallion. Barry grasped the reins of the remaining horse, swung himself up and kicked him into action. The three galloped swiftly away over the coarse grass, with White Hawk bounding beside them.

The men suddenly realised what was happening. There was great confusion while they gathered up their own mounts. The three prisoners reached the cover of distant trees where in desperation Tansy blew her horn again. This time it was answered and Tansy looked down at the wolf. "Go on, White Hawk. Show us the way."

CHAPTER 5
REUNION WITH THANE

"Which way?" Barry reined in his horse and stared at the impregnable wall of greenery before him. It looked more like a jungle than a forest. Tansy slithered to a standstill, her eyes looking for a possible way through the tightly packed trees. Sue cast anxious glances over her shoulder. She was more worried about the soldiers in pursuit of them. They were getting too near for comfort. They dared not lose what little lead they had.

"Did you notice which way White Hawk took?" It was Tansy's terse voice which broke the silence.

"I thought he went down that hole by the pine trees," said Sue, unhelpfully.

They took a closer look. It was a path, but to get down to it was a steep drop. The route was definitely unsuitable for horses. Then she saw White Hawk down below. His golden eyes gleamed in the semi darkness. He was waiting for them to follow him, so Tansy swung out of her saddle and said,

"I don't like doing this, but we're lost without White Hawk. He is the only one who knows the way back. For the moment, while we're out of sight of the soldiers, we must let our horses ride on without us. We're going to slither down this drop and join the wolf."

"But the soldiers will catch us," Sue retorted. "The horses are our only hope to outdistance them."

Barry was already on the ground, pulling the blanket off his horse. He tugged at his sister's leg urgently. "Tansy's right. The soldiers are thick-headed enough to follow the horses and by the time they realise we're not on them, they will have lost us in this dense forest."

Reluctantly Sue dismounted. They collected up the water bottles and blankets, slapped the horses' flanks smartly and watched them as they crashed through the undergrowth, finding a path of their own. Tansy threw one blanket over Sue's shoulders.

"That's to stop your gown fragmenting on the branches. Come on, we don't want to give the soldiers a lead. I'll go down first, Barry, and you follow, Sue. Your job, Barry, is to make sure we've not left any clues behind. Be careful, all of you. The drop is rather steep. Quickly. It won't be long before they're here."

Tansy slid down the bank with one or two muffled words, which the other two could not understand. Sue followed awkwardly, catching hold of roots and branches. Then Barry followed, recovering small pieces of Sue's gown which would be a giveaway of their whereabouts to a good tracker; not that they thought for one minute that the pursuing renegades had the sort of ability to see anything, but the officer with them was a lot more shrewd.

In the ditch, they covered themselves up with dead leaves and bracken just as the soldiers crashed by above. As they anticipated, they followed the runaway horses, sounding in high spirits, singing bawdy songs. It had not occurred to them they were not going to catch the prisoners.

The escapees remained crouched where they were, until the sound of the soldiers' voices diminished, and then they shook the leaves from their clothing. Each one took a blanket and a water bottle, and then they urged White Hawk on his way. The wolf kept to the ditch for some time, although it was waterlogged. This brought back memories to Barry which he would rather forget of his first time coming to Therossa. They could hear the sound of birds in the trees above, but in their lowly position they were surrounded by silence. At long last, White Hawk climbed upwards and, much scratched and bruised, the others scrambled after him.

By now the birds were roosting and rabbits were venturing from their burrows. They looked around and could see nothing but trees and shrubs in all directions. It was impossible to know which way to turn. They were completely dependent on the wolf in this wilderness of green. It didn't help that the sun was sinking fast. They looked around in despair. Barry asked Tansy why she didn't blow the horn again, when the last time she did it she had received a response. To which she carefully replied, this time it would tell the wrong people where they were.

"Well not many people use this forest – do they?" asked Barry.

"What makes you think that?"

"There are no pathways."

"Pathways can be dangerous, and if you don't mind, Barry, please stay perfectly still and I'll try and catch a rabbit for supper before they're all gone."

Then the forest suddenly became silent. It was unnatural. Nothing moved. The rabbits vanished. A shiver ran down Sue's spine because she remembered the last time this had happened. The branches on the trees had stopped swaying. The twigs reminded her of rows of soldiers. There was no wind, but through the trees came the first wisps of mist. The sight brought a strangled gasp from her as she watched it advance stealthily towards them. She knew the Priest was about to ensnare her for a second time. Her frenzied look around showed the mist was circling them, cutting off all escape. Barry and Tansy still had their masks. They quickly put them on, but the tracker untied the gossamer drape round her head and tied it firmly round Sue's mouth and nose. She called White Hawk to her side and his intelligent eyes were fixed firmly on her face.

Tansy said to Sue, "Get on White Hawk's back and ride him as you would a horse. It's got to be you because you are the most vulnerable one. Hang on to his ruff for dear life. Don't argue," she said as Sue opened her mouth, "because he's strong enough to carry you." And as Barry helped her up onto his back, she commanded, "White Hawk, go back to Thane."

The wolf bounded away with his burden. The others watched until he disappeared amongst the trees. Letting out a sigh of relief, Tansy turned to Barry.

"Hold on to me and keep your eyes skinned for unfriendly visitations."

* * *

As unerring as a dart, the wolf raced along with his belly low, through the tangle of foliage. He moved along much quicker than any human being could. His inborn homing instincts were well tuned and directed him the quickest way possible back to the camp and his master. Sue was no weight on his sturdy back. As wolves went, he was half as big again as an ordinary wolf. He hardly noticed her arms clasped round his thick neck as she clung on like a limpet. The mist was thickening with every passing minute. It moved in such a way one would be forgiven for thinking it was being directed by a master hand. White Hawk being so close to the ground missed the worst of it.

Tansy and Barry were caught in its thick density. It swirled viciously about their bodies, but thanks to their masks, it had little or no effect upon them, except to burn their skin. Barry's glasses were rendered useless as the droplets of water misted over his lenses. Half the time he was going along blind, so Tansy reached up and removed them, placing them in her pocket.

She mumbled indistinctly, "Can you see now?"

"I'm fine. I can see you perfectly," he replied.

"Then what do you wear them for?"

"Reading."

Tansy felt exasperated. "Then you don't need to wear them now, do you? Come on – let's get moving."

It did not help them that darkness fell. As they wandered along they felt the cold clammy moisture all around them. It stung the unprotected parts of their skin and they knew it could affect their minds. They had a certain amount of satisfaction, however, knowing Sue had escaped.

As they hoped, White Hawk outran the mist. Whoever was responsible for it did not know about him. The trees thinned out and they were in open countryside. Everything was going well until a shrill whistle pierced the air. If the cloth had not been tied firmly round her face and ears, it would have deafened Sue. As it was, the wolf stopped moving and without warning, cowered to the ground. There was enough light from the moon to cast an eerie light over the surrounding area. The place was deserted. Little whimpering sounds came from the wolf, but he made no attempt to move. Sue rolled off his back and crouched beside him, wondering what had happened. Something was ailing White Hawk. Had the mist got at him?

She lifted his heavy head and rested it on her knees, gently stroking his head. At the same time she ripped off the stifling gag from her face. There was no sign of the mist and she felt she could do without it. Her hair shone like silver where the light of the moon caught it. The wolf was perfectly still and his eyes closed. She hugged him tighter, tears of desperation filling her eyes. He was her best friend. She could not lose him, and Thane would never forgive her.

"Please don't die on me, White Hawk," she whispered in his ear. "I wasn't that heavy, was I? What am I going to tell Thane?"

In her misery she neither heard nor saw the dark figure come up to her until a hand touched her shoulder. With a startled gasp, she looked up, tears running unchecked down her cheeks. The figure was swathed from head to toe in a loose robe. A dark cowl covered his face. She could not see any distinguishing features and the moon made shadows darker, but one thing was certain – by the touch of the man he was nothing to do with the Drazuzi.

Yet thoughts of the Priest were so fresh in her mind it made her shudder. He had many disguises, and this could be he, posing as a benevolent friend. She cowered back, showing her distrust.

He bent down and, ignoring her agitation, pulled her to her feet, leaving White Hawk's limp body on the ground. The wolf seemed to be dead and no longer able to help her. Sue tensed. From the blackness where the face of the man should be, she felt his eyes were staring at her intently. He raised his two hands to her face and she stood transfixed. He placed a hand gently on each cheek, and at his touch her fear abated slightly. The hands were soft and warm, almost pulsating with energy as they roved through her hair. He said but one word, "Sonja."

"You know me?" she managed to whisper.

"It's like looking at your brother," was the startling reply.

He dropped his hands away from her face, but not before she caught sight of a serpent entwined around each of the man's wrists. They had red eyes and held their tails in their mouths.

"Who are you?" enquired Sue.

He ignored the question. He may not have heard it because from the distant trees came a chorus of howls which drowned her words.

"Sonja," the man said, "I must go, I have no time left. Your brother's life is in danger. I see you wear his ring. Use it to find him. Thane will help you just as his father helps me. He will keep you safe because danger also follows you. Go quickly now."

He bent down and touched White Hawk. Before she could reply he had vanished as quickly as he had appeared and the wolf leapt to his feet as though nothing had happened to him. The howls drew nearer. White

Hawk whined and, understanding what he wanted, Sue quickly resumed her position on his back. In a flash White Hawk was on his way and the cloaked man forgotten.

They raced across the moon-flooded meadow ahead of a pack of ferocious wild wolves. Sue lost her covering blanket as they passed the first spiky bramble bush. The cold night air touched her bare arms and brought up many goose pimples. She had no time to take in the beauty of her surroundings, it was a matter of life and death to keep ahead of their pursuers. The wolves were hungry and had numbers on their side. Their hideous howls filled her ears and seemed to be getting closer.

For a brief second, a slight rise in the ground obscured what lay ahead. She could only hope it did not conceal a sudden drop. White Hawk was slowing. He had her weight to contend with. A row of bushes appeared in front, getting larger as they drew near. She blinked her eyes in disbelief. She must be hallucinating. The bushes were moving. Then the clear sound of a horn cut across the wide-open expanse. Her relief that someone was near at hand to save them turned to horror as an arrow whizzed past her head.

She lowered her face into the wolf's thick ruff. The howling behind them ceased abruptly. White Hawk slithered to a standstill. Sue raised her head and saw a thin mangy wolf lying in its death throes within a short distance of them. Two arrows were protruding from its chest. Even by the light of the moon, she could see death glazing its eyes. It looked mean and hungry. The rest of the pack, equally thin and mangy, were milling around some distance away. But one wolf flung himself forward, teeth flashing and snarling defiantly.

Sue was flung to the ground as White Hawk leapt up, springing at the chest of his assailant, his teeth clamped in the throat of his adversary. They rolled over and over again on the ground – a heaving mass of snarling, snapping, furious animals. Their muscles rippled as each sought an advantage over the other. Sue screamed out in terror, not hearing the sound of horses as they came alongside and she was swept up in strong wiry arms. Her indignation at being forcibly removed from the scene of White Hawk fighting for his life was cut short as a gruff voice muttered in her ear,

"This is no place for you, Miss Sonja." Sue recognised the voice and shouted, "Amos, put me down this instant. White Hawk needs some help. He will be torn to pieces."

Amos mumbled "Humph."

Sue remained silent, staring aghast at the carnage around the horses' feet. The adversary was dead and White Hawk, standing with his feet on either side of the body, raised his head to the sky and gave a primitive howl of victory. The pack of wolves fled. Not one of them sought to challenge for leadership. Before Amos could stop her, Sue slid from his grip and knelt beside White Hawk. Blood covered her hand as she touched his ruff and, undeterred, she hugged him tightly. He responded with a snuffle at her cheek.

Another rider appeared, dismounted and threw a cloak over Sue. She did not realise that to him she looked like a mythical creature in her indecently short gossamer dress and halo of silvery hair. As he lifted her up, he said in a controlled voice, "I'm taking you to Annalee at once. She will have something more fitting for you to wear. What will the men think about you, seeing you dressed this way?"

"Thane." Sue ignored his words and wound her arms round his neck, kissing him on his cheek – much to the amusement of the men watching. "I can't go back yet. Barry and Tansy are somewhere in that forest and the fog is coming back again. I'm going ..."

"You're coming back with me," Thane cut in roughly. "Annalee is waiting. Amos and the men will find Barry and Tansy."

He threw her up onto Saturn's back and swung up behind her. With a nod to Amos, they parted company. White Hawk decided to go with the horse trainer and Amos rode off with an unexplained feeling of happiness in his heart. He knew his instincts were right. Sonja had returned.

* * *

The towering cliff face with its many cave openings was the first thing Sue saw in the moonlight. An unexpected emotion caught at the back of her throat, Thane's arm round her tightened, and as they rode to the dwellings of the cave people, she felt this was a turning point in her life. She had come home at last.

Late though the hour was, many of the inhabitants were still up and moving around, having previously been alerted by the horn blowing that she had been found. The fire in the communal clearing had been built high, and could be seen for miles around. From certain points high in the mountains, a reflected glow came from beacons burning there. Very soon, even further afield, more beacons would be passing on the message that Sonja had returned home.

Many willing hands were waiting to attend Saturn as he trotted up to the picket line. There were many more who wanted to assist Sue down, but Annalee got there first. She hugged Sue like a long-lost sister, and then asked where Tansy and Barry were. Sue had never felt happier. She wanted to talk but couldn't understand why Thane was itching to get her out of sight. No one missed the twitching of her nostril, but she couldn't help it. She had smelt the food cooking.

A pathway miraculously appeared before them and a seat was provided in front of the fire, the heat from which dispelled the chill of the night. The Shaman came personally to greet her, Neela and Tug either side of him. Away from the Gypsies, Tug had changed almost beyond recognition, no longer looking like the skinny boy she first knew. Good living and plenty of food had filled him out. An aura of dignity now surrounded him like a cloak. As his eyes made contact with Sue, they both remembered the hell they had lived through. The Shaman stepped forward, firelight dancing on the dome of his bald head. He placed his withered hands on her shoulders.

"Welcome home, my child," he said. "Word has been sent to the Queen of your return to this land. This has come at a time when she is in need of some good news, having just heard that her husband's best friend is missing." A silence fell around the people. Everyone there knew he referred to Thane's father. Giving a slight cough, the Shaman continued. "Raithe is on his way to greet you. Obviously something has held him up because he should have been here by now. There is much rejoicing in the city where the Queen now lives. When Amos returns with Tansy and Barry we shall celebrate having you all back again – no matter how late the hour. Meanwhile," he turned to Thane, standing with a protective arm around Sue's shoulders, "you must accept my apologies, Thane, but I wish to take Sonja away for a while so that I can make sure no harm has befallen her at the hands of the Drazuzi."

"Then I'm coming with you," Thane insisted. "Every time she moves out of my sight, I lose her."

The Shaman's eyes twinkled. "I wonder why that is." Then his face sobered up. "No, Thane." His refusal was like a douche of cold water. "You remain here but your sister may come in your place."

He left Thane smouldering and Annalee elated, because etiquette decreed the Shaman should always be obeyed; Annalee removed the cloak from Sue's shoulders and handed it back to her brother. She placed her own jacket over Sue, and went with her and two acolytes to the Shaman's private domain.

There was no formality. Sue sat on a bed in the empty sickroom and first of all allowed Annalee and Neela to strip off the remains of the gossamer gown and cover her with a healer's tunic and pants. It was all that was available at such short notice, but Sue felt much more comfortable in these. Except for being minus the row of pouches Neela wore with pride, and having different coloured hair, she looked exactly like the young acolyte. Annalee grinned as she surveyed her friend.

"Wait a moment, I know exactly what is missing." She dashed out of the cave, to return seconds later with a bow and quiver of arrows etched with the royal insignia. "I thought these would make you feel at home, your Highness."

"You can pack that up right now." Sue aimed a cushion at her, which missed Annalee and struck the Shaman in his stomach as he moved back through the tapestry. Sue clamped her teeth tightly in case she laughed. The Shaman, however, dismissed the missile as a nonentity and sat on the bed facing her. He leaned forward and said, "Now tell me what happened to you. All of it."

There was no formality, although Sue knew this questioning was serious. It crossed her mind that the Shaman was supposed to have powers that meant nothing could possibly happen without his being aware of it, and then she wondered fleetingly if he was fluent in thought-reading. At his raised eyebrows she decided he was. But Sue made a point of choosing her words carefully when speaking about the Drazuzi people because she didn't think they were the enemy.

"The Priest must have some hold over them because he and his followers treat them like slaves. How he manages to do so I don't know because the Drazuzi are not without power. Losing my memory was all due to the Priest. I'm quite sure he produces the mist and is devious enough to let the Drazuzi take the blame for its consequence."

"Are you quite sure?" The Shaman looked at her closely.

"Positive. He sent the mist again when I escaped. It wouldn't have been in the interest of the Drazuzi to do so when they had just helped me get away. They have a different power. They can paralyse one by the touch of their hands. That is only confusing for a while." Sue looked at the old man who was devouring her words, and asked guilelessly, "Have you ever seen a Drazuzi, Shaman?"

The old man looked startled for a moment. "I can't say I have, but I do know the Priest from long ago. Now tell me more about the people, my dear," and he artlessly changed the conversation, knowing that would get her to continue. It wasn't until she mentioned Lex Ansell that he became alert. His lips tightened. "This makes it perfectly clear why you were captured, Sonja. The renegades need money, and the Priest wants his power, evil though it is, to be openly recognised by the country. Both groups of people need you as a hostage to make the King pay."

"The Priest was very interested in my ring."

Sue held it out for inspection. Raithe's ring glowed dully on her finger. It looked no more interesting than a piece of glass. "The Priest wanted it. He ordered me to remove it and give it to him for safekeeping. When I refused, he was angry and tried to take it by force – but the ring has magical powers, which repelled him. It was after that that I was never left alone. I have no idea what would have happened to me if the Drazuzi had not planned my escape with Barry and Tansy; and if the renegades had not been waiting for us at the top of the shaft. The entrance closed as we got out. The mist would have ensnared me again and I'd be back in his clutches."

Sue actually picked up the Shaman's unspoken thought of, *I wonder why they were there*. The others only saw him purse his lips. Eventually he said, "It was like jumping from one opposing camp to the other. I am interested how you escaped from Captain Ansell. He is not an easy man to fool."

"His horse threw him so he was hurt and out of action. Tansy soon worked out the mentality of his men and organised our escape. Also we were lucky to have had White Hawk. I escaped by riding on his back, as you know, and Thane found me."

The Shaman looked at her with a frown. "And that is everything?" he asked.

"Yes."

For many seconds the Shaman stared at her and she began to feel uncomfortable. His eyes were stern and unyielding. He knew she was withholding information from him, but Sue felt her mouth clam up and words she would have spoken were strangled in her throat, making speech impossible. This phenomenon puzzled her. She had no idea why she could not speak about the strange cowled man who appeared to her before the pack of wild wolves attacked. She swallowed nervously, saying,

"May I go back to Thane?"

For a brief moment the Shaman held her gaze, then he touched her gently, saying, "go my child – but remember, you will not go far wrong if you trust him. No one is forcing you to say anything."

Annalee stared from one to the other, confused. "Sue," she began, but Sue stumbled to her feet. "Please take me back, Annalee."

The Shaman watched them go. He was trying to work out what information she had withheld, and was a little piqued she had learnt how to mask her thoughts.

CHAPTER 6
THE COWLED MAN

The following morning the soldiers were on the move to cross the mountains and deliver Sue to her mother. There was a lot of activity and since Sue's help was not required she stood alone on the slope of a hill, gazing towards the mountains, daydreaming. Clouds had accumulated since dawn, but there were still gaps wide enough to see the rugged peaks beyond. She wondered which way they would be travelling since the sky-bridge no longer existed and their destination was the city of Therossa. She was longing to see this city she had been told was full of beautiful spires, towers and lavish parkland; also eager to arrive there and see her mother and Raithe again.

She lifted her hand to inspect the ring placed there by her brother. 'A small trinket so that you will never forget me,' he had told her. It was more than a trinket, it had magical powers, which could speak to her, and right now it was burning her finger to attract her attention. Why? Was Raithe in trouble? He should have been here to meet her but had not arrived. The facets were dazzling her eyes. Gently she rubbed them with her finger. She was so absorbed, she did not hear Thane approaching behind her. He stood a few paces away and paused to watch. When he heard her low voice whispering words, he was surprised. He had not fully believed what Annalee had told him. He took one step nearer and heard, "Speak to me, Raithe. Are you there?"

Thane never heard any answer, but nevertheless knew without a doubt that the ring was magic. In the silence that followed, he heard Sue utter a small cry and wondered what it was about.

Sue had seen her twin brother with water falling at his back. His hands were bound behind him and a gag was over his mouth. As she watched, something fell from high above and hit his head. Like a fragile blade of grass, he crumpled to the ground. Two heavy, fur-covered men hauled him to his feet and virtually dragged him through the water.

Then the brilliance of the ring dimmed and Sue's control of it was lost. She stood, unable to move, her eyes wide with shock. Hypnotised, she still stared at her hand. Thane came alongside and peered over her shoulder. He expected her to jump, but she didn't move. Then he remembered what the Shaman had told him, about the extraordinary powers of the ring. It did not work on its own. It had to be in conjunction with another ring or artefact to work, and only Sue would be in tune with it. Thane still found this hard to accept.

"Is there anything wrong?" he enquired. His concern reached her and slowly she lowered her hands. The excitement of the morning had vanished. The mountains no longer looked welcoming, but dull and threatening. Furthermore the sky seemed full of rain. It took some time for her eyes to focus on Thane properly and by then he was truly alarmed. Events were taken out of his hands because Tansy, Annalee and Barry came towards them. The moment when he should have tackled Sue had passed, and colour came back to her cheeks. Barry was excited.

"We're travelling on the river since it's almost impossible to cross the mountains. I've told the others you can swim like a fish so there's no need to pump you up with air."

"Is it a calm river?" Sue never knew why she asked that question, but no one seemed to find it strange. Tansy remarked carelessly,

"Depends on what you mean by calm."

"Are there any waterfalls to negotiate?"

The others fell silent, remembering what the Gypsies did to her. Thane put an arm round her and gave her a playful squeeze. "No waterfalls," he said, "but plenty of rapids, white water and strong currents. You can rest assured you will be perfectly safe and we shall rope ourselves together so no one can fall out. Our boat will be full because we're carrying Cailli, Amos and believe it or not, White Hawk. The horses, I'm afraid, will be travelling a lot slower. Does that suit you, ma'am? Or would you rather ride a horse along the dangerous rocky terrain?"

Sue gave him a punch. He was just like his sister. "You can stop that right now or I shall refuse to go with you. Is the Shaman travelling on the water?"

"No – he will remain at the camp until Raithe turns up," Thane answered.

"Then that's a waste of time. He won't do that." The words were out before Sue could stop them. She felt four pairs of eyes on her and her face turned red under their scrutiny. Barry broke the uneasy silence by asking, "Don't tell me you're into telepathy, Sue. I know some twins have that kind of ability, but…" His voice trailed off.

"What I meant to say was..." Sue also broke off because Annalee said with a laugh,

"We all know what a rotten timekeeper Raithe is. I expect he's changed his mind and is waiting with the Queen. Come on, let's get going."

They moved off, but not before Thane saw how anxious she was. Then he saw his sister watching them. They moved back to the centre of activity and the incident was forgotten, but Annalee hung back and caught hold of Sue's arm. Sue eyed her warily. Annalee came to the point at once. Her voice was low so that the others could not hear.

"Do what the Shaman told you to do," she said. "Trust Thane. You've had a message from that ring, haven't you," she accused.

Sue was about to deny it, but seeing the other girl's expression, nodded her head.

"You're right. I'll tell Thane later."

"Then let's hope it's not too late," retorted Annalee darkly, and quickly caught up with the others.

* * *

Sue paused near the bank of the swiftly flowing water and felt fear; it had nothing to do with the journey, because she was as keen as the next person to go. From where she stood, the boats did not look safe, they bobbed alarmingly at the end of their tethered ropes. The sterns swung out of control and the current did its best to sweep them away. The rushing water looked dull and ominous. Clouds were building up and the weather looking decidedly unhealthy. She thought there was rain in the air, but Barry, as he passed with his arms full of packages, remarked carelessly it was spray. She could not help noticing how happy he was here. The people had taken to him, with the exception of Amos. Watching the swiftly rushing river break into waves, she became aware of the submerged rocks, unseen below the water level.

With a shudder, Sue turned her back on the activity and found a rock to sit on. She needed to work out why this unreasonable fear assailed her. Pulling the cloak tightly round her shoulders, she raised the hood and covered her bright hair. She was still wearing the garb of an acolyte, and to all intents and purposes, she looked exactly like one. No one gave her a second glance. Acolytes led solitary lives. In another two hours it would be dark. Thane made it common knowledge where he was camping for the night. Sue sighed dejectedly; she had to face this situation at some point. She seriously contemplated asking if she could travel with the horses, even though she had been told this way was almost impossible.

Unbidden, another hooded figure came and sat beside her. There were many attendants of the Shaman here. She pretended to be meditating, in the hope they would go away if she did not speak. Unhappily for her, that was not the way it was going to be. This hooded figure obviously had the same idea as she had.

"I say, has anyone seen Sue?"

Barry's voice floated over the hustle and bustle of movement. She did not want him to find her. Then she heard Annalee's answer: "You'd better start wearing your glasses again if you've lost her. But I must say, Barry, you look quite handsome without them."

General laughter made Barry forget who he was looking for. The others forgot about Sue as well. From the depths of the other cowl, Sue heard a familiar voice say, "It's hard not to speak, isn't it?"

"Tug," Sue exclaimed, swinging round and managing to keep her hood in place. Her hair would have given her away. "Don't you have duties to perform?"

"Of course, and I'm doing them," was Tug's answer.

"What do you mean? You're sitting here."

"That's right, and so are you."

Sue digested that remark in silence. It did not take many seconds for the truth to hit her and she felt resentful. "You've been sent to keep an eye on me," she accused. "Who sent you – the Shaman or Thane?"

"Neither. I just happen to know you fear the boat, and you're right to do so."

Sue immediately visualised the boats capsizing and everyone floundering in dangerous water, but Tug's hand stayed her when she would have leapt up. She relaxed. His grip was firm and strong. Almost as though he read her thoughts, he said,

"They are not going to sink, but they will meet trouble. Both the Gypsies and the renegades know which way you will be travelling. They have their spies, you know, even though sometimes they do not realise they are spying. The Queen's enemies are cunning and they are the people you least suspect. It is imperative you do not go in the boat, Sue. It is you they are looking for and the reason this ambush has been planned. They are desperate men. They did not expect you ever to escape from the Priest."

Tug's words sent a shiver through her. She looked distressed. "Tug, we must warn them. We can't allow our friends to go sailing into danger. You know, and I suppose the Shaman knows. Why doesn't he do something about it? Let's go..."

"No." Tug rose to his feet and stood over her. He seemed to have grown a lot since leaving the Gypsies. "You are the one who is important at the moment. They have the King in their power already and lots of good men have been lost… Thane's father included. We are almost sure they have the Prince as well. He used to be a friend of theirs and they brainwashed him about your coming, telling him that you were a threat to his well-being.

"When Raithe actually met you…maybe not at first…he liked you. They will never forgive him for that. Please understand, Sue, the renegades must not get you, otherwise the Queen will be forced to abdicate and this unruly band of men will take over the land. Your friends will not be harmed, but believe me, you will be if they get you."

"How do you know all this and what do I have to do?" Sue was completely dazed. Tug seemed to know a lot about Raithe. Things she had never told him. She had not spoken about his captivity to anyone. She wanted to warn Thane. She hated the sudden thought that came into her head. Was Tug to be trusted? Tears filled her eyes at that thought and Tug saw them. He bent his head close to hers.

"You have always been my friend, Sue," he said, "this time I mean to save you. There is another way to the city of Therossa, but it is long and dangerous and your antagonists will not expect you to take it. Directly the boats leave, I shall guide you to where the horses are waiting, already saddled for a long journey. I shall travel with you, but the ambush of your friends must go ahead without any interference from you."

"Haven't you forgotten something?" Sue asked softly.

"Like what?"

"I shall be missed when I'm not in the boat."

"That's all been arranged," answered Tug.

"Oh," Sue was nonplussed. "Does the Shaman not know you are here, speaking to me?"

Tug was saved from answering because a cry filled the air calling for Sue. "We're ready to cast off. Where are you?"

"Neela!" Tug twisted round and called for the acolyte. Neela stepped from the bushes. Completely covered from head to foot, she looked exactly the same as Sue. In passing, she pressed Sue's hand.

"You're doing a brave thing for this country. Good luck on your journey. You should be well away before you are missed."

Giving one of her lovely smiles, she pulled the covering hood closer to her face and moved away to join the throng boarding the boat, replacing Sue. Sue watched her anxiously. No one around the boat noticed anything different. Neela was accepted. Remaining well covered, she took her seat. As usual, Barry could not resist butting in.

"If you're afraid of getting wet, Sue, you're in the wrong place. Want to change places with me?"

"Leave her alone." Sue recognised Thane's voice and it felt like a sharp pain in her heart as she saw him sit next to Neela. Neela lightly squeezed his arm and continued to stare upstream. Sue exhaled slowly. Thane seemed happy with that gesture.

There was very little daylight left now and the pins and needles in Sue's legs from crounching in hiding were beginning to become a nuisance. At last the boats left their moorings, disappearing round a bend in the river. The watching people made their way to the communal fire for their evening meal. Tug pulled at Sue's sleeve.

"Come on," he whispered, "we've got just enough light to cross the water further up in the other direction – but we must not be seen."

Sue looked around anxiously. "Where are the horses?" she asked.

"On the other side of the water," Tug answered blandly, "so follow me."

* * *

To Sue, there did not seem to be enough bushes near the riverbank to give cover. Some gaps were lengthy and this worried her. Surely they would be seen by one of the lookouts. This was all too easy. What Sue failed to realise was that the mundane acolyte cloaks were a perfect camouflage in this half-light. She felt sick in the pit of her stomach, wishing she were in the boat. She was also battling with uncertainty about Tug in whom she had been forced to put her trust. How was it he knew everything if he wasn't a spy in their midst? Then she remembered other occasions when he had unstintingly put his life on the line for her. She had to give Tug the benefit of the doubt, so she pretended she was happy with this arrangement. He must never suspect how she felt.

Passing the camp was easier than anticipated. Tug stopped near an inward curve of the river. All that was visible was turbulent water. The sight of it did little to settle her stomach. The banks on either side were already covered in shadow and behind them the glow from the communal fire lit the sky.

"We cross here," Tug indicated, stopping.

Queasily Sue looked from the watery moon to the dark threatening river flowing past her feet. She couldn't see any way of crossing easily.

"There are stepping stones," explained Tug's soft voice when he noticed her uneasy expression. "All you have to do is remove your shoes and jump from one to the other."

"But I can't see them." The wind gusted round her body and her cloak billowed out. Sue made no attempt to remove her shoes.

"Then use the ring," Tug commanded in a flat voice.

"What do you know about the ring?" she burst out apprehensively, and spun round to stare at him. Then she remembered he was with the Shaman when she had been talking. She bit her lip, feeling foolish.

Tug watched her carefully. "Sue, everyone knows that the ring contains magic. Your brother from the other world, and Tansy, have made no secret of the fact that light from its stone showed them the way out of the Drazuzi caves. Don't you think it is feasible for us to use it now?"

Ashamed of her suspicions, Sue made an effort to be helpful. Everything he said was perfectly true. Her hand was cold and the ring a dull green. Doubtfully, she rubbed it, and nothing happened. If anything, the darkness around them deepened. Tug's dark eyes were inscrutable.

"Ask it for light," he suggested with an air of superiority, and the tension between them built up.

"I need light to cross the river." Sue's voice was barely audible and the ring remained static. It looked just like a piece of worthless glass and Sue was pleased. "That's it. I guess we'll have to wait until morning."

Tug suddenly appeared much older than his years. His manner became assertive. He reached out and gripped her arm. "I know the way," he assured her, "even in the dark. Jump with me. The stones are big enough to take the two of us."

"No!" she shouted, stepping back. This was all wrong. How could he possibly know about the stones? The Gypsies had brought him up. That must be why the ring wouldn't work. "Let go of me. I'm not going. The boat will be back in the morning."

"Don't be such a fool, you're playing into their hands. You've got to come..." Tug's voice ended in a high-pitched scream. From the darkness something leapt for his throat. With arms flailing wildly, Tug fell to the ground. Sue's involuntary scream was even louder. She could not see what type of animal had attacked him, but she braced herself for another one to assault her. The ring flared brightly, piercing the gloom, exposing the mangy wolf. The intensity of the light made it back off, its wild eyes reflecting the glow. Tug lay unconscious, a nasty gash down one side of his face. Repelled by the ring, the wolf seemed to be transfixed to the spot, saliva dripping from its maw. It pawed the ground nervously. From the campsite floated the sound of a horn, and cries of alarm filled the air. A row of men carrying burning torches were heading in Sue's direction. Before they covered half the distance, a shadowy figure emerged from behind her; she was unaware of him until with one swift movement of his arm, he slew the wolf and Sue saw the serpent on his wrist. As the wolf died, the ring dimmed. Before Sue could collect her thoughts, he lifted her bodily from the ground and carried her across the river. There she was dropped unceremoniously at his feet. The horses grazing there shied back.

"Mount one of them," ordered the cloaked man. His voice sounded cold and dismissive. This was not like her last encounter with him. "You must get away from here."

"But Tug…" she began, feeling dazed and looking back over the water. "He needs help."

"And he will get it," came the unfeeling answer.

The men carrying their torches had almost reached them. There were exclamations of disbelief when they saw the wolf. Her companion did not ask a second time. He picked her up and threw her onto a stallion's back, leaping up and mounting another one himself. Then with a strange cry, the horses galloped off into the darkness.

*   *   *

Anger, disbelief and fear all fought for supremacy in Sue's mind. Automatically, self-preservation came to her rescue and her hands stretched out to catch hold of the horse's reins. It had nothing to do with obeying orders; she was terrified of falling off this great moving beast. Things were happening too fast. There was no time to think. The hooded man was moving swiftly away, barely visible. His mount appeared nothing more than a shadow merging into darkness. He ignored the fact that Sue was trailing in his wake, and galloped off at a speed that was highly dangerous under such conditions. He might know where he was going, but she did not.

The people holding flares who had surrounded Tug were soon left far behind. Sue bent low over the horse's withers and, gritting her teeth, clung on. A strong wind pushed back her hood. The acolyte's cloak billowed out like a tent. A few spots of rain touched Sue's skin, and she felt this was a bad omen. The watery moon disappeared behind ominous clouds, leaving the sky a sheet of inky blackness. Another stallion, with no rider, kept pace with her. Sue screwed up her eyes, trying to blot out the denser shadows which sped by with alarming regularity. She was completely at the mercy of her horse.

The wind roared in her ears sounding like a continuous thrumming, only to be joined by an almighty clap of thunder. Through the lids of her closed eyes she saw the blinding flash of lightning. She opened them with a start and stared fixedly ahead. The rain fell heavily and the wind lashed against her skin. Before long her hair was plastered to her scalp and her tunic soaked through. Sue blinked as lightning again forked across the sky. For a brief moment, the outline of the man and horse were illuminated. Another deafening boom of thunder filled the air. Darkness once again reigned supreme.

Still the man galloped onwards. He was evidently determined to reach some destination unknown to Sue. His speed never faltered. She felt the rain running down her face in rivulets; it filled her mouth before continuing to dribble down her chin and then it disappeared through an opening at the neck of her tunic. The wind-chill touched her like an icy blast. She shivered, feeling decidedly bedraggled and uncomfortable. She collapsed on the stallion's back, trying to grab a handful of mane and to hug him close for warmth.

Sue knew instinctively no one was following, so why didn't the man stop? Surely they could find shelter somewhere from this weather. What kind of a man was he? The thunder and lightning overhead was continuous. Unbidden, the thought came to her of Thane and the others. With a cloudburst like this, their boats would be swamped. Then suddenly the storm abated as quickly as it had come and the watery moon decided to reappear. Thunderclaps still reverberated in the distant mountains, and when lightning flashed, its brilliant light showed her a glimpse of towering peaks. It also showed her she was completely alone.

With a supreme effort she pulled the horse up. It slithered to a stop. The rider-less stallion continued onwards. Sue waited patiently for another flash of lightning to make sure her assumptions were correct. Sitting on the horse, she felt like a sack hung out to dry. Water oozed from every part of her body. It dripped from her hair, down her legs to swamp her boots and round her wrists to numb her already cold fingers. The cowled man had vanished. Unbelievably she was on her own in this wild and desolate land.

The horse was restless. Sue was too upset to wonder why. She was trying to work out her next move but her mind became almost as numb as her fingers. A wolf howled hungrily in the distance, only to be followed by another. Her flesh crawled when they started to come from all different direction. It was madness to stay here. She picked up on the stallion's nervousness. He was pawing the ground, showing clearly he wanted to go forward. Sue wished she knew what lay ahead. Her eyes inadvertently fell on Raithe's ring and she was filled with confusion. Was this a sign? Another howl rent the air, much nearer now. Fear started to take control. Uncertainty made her wonder if she should call to Raithe for help via the ring. He had helped her before. Would he help her now? As she glanced around, her throat restricted. Several pairs of eyes were surrounding her in a circle. In sudden frenzy she clutched the ring and called.

"Raithe… Raithe… Can you hear me?"

The gem flared brightly. Her hand shook as she held it close to her eyes, but no way could she see her brother – no matter how hard she looked. But if nothing else, the ring had stopped the wolves' advance. Her moment of satisfaction shattered. Like a whirlwind her horse-riding companion was back. His face was completely covered by his hood. He leant forward as his horse slithered to a standstill and he covered Sue's ring with his hand. Fury filled his voice as he shouted,

"My God, girl – have you not been taught anything? Dim that ring at once! Its magic works two ways, for and against. If you don't understand it, you should not be wearing it. Now buck up your ideas and follow me. I have a place for you to dry out in."

Sue did not have the power to move after that berating speech. She expected him to gallop off again, but instead he sat, silently contemplating her. Her lips trembled. The wolves were watching from a safe distance.

"The ring has always helped me before," she choked, and her voice quivered. He relented at once and now he was gentle when he spoke. "I believe you, Sonja. What you do not seem to know is that each time the ring flares on your hand, the enemy know where you are." He reached out and took the reins from her cold hands and started to lead her forward into the night.

CHAPTER 7
OUTWITTING LEX

When the rebuke came from Tansy, it was unexpected, especially to Barry.

"For goodness sake sit still. With the light going we need to be alert on this stretch of the river. What we don't need is you to be moving about."

Barry eyed Tansy, his face full of hurt surprise, wondering why she, above everyone else, did not realise how jubilant he was feeling. Riding the rapids was every lad's dream. He glanced at the river as the strong current swept the craft along. His adrenaline soared every time they swirled dangerously around submerged boulders – only noticeable by white water. Their boat missed projecting rocks by inches and dived steeply down small cataracts. As the craft righted itself, he was stimulated.

The sturdy craft was well built and not likely to break up. It was unlike anything he had ever seen before with very low sides, which enabled the occupants to do some effective paddling. Although water occasionally slopped in and covered the base of the craft, White Hawk sat in the middle like a lordly figurehead, daring anyone to move him. Barry gave Tansy a lopsided grin to keep the peace. "Sorry, this is all new to me."

Tansy pursed her lips and continued to paddle. The trouble with Barry was he never did look sorry. Thane glanced up from the gruelling task, long enough to stare at the lad.

"I can assure you it won't stay new for long," he cut in dryly. "By the time this journey is finished there will be blisters on your hands."

"He'll have them somewhere else if he doesn't pick up a paddle," Amos interjected grimly. "Come on, lad. Jump to it. You can't leave it all to the women."

Although aggrieved, Barry complied, and bent forward to pick up a paddle from the floor. A warning growl came from the wolf because he was now sitting on it. The way Barry felt at that moment, he didn't care and yanked it away. It was then he noticed, in spite of Amos's cutting remark, only Tansy was paddling. Annalee and Sue were blissfully ignoring everyone and watching the banks fly by. Barry was a great believer in sharing work. With brotherly love, he deftly retrieved a second paddle and, collecting another warning growl from White Hawk which he disregarded, he deliberately poked his sister in the small of her back, saying,

"Why don't you do a spot of work? I'm not the only able-bodied person here. Even White Hawk is moving more than you are."

Sue behaved as though she never heard him, but Barry yelped as a stinging blow made contact with his head. He turned indignantly, meeting the angry face of Amos, who said in an icy voice,

"We do not expect Sonja to work – now, or ever. Have a care as to whom you are addressing."

"I'm speaking to my sister," retorted Barry hotly.

"She is not your sister," replied Amos. "In this world she is a Princess, so it's best you remember that in future, lad. Now suppose you do some work."

Barry fell silent, feeling all eyes were on him. He glowered resentfully at Sue's back. The least she could have done was to stick up for him instead of acting as though he were not there. Amos had already lost interest in him, but Barry's stinging ear made him very much aware of the old man. Angrily he dipped his paddle in the water, and the fierce current came as a surprise. Before he was aware of it, the paddle was jerked from his grasp and carried away to midstream. There it bobbed tantalizingly out of reach. Mortification filled him. Cailli's guffaw caught him on the raw. His colour mounted with his temper. Clenching his teeth, he was about to pick up another paddle, when Annalee's hand shot out and caught his wrist. He could barely make her out in the gloom, but felt her eyes staring at him intently.

"Leave it, Barry. If Cailli's so good at it, let him do it. You and I will have a go when he is tired."

Barry was grateful for her intervention. She had given him the chance of backing down gracefully. He acknowledged her words with a smile and from then on he copied his sister. He ignored the others, but his enjoyment of the day had evaporated. Total darkness was nearly upon them. Signs in the sky boded ill. Everything warned of approaching bad weather. Heavy ominous rain clouds were building up. The watery moon did not stand a chance. Storm clouds gathered over its feeble light, obliterating its presence from the heavens. It was hard to tell whether or not it was raining as so much spray blew over the seven occupants of the boat that they were already wet. A blinding flash of lightning took them unawares. Immediately it was followed by the explosive bang of a thunderbolt. As they jumped in alarm, the heavens opened up and with no warning, the clouds emptied their contents.

Blustery winds and lashing rain had them drenched in seconds. The crafts ahead could no longer be seen. The rain had extinguished their lights. The river took on a fury not often seen. What at first had been choppy water was now waves, big enough to come over the sides of the boat and swamp them.

"This is foolish," Amos yelled. "Make for the bank."

"I disagree," shouted Cailli from the back of the boat, "keep going, at least until we get round this bend."

"You're a fool, man. Look at the water. We've got ladies aboard," roared Amos, "head for the far side, Thane."

The river raced ahead at a furious speed. Their paddles were not much use against the current. Thane set his jaw firmly, and with the help of Tansy, tried to guide the craft across. Darkness was a hindrance, but the further bank could be seen with every successive flash of lightning. Annalee helped Cailli at the back. It became noticeable that Sue was the only one not doing anything, and it embarrassed Barry, especially when he knew she deplored idleness. While no one was looking, he worked his way along to be behind her but he accidentally tripped as the boat tilted. He clung to his sister for support and her hood moved slightly as she turned to face him. With so much noise from the storm, no one heard his quick intake of breath. The next blinding flash of lightning revealed Neela's face to him, and her dark expressive eyes pleaded with him not to say anything. Thane towered over him, pulling him away.

"Leave Sue alone," he shouted angrily, "and give Tansy a hand to hold the paddle. You'll have Amos having another go at you in a minute."

Bemused, Barry turned to the tracker, his mind working furiously. He knew something was going on here. The subterfuge had been carefully constructed. He could not believe Thane had sat beside Neela all this time and had not known it wasn't Sue. He thought that everyone in the boat must have known about it, except him. Barry breathed hard, his chest tight. *Right*, he thought – *if that's the way they want it, two could play the same game*. He was determined to find out where Sue had gone, without their help.

* * *

The craft shuddered out of control and tilted as it came into contact with hidden objects. At last the men succeeded in bringing it to a halt; and before the fierce current could break it free again, Thane disregarded danger and plunged over the side. Through heavily falling rain he was able to make out a rock and caught hold of it. He swore as the sharp flint cut into his hand and held on, managing to stop the craft. He swayed drunkenly as the current endeavoured to sweep his feet from beneath him. His muscles bunched, and sinews in his arm tightened with the strain. Cailli was beside him and caught hold of the mooring rope, lashing it to a tree that leant drunkenly from the bank. They both heaved on the taut rope, working against the pull of the river, and fought to bring the craft alongside the bank.

Amos gave no thought to his age as he jumped over the side of the boat to help. He considered himself the only other able-bodied man there. Barry did not count, other than being a nuisance, and had he offered to help, he would undoubtedly have been told off for interfering. With determination, Amos held both bank and craft. The water swamped him as it raced by. Gritting his teeth, he looked grimly at the remaining occupants and shouted, "Get off quickly."

Tansy was off like a shot and leapt nimbly to land. Annalee followed at the same time as the wolf. He didn't wait to see what happened but quickly vanished into the darkness. With the strain bringing perspiration to his lined face, Amos glowered at Barry who hadn't moved. He was in no mood to play games. "That means you as well, lad," he snarled angrily, "or didn't I say please."

Barry's head still smarted where the cuff had landed earlier. Much as he respected Amos, at the moment he didn't care if the old man pushed them adrift.

"Before I leave," said Barry, "I will help my *sister* off," and he emphasised the word 'sister', so that it was not missed by anyone.

"Let me help. You're not strong enough," Cailli called. Amos looked as though he might break a blood vessel. Thane beat him to it by clambering back into the boat. "I'll give Barry a hand since I'm nearest," he shouted.

Thane kept his balance with difficulty. Barry watched his approach warily. Deliberately he put his arm round Neela and felt her stiffen. Thane came right up to them, his expression tight. He paused, glancing first at Neela, whose face was completely covered with her hood, and then at Barry. The expression he saw there was one he never expected to see on Barry's face. It was almost hate. Thane swore softly under his breath, wondering why the lad had left it till now to take a stand, but deep down he knew the fault was his. He had always treated Barry as a kid. He should have accorded him the status of an equal. Annalee had warned him he was being too hard on the boy.

"Barry," he said tentatively, "let me..."

"Keep away," shouted Barry, his anger barely under control. "I can manage by myself. She may be Sonja to you lot, but first and foremost, she is my sister," and he tightened his hold round Neela.

Thane exhaled sharply. He swallowed back the rebuke on the tip of his tongue because he caught sight of the ironical look on Amos's face. He growled ominously, "No one is stopping you, but if you don't get off right you're going to be washed away by the river."

Barry knew he spoke sense. More and more water was filling the craft. He helped Neela to the edge and held her there. Thane tensed, but made no move to help. When Annalee and Tansy stood by Amos, Barry squeezed Neela's arm and said in a low tone, "Are you ready to jump?"

She nodded, gathering her cloak about her body. Barry looked across at the girls on the bank. "She's coming now," he called and Neela jumped.

* * *

The rain clouds dispersed as the wind drove the storm into the mountains. There it continued to flash and rumble. The rain cleared, allowing a watery moon to reappear. Its faint light was better than none at all.

Huddled beneath the boughs of a tree thickly clothed with an abundance of leaves, the group from the boat were wet and bedraggled. They stared morosely around the clearing. They were all unnerved at the speed events had changed their original journey. It was Tansy who pointed out that it was drier in the open than standing beneath a tree continuously dripping water. Apathetically they moved to the middle of the clearing. Amos clucked his tongue in annoyance.

"What we need is a fire. It seems to me to be the only plausible solution to our predicament. We're not going anywhere tonight." He glanced round the group, unsmiling. "Let's see how good our fire-makers and trackers are."

His voice died away. The noise from the river took over. It roared by, looking extremely dangerous, carrying double the usual amount of water. Although their craft was securely tied to a tree, it still strained at the mooring rope, trying to get away and go with the current. Barry stood apart from everyone and remained silent. His mind was too full of confusing thoughts. The biggest of which was, where was Sue? At Amos's words, Thane looked towards the two girls, Cailli as well, and called out,

"It seems to me you've been issued with a challenge. How are you going to make a fire? Everything you lay your hands on is going to be soaked."

"You haven't much faith in us," retorted Annalee. "In five minutes I can guarantee you will have your fire." She moved off, accompanied by Tansy, but Cailli made no attempt to follow. The girls looked at him reproachfully, and he had the grace to flush. With raised eyebrows, Thane asked him bluntly, "Aren't you up to the challenge, old boy?"

Cailli shrugged. "I thought I could be better employed helping you build a shelter. They can take Barry with them. Barry looks as though he needs something to do."

It was on the tip of Annalee's tongue to say Barry would not know what to look for, when he suddenly asserted himself by saying. "I can't think why you're all bothering. I can smell wood smoke. Someone nearby has already got a fire. Why don't you track that down?"

A silence fell over the group. They became tense. Amos lifted his head and breathed in deeply. Begrudgingly he looked towards Barry. "The lad's right," he agreed. "It's not too far away either."

Cailli pushed himself to the front, ready to lead. He looked at them questioningly. "Well, come on. What are we waiting for? Let's find it. I expect it's our men from the other boats who have lit it." He took a few steps and Thane's voice halted him.

"Keep where you are," he snapped. "I don't like this. It's not our men. They wouldn't have had time to light a fire yet. The one we can smell is well established. It could belong to anyone out here. Perhaps it's a trap."

"A trap?" questioned Cailli, and he laughed. "No-one in their right mind would be here in this kind of weather, as you well know. You're getting paranoid, Thane. Come on, Amos, let's you and I investigate."

Cailli was chagrined when he found himself ignored. Instead of complying with him, Amos did the exact opposite and signalled everyone to bunch together. At his nod, the girls fixed arrows to their bows and stood ready.

When they heard the crunch of twigs and other debris underfoot, they strained their eyes to look in the direction from which the noise came. It was the thud of horses' hooves, which told them they had no need to go anywhere. Whoever had lit that fire, was searching for them.

By the light of the moon, they saw several shadows break cover from the trees. These solidified into mounted soldiers holding drawn swords. It was obvious to the watchers they meant business, and their little party was at a disadvantage. They looked aggressive, nothing at all like the renegades led by Lex Ansell, so it came as a shock when they heard his voice. The two girls lowered their bows on hearing his cynical words.

"Well, well, well," he taunted. "It seems we've come across the royal entourage out on night manoeuvres. Got caught in the storm, did we?"

"You're a little off course, aren't you, Ansell," snarled Amos, not masking his hatred. "What brings you to this particular spot with your followers ready for a fight?" He stared balefully at the naked blades.

"Well actually you do," Lex Ansell replied. "We have come to relieve you of Sonja. So hand her over and then you can go home and get dry."

No one heard Barry gasp, except the girls.

"Over my dead body," Thane exploded furiously, but Lex cut in, "Be careful what you say because that can also be arranged, though I would rather not shed blood in front of the Princess. I don't know how squeamish she is."

Amos moved up to the head of Captain Ansell's horse and caught hold of the bridle. The rider stiffened, but did not back away. He glanced down arrogantly, knowing the cards were stacked in his favour. "Is there something I can help you with, Amos?" he enquired.

"Yes," the older man spat out. "Aren't you a little off course? Who on earth told you Sonja was with us? Do we look foolish enough to take the Princess on a river trip in weather like this? Ask yourself that question."

"No need. You're stupid enough to do anything. I wouldn't put it past you. Now let's cut out this useless waffling. There is nothing you can do to stop us. We know she is with you disguised as an acolyte. Your first mistake, old man, is that acolytes don't go out on the river at night. Unless you want trouble, I would suggest you let us take her. We are much more able to escort her than you are."

Amos still held the horse. His blood was at boiling point. "Where did you get your information from?" he ground out through clamped teeth.

"That would be telling and I'm afraid you will never know, but thanks all the same for delivering her." Ansell smiled at him. "We've got a nice cosy place ready to put her."

Thane stepped closer to Amos and drew a knife from his belt. He ignored the soldiers who raised their swords at his action and pointed them at his heart. Barry was galvanised into action and drew the dagger Raithe had given him. He glared defiantly at the Captain.

"You're not taking my sister anywhere. Lay one hand on her and I'll..." His voice trailed off because Lex made a signal and his men spread out, making a circle round the luckless group. Then he looked down on Barry, his voice cold and dismissive. "I've met you before, haven't I. Put that plaything down before you cut yourself." His eyes scanned the group, noting with satisfaction that the two trackers had moved closer to the hooded figure, and Cailli was trying surreptitiously to melt into the shadows. Then unexpectedly he asked, "Where's the wolf?"

He got no answer. From the shadows came the sound of more horses approaching. Lex Ansell had reinforcements and meant to capture Sue. Barry's initial bravado left him. He realised how badly he had misjudged his companions. Thane had known this ambush was imminent. That's why Neela was taking Sue's place. No matter what happened to her, she had the Shaman's power to protect her. Making up for his former hostility, he walked up to Neela and placed his arm round her shoulder. His voice rang out clearly. "If you take my sister, then you take me as well."

The Captain laughed, and a few of his men joined in. "What brave words, sonny. Well, I've got news for you. I don't want you. I only want Sonja. Take her, men." He nodded curtly to his soldiers. The group were easily overpowered and Barry was viciously thrown to the ground. Thane watched helplessly while Neela was grabbed by brawny arms and carried to the Captain's horse. She was more worried about keeping her cloak around her and if Lex was surprised she showed no resistance, he concealed the fact. It was a bonus as far as he was concerned. He sat passively while his men lashed her to the saddle behind him. Then with a mocking salute to Thane and Amos, he shouted, "Enjoy your river trip."

Flicking his whip with unnecessary violence to make his horse rear, he led his soldiers away. The bedraggled party watched them go. Barry picked himself up and glared at the immobilised gathering. Without giving any thought to what he said, he shouted furiously,

"What's the matter with you all? You can't let them take Neela."

"Neela!" exclaimed Cailli, crashing out of the bushes. He was the only one to answer Barry. "Neela! Are you trying to say that wasn't Sue?" The others turned to eye him, questions hovering on their lips. Cailli's face became damp with perspiration, sensing something was wrong.

"I'll follow them," he declared and made to move away, but Amos stopped him dead.

"How? How are you going to do that? They are on horseback, man."

Thane exchanged a grim look with Amos, and then nodded. Before Barry realised what was happening, he felt himself pulled into the shadows. While Amos and Annalee confronted Cailli, Tansy moved quickly after Thane. Barry's indignant protest was smothered as a firm hand clamped his mouth. The grip was like a vice making sure he could not escape. He was compelled to listen while Thane spoke to Tansy.

"Go back to the Shaman and tell him it all worked perfectly. Much too perfectly, I'm afraid, for my peace of mind. You and Annalee can track us later if you like, but right now I've got to leave."

He looked down on the squirming Barry and asked sternly, "Are you going to keep quiet if I remove my hand?"

Barry nodded and the pressure on his mouth relaxed. Thane studied him before saying, "I appreciated your acting back there. You made that farce very convincing. Now, do you want to come with me to find your sister?"

CHAPTER 8
THE SNAKE PEOPLE

Sue and her abductor rode through the night for thirty minutes, or it could have been much longer. It seemed all the same to Sue. So much had happened to her in one day that her mind could no longer cope with it. All she wanted was to remove her wet clothes and stop shivering. The hooded man relentlessly led her through the darkness. For all the notice he took of her, she wondered if he had forgotten she was there. The watery moon gave little light and the night was full of animal noises. On her own, she would have been scared, but with this strange companion who had snakes round his wrists she felt safe. She had no idea who he was nor where he was taking her. He mentioned something about a warm place to dry out in, and those words lured her to accompany him. She believed every word he said. It was just as well Barry did not know what she was doing, he would be the first to tell her she was mad to be so trusting towards a stranger. But Sue did not put this man in that category. She felt she knew him.

She sat slackly on her mount and the hooded man continued to hold the reins. The rain had stopped, but now the wind was getting up and blew coldly on her body. Her wet clothes chafed her skin. Then the sound of a galloping horse behind them jerked her back to awareness. Someone was following them, but her guide showed no sign of unease, even though he must have heard it. A rider-less stallion made a wide circle round them and took up its position abreast of them. He still did not turn.

"How much further are we going?" Sue asked wearily.

Sue meant her question to be light-hearted, but her voice cracked. This time the man did stop and he wheeled his horse around. With one look at her he realised the distress she was feeling.

"Forgive me, Sonja." His voice was contrite. "For a while I had forgotten how inadequately you were dressed. We must speed up."

"Then may I hold the reins?"

She was sure he smiled, yet when she looked at the place one would expect to see a face, there was nothing but black emptiness. He pressed the reins into her cold hands and the warmth that radiated from his fingers startled her. With a jerk he broke the contact and uttered a few strange words, whereupon his mount sprang forward and disappeared into the darkness. Before Sue could grasp the fact that he had abandoned her again, her own mount seemed to sprout wings and speed after him. With an inarticulate cry, Sue clung on and closed her eyes against the biting wind. She felt as though she was flying through the air. A sensation of weightlessness ran through her body, bringing with it a feeling of exhilaration.

It was a shock when the neigh of a horse and the gentle pressure on her arm aroused her from the dream-like trance into which she had fallen. Her eyes encountered total darkness which pressed down and felt overpowering. Trying to see was like looking at a solid black wall. Gone were the watery moon and the feel of the wind on her face. By the smell that assailed her nostrils, she assumed she was in a stable or a cave. Her clammy clothes stuck to her skin, making her feel uncomfortable. The shivering returned. Where was her guide? His habit of abandoning her was disconcerting, but the neigh of a horse calmed her down, even though she couldn't see it.

"Where am I?" The suspicion of a tremor was in her voice.

A light flared in front of her. The unexpectedness of it hurt her eyes. Automatically she lifted an arm to shield her face.

"Accept my apologies, Sonja." Her companion's voice came from beside her. At once the light dimmed to a pleasant glow. Sue could now make out the cave in which she stood. Several horses stood bunched together. A few were eating from a long narrow trough, and hay was strewn over the earthen floor. They were well catered for.

A human figure moved in a far corner, but directly it became aware of Sue's scrutiny, disappeared into the shadows. Her guide stood motionless by her side. He was still hard to see because of his dark garments, but in his hand he held an incandescent stone and this clearly showed the snakes encircling his wrist.

"Where are we?" Curiosity got the better of her as she looked round the makeshift stable, but overpowering fatigue threatened to swamp her. Unconsciously she drew nearer to the stone because as well as light, it gave off heat.

This small action was not missed. Instead of answering, her guide gently grasped her arm and propelled her forward, saying, "You need warmth, dry clothes and sleep. I hope Deena can help you. Come this way."

With the aid of his stone, Sue could see several tunnels leading off from the cave in which they were standing. Although she moved readily with him, the atmosphere of the place brought back memories of the Drazuzi and unconsciously her body stiffened. Her unease filtered through to the man. He paused, half inclined to do something else, but changed his mind and continued along the tunnel that ended in another spacious cavern.

Warmth engulfed them. The place was abundant with glowing stones, placed strategically round the walls. It was furnished with costly artefacts, tapestries and low comfortable couches. She expected to see the Priest materialise before her. The shock made her reel. Everything started to spin round and she could feel herself falling into an abyss.

* * *

Deep in the depths of the mountain, a group of young girls huddled together and spoke in excited undertones. Every so often, one would shriek and the high sound jarred on the ears. It brought unwanted attention in their direction. The room was dank and unpleasant in spite of the stones, which gave off light. It was a workroom, kept at a low temperature for just that reason – to make them work.

A few more mature members of the community looked up and shook their heads in despair. They had been brought up the hard way and taught to keep their thoughts to themselves, no matter what happened above ground to trigger off dormant emotions. They were so old now they had forgotten what it was like to be young and see an adventure in every incident. Yet still, they eyed the younger generation with pride and felt honoured that these girls had been chosen for this task.

It was Deena's voice that broke up the illicit meeting. Deena, who was powerful and had absolute control over everything in the underground domain. She was chief of the tribe and had been so for aeons. Unobtrusively she entered the cave and watched for a while before speaking to the small group of girls.

"Are you four ready?" Her voice was guttural. "The Master is waiting."

With amazing dexterity, the four girls sprang to their feet. Their dusky faces became serious. They knew the reputation of the tribe was resting on their shoulders. Quickly they moved over to where Deena stood. She was resplendent in her shimmering silver gown and sparkling snake-like ornament which was entwined in her black, coiled hair. She cast a critical eye over the girls, making sure their tunics were clean and their hair tidy. A red band of office was fixed tightly round each smooth forehead.

Nodding approval, Deena led them from the room into the tunnel outside, where the temperature rapidly changed. Out here it was gloomy and damp, but not cold. The air was warm and humidity high. Along the base of the rocky wall, where water gathered, there were masses of long thin black serpents, with glittering red eyes. They slithered over each other. Their bite was lethal, but not to the inhabitants of the lower caves, who were immune to their venom. To them the serpents were a symbol of power and protection. The girls handled the reptiles and hung them round their necks as decoration, especially in certain rituals. On each of their arms a snake was tattooed around the wrist. This was a sign they had reached womanhood.

Deena showed no sign of her great age as she led the girls up a winding staircase. At a small door she paused, allowing time for her charges to settle down. Then she pushed it open and a dazzling glare of light hit them. They all glided silently into the room. Automatically the door shut behind them with a click. It was not the first time they had been in this particular room, but certainly it was the first time with the Master in residence.

The click of the door alerted him. He rose to his feet, watching the band of women coming towards him. Dressed in his customary black hood and cloak, he looked impressive. They barely reached the height of his thigh.

These tiny people, who lived in the heart of the mountains, were fiercely loyal to him. They had initiated him into their cult. He was the only man in a society of women. In spite of their size, they were immensely strong and ruled over by Deena who was so old he would hate to hazard a guess at her age.

"Welcome, Deena." He bowed low, holding out a hand to the proud old woman. Her lined face wreathed into a smile, showing broken yellow teeth. She kissed his proffered hand with her thin hard lips and caressed the snake wound round his wrist with a bony finger. Her small dark eyes were bright and full of wisdom. She came to the point at once.

"I have brought the girls you requested. You will not be unhappy with them. They will do whatever you ask," she said, and stood to one side.

He glanced at the nymph-like creatures behind her, standing in a straight line and staring at him with solemn eyes. A puff of wind could blow them away. Their dusky faces, soft and unlined, were beautiful. Long lustrous black hair fell to their waists, and in their eyes was the desire to please. It was only when they spoke that the illusion of beauty shattered. Their vocal chords sounded as though they were trapped in gravel.

"The Princess Sonja is in the next cave." The man spoke in a stern authoritative voice, and although the girls did not notice, his eyes flickered over them appreciatively. "She will sleep for a few hours," he continued, "long enough for you to do what I require. I shall not be here when she awakens and I have no idea what her reaction will be." He turned to the very old lady, saying, "Keep her comfortable, do not touch any of her belongings, and most importantly, prevent her from leaving."

Deena bowed, masking her thoughts. "Yes, Master."

"I shall not be gone long. Just be aware her enemies are searching for her."

"Yes, Master," acknowledged Deena. Turning, she snapped her fingers at the young girls. They almost ran from the cave, eager to see the Princess. A cynical smile lurked at the corners of Deena's mouth. She was looking forward to this. Her wily brain soaked up events and never forgot them. She remembered Raithe's last visit here. His sister would surely react the same as he.

*   *   *

In contented bliss, Sue turned in the soft bed, enjoying the warmth about her body. But before long, it was the quietness that disturbed her and she wanted to know what was going on in this cell-like room. Parts of it were obscured from her view. As her eyes moved around the little she could see, she endeavoured to put her disjointed thoughts into some sort of order. Two large pedestals stood on either side of the bed, balanced on top of them were two stones that gave off a rosy glow and were the source of the heat she could feel. The cave walls were covered with tapestries, which reminded her of a place she would rather forget. It was certainly time she made a move to find the man who had brought her here and ask for an explanation.

Struggling up from the mattress, she nearly fainted with shock. She became aware her clothing had been changed. The flimsy garment covering her body was even worse than the gown that the priest had made her wear. Flimsy and impractical; to her mind it was indecent. How could this have happened to her without her knowledge? Was she a prisoner here? Had that hooded man removed her clothes? Her face burned with embarrassment at the thought.

Desperately, she scanned the floor, hoping to find her own clothes piled up there, and in doing so saw something move in the far corner. She stared transfixed at the apparition, which rose to its feet and was no higher than three foot. Sue doubted its head would reach her waist. The dwarf-like person was a very old woman who held herself proudly. She looked bizarre, dressed in a shimmering silver gown, and Sue noticed that her black eyes were scrutinising every move she made.

In spite of her great age, the woman's hair was black, and entwined amongst the heavy coils was a snake. Sue looked down to the dwarf's hands and her suspicions were confirmed. Snakes were there as well. Sue immediately thought she had been brought to a snake cult. She hated snakes. The very thought of being amongst them filled her with terror. Her tongue clove to the roof of her mouth, rendering her speechless.

The old woman drew nearer to the bed. She knew exactly what impression her appearance had given the Princess Sonja. She exulted in this until she realised the Princess had not got her brother's arrogance. Deena knew she would definitely look after her, but not quite in the same way as the Master expected. If the Princess had enemies, she knew exactly what to do to enable the girl to defend herself.

"I am Deena."

The sound of her voice made Sue flinch away. The old woman's lips tightened. She ignored the apprehension in Sue's eyes and said, "Now that you are awake, would you like some food?"

The way she pronounced words made Sue want to clear her throat. Then she realised she was staring. The woman's mundane question released Sue's tongue and she said, "Yes please, but may I have some clothes first?"

Deena glanced at the diaphanous gown she had deliberately dressed Sue in and watched the girl's hands try ineffectively to cover herself. "It is very warm in here. Do you not feel it? You will not need any other clothes until you leave here."

"But… but…." Sue stuttered, uncertain of how to continue since she did not know the name of the man who had brought her there. The old woman's impassive face, watching for her reaction, put her at a disadvantage. "If my friend comes in here," she said at length, "the man who brought me here last night. If… if he sees me… he, he.." Her voice trailed away and Deena swept aside her explanation as though it were nonsensical and said,

"You fret too much, child. The Master is not here. He left at an early hour. You are in my care. I shall have a cloak brought for you. Do not be concerned about your appearance. Only women live here."

As Sue digested that information, the old lady clapped her hands. The girls must have been waiting outside, because two of them entered and Sue caught her breath. After having looked at the grotesque form of Deena, these came as a shock. Their petite, elfin loveliness was a complete surprise. They smiled at her shyly until a harsh order from Deena sent them scuttling away. Immediately, two more entered. As far as Sue was concerned, they seemed replicas of each other. Their strength was astronomical, because between them they carried in a table that was bigger than they were, and it was laden with dishes of food. Sue, looking at them intently, saw serpents encircling their wrists. She turned her eyes and met those of Deena. The two young girls backed out and when Deena and Sue were alone, Deena asked bluntly,

"You have a question you want to ask?"

Sue realised she had been staring again. Swallowing hard, she blurted out, "I didn't mean to be rude, but I was intrigued by the snakes you all have marked on you. Do you have a cult here?"

Sue thought she had annoyed the old lady. But without warning, a smile covered her face which changed her personality completely, making her much more approachable. She drew herself up regally. "We are the snake people and I am Deena, the snake Queen. We have lived in these mountains for centuries, where we nurture the snakes who protect us."

Sue felt herself go cold. "That sounds so barbaric. Do the girls handle them as well?"

"You saw the snakes on their arms," replied Deena. "That means they have been initiated into womanhood. We have ceremonies here. Maybe you would like to witness one?"

"I think I shall be gone before that," Sue answered quickly. Then suddenly a thought occurred to her. "The man who brought me here has snakes on his wrists, but you told me there were only women in your cult."

Deena smiled secretly. "The Master is an exception."

"Who is he?"

The old lady moved to the food and uncovered it. Sue thought Deena was not going to answer, but as she turned to leave, she looked at the girl. "If you do not know who he is, it is not my place to tell you," she said, and after that ambiguous remark, she left the cave.

* * *

The rain-washed countryside looked bleak and uninviting, making the subterranean caves seem the best place to be. With a cloak wrapped tightly about her, Sue stood at the cave entrance, disappointed there was no one to be seen. The sweet smell of hay tickled her nostrils, but frustration arose when she found the cave was empty. Every horse had vanished. Just for a moment she stood alone, and realised why she had been allowed to come here. Deena had read her mind. No attempt had been made to curtail her movements, but her hosts were very much aware she would escape if the chance presented itself. Escape was the wrong word because she was not actually a prisoner. From the entrance where she stood, there was nothing to be seen except rolling hills and a vast landscape of waving grasses, which stretched for miles in any direction. One could see forever, and anyone approaching would be spotted at once.

The man who had befriended Sue and brought her here had not returned, and by now she was getting anxious. She needed to be on her way and find Raithe. She knew he was in danger, a prisoner somewhere. Ever since she saw the picture of the waterfall in her ring, she knew it was there she had to go. In this place, the green stone was treated as nothing more than a piece of glass, a pretty trinket to be worn on the finger. She had not forgotten the warning about her ill use of its powers so she left it strictly alone, although at times it irritated her hand. Maybe Raithe was trying to contact her. Whenever she mentioned his name to Deena, she received a negative response. Raithe had obviously not put himself out to create a good impression.

Two days of wandering round this complex of caves had revealed nothing of interest. They were beautifully furnished and very warm. Sue had questioned the old lady about the hooded man, but she was not forthcoming with any information. Sue had the impression she should know him. Deena found the fact that she didn't highly amusing. Sue's desire to be on her way was gnawing at her continuously. It was all very well being here, but she missed Thane and wanted to see her mother again. Why was it that she could not make these dwarf-like women understand that she had friends who cared for her and must be worrying about her whereabouts. Her melancholy thoughts were interrupted by two of the elfin girls, coming up to her and standing on either side. They came to their point at once. One said, anxious not to offend,

"Forgive our intrusion, Sonja. Deena would like you to attend a ceremony."

Sue shuddered, unable to help herself. "What ceremony?"

"The initiation of one of our sisters," replied the girls.

Coldness descended over Sue. "If there are snakes involved – no!" she said decisively.

The two girls were perplexed, not understanding her reaction. "There is nothing to be afraid of," they assured her. "The snakes are our God. Deena does you a great honour by asking you to be there."

Sue inhaled deeply, not wanting to refuse because they had all been so good to her, yet something screamed within her to run. She had no wish to come into contact with slithery serpents, not that she had seen any. A sharp clap of hands made her jump. The two girls melted away at once and Deena herself stood facing Sue. She had changed from her silver dress into a red one that fell to the ground in shimmering folds. There was a long slash up the front where her legs could be seen, and they were not the legs of an old woman. The coils of her hair were now adorned with scarlet feathers. She held herself like a queen and her black eyes studied Sue's apprehensive face. She spoke in measured tones and said, "So it does not appeal to you to honour us with your presence,

Princess Sonja. I speak for everyone when I say we shall be disappointed, but nevertheless we understand the way you feel. Do not give it another thought. Come and have refreshments with me before I have to leave you."

Deena walked away with those words and Sue reluctantly followed, back to the cave where the table was spread with red berries and bowls of liquid. She sat on the edge of her bed and only momentarily closed her eyes in relief, thus missing the swift action of the old woman as she dropped something small into the bowl that was nearest Sue.

"Eat some berries, Sonja, they are very sweet and you will like them," Deena said unemotionally, "then you will enjoy the drink much better."

Sue jerked her thoughts back and took a firm grip on herself. As requested, she picked out a few berries and stared at them curiously, never having seen such berries before. "What are they, Deena?" she asked with interest, because she really wanted to know. She put one in her mouth and it was sweet, almost moreish. Before she knew it, the small pile before her vanished. The old lady hardly touched hers, but lifted up her bowl and drank. Sue immediately copied her but after the first mouthful gave a shudder, complaining it was bitter, and put it down resolutely. Deena eyed her in surprise.

"I dare say you think it is bitter," she said, "but that is because you have just eaten all those sweet berries. Try again. It will taste better."

It was a reasonable request so Sue lifted the bowl again and put it to her lips. Her face showed instant distaste, but seeing Deena watching her, she took another mouthful, to show she was not being awkward. "I still do not like it," she said firmly, putting the bowl down with a thud and Deena gave her one of those rare smiles and said, "very well, do not drink it. I must go and prepare for the ceremony. Would you like some more berries?"

Sue tried to say 'no', but could not speak. A surprised look flared in her eyes. The old lady moved closer to her. "Do you not feel well, Sonja?" she asked.

Sue found it difficult to open her mouth. Her mind was reeling. What had Deena done to her – that bitter taste, there was something in her drink. She tried to leap to her feet but her limbs would not support her. It was the last straw when she saw the look on Deena's face. It was just like the cat that had the cream.

The old lady clapped her hands energetically. All six girls entered the room and they held a gown, which sparkled with gold dust. They surrounded Sue and stripped off her cloak, then with deft fingers dressed her in the gown. Sue was unable to stop them. All this time Deena watched and Sue was feeling sick. She knew they were going to take her to the ceremony.

CHAPTER 9
FOLLOWING THE TRAIL

There was no pleasure in scrambling over rough ground and following a river by moonlight. Not only was it dark, but for Barry every leaf he passed seemed to be carrying a load of water, and he was the unfortunate recipient who got slapped in the face by branches that Thane carelessly allowed to swing back. After the fourth time he received a mouthful of wet leaves, he stopped in his tracks and declared, "I'm going to walk by the water's edge, Thane. It will be a lot better than following you."

Thane hardly paused in his stride. "I shouldn't do that if I were you. It's not safe. What happens if you fall in?"

"Then I shall get wet, which I am already, thanks to you."

"Well if you fall in, I'm not fishing you out. So be warned. We need to push on."

Thane had a lot on his mind and was already regretting having Barry with him. Barry felt aggrieved that Thane didn't have the decency to say sorry. So a stubborn streak made him deliberately venture nearer to the bank when normally he would have kept to the path. His change of direction was not a good move. Water rushed by at an alarming speed. In the dark it looked black and foreboding. The storm had undermined parts of the bank that had collapsed and been washed away. The ground was soggy. Barry squelched along; his feet soaked and bogged down in mud. He found the going slow and hard work. From what he could see, the way ahead was a quagmire. Instinct warned him to turn inland, even if it meant he would have to put up with Thane's 'I told you so'. But Thane was already out of sight, not giving the boy a backward glance.

Barry tried to retrace his steps to where he thought the path was, but he couldn't find it or lose the roar of the river in his ears. However, he was not going to be beaten by such a triviality.

He pushed himself through a few water-saturated bushes that ensnared his clothing and scratched his face. His feet sank in mud. What had started off as an exciting adventure was now turning sour. He swore softly to himself when the thick bush in front of him failed to give way. He battered at it with his thighs. After a few shudders it gave way. Unprepared, he fell forward with nothing to stop him. With one yell and an almighty splash he landed in a stagnant pool that was bypassed by the river. As his body disturbed the water, a sickly stench arose and made him want to vomit. The mud beneath his body felt like a sponge, but it held him in a vice-like grip. The impression of sinking was very real and could not be ignored. He had no way of getting out unaided. It didn't help that he knew lots of things could be lurking in the surrounding undergrowth. Swallowing his pride, he shouted,

"Help! Thane! Come back. I'm sorry I didn't listen to you."

Because of the trees, it was dark where he had fallen, but he felt that the bushes near him had moved. Water droplets fell around him, and common sense told him it wasn't Thane. Instinctively he knew something was near and weighing up the situation. Because no word was spoken, Barry moved impatiently, and with that move he felt himself sink deeper. Then a gruff voice he didn't recognise, spoke. "Stand up, boy. The water isn't deep."

Barry took in a deep breath which he instantly regretted. "I would if I could but I'm stuck."

"Then try a little bit harder. Don't just sit there." The answer was unsympathetic.

The water circulating round his waist made a peculiar noise every time he tried to lift his legs. Bubbles rose to the surface. In spite of the seriousness of his position, Barry was curious. "I don't need a lecture. I want to get out of here. Who are you? I can't see you."

"Well, I'm certainly not Thane." There was a humourless laugh. "But does it matter, if you need help?"

"I suppose not." Barry tried to penetrate the darkness. It was a waste of time because the shadows were dense. The chill was getting at him and so was the roar from the nearby river. "Are you going to get me out of here before I sink?"

"Of course. Bear with me for a moment."

The moment turned into several minutes and while he waited, Barry swore he was slowly being sucked down. A rope struck his shoulders. From the bushes, a hand appeared. "Tie this quickly around yourself and under your arms. When it's secure, I'll pull."

Barry complied with feverish haste, keeping his fear bottled in. Then the unknown man pulled and heaved and as the rope grew taut lots of grunts and heavy breathing escaped from his mouth. From the water came a sinister sucking sound as Barry felt himself moving forward, bubbles broke the surface and burst and an obnoxious smell filled the air. Barry felt as if he was wading through treacle. As he neared the edge of the bank, the hand dropped the rope and caught hold of Barry's arms. With a stupendous heave, he had him out, floundering on the bank. Barry gasped, trying to see the person who still had a grip on him, but he blended too well into the surroundings.

"What on earth were you doing in there?"

That caught Barry on the raw. "Taking a bath," he retorted, thinking what a darned silly question that was, but the man gave a low laugh. "Well you don't smell very sweet to me. Where are you heading, lad?"

"Err – ." That stumped Barry, and he wondered what to say. He had to think quickly. He could hardly say 'tracking Sue'. She had far too many enemies, and this might be one of them. "I – I lost my path."

"Well I'd gathered that much," the man said. "You're lucky I came this way. But I repeat, where are you going?"

"I don't know." Barry felt foolish. "I was following my friend Thane."

"Thane," said his rescuer thoughtfully. "You mean Thane and White Hawk?"

Barry just nodded.

"Then I should say you were heading towards the village. I shall put you on the path if you promise me not to leave it again."

"Thanks. I'm in your debt," Barry mumbled.

The man, completely shrouded in something dark which disguised him perfectly, drew Barry away from the turbulent river and said casually, "you had a very lucky escape, lad, a little more to your right and the current would have swept you away. On the other hand, a little more to your left and you would have sunk without trace. That is a very infamous bog you have just made contact with. I am surprised Thane never warned you, being as you are a stranger to this land."

How did he know that? Barry felt an icy shiver run through him. The stranger seemed to imply Thane had tried to do away with him. "It was not Thane's fault," he blurted out, "he wasn't to know I'd be stupid enough to go near the bog."

"Be that as it may, here is the path. Keep following it…Blast!" He ended with a muffled oath as something lit up within the folds of his cloak. "I have to go. Someone calls me away," he said.

Barry had no chance to say any more because the figure swung around and vanished from sight. A few seconds later came the sound of a galloping horse.

"At least you could have given me a lift," he shouted after his disappearing rescuer. Then the awful smell about his person rose up and hit him. Who in their right mind would want to give him a lift anywhere? With a shrug he proceeded along the path. It was hard to get along at times because the shrubbery had encroached to the extent of obliterating the pathway. At other times, indentations were filled with muddy water and it was wiser to go round them. But at last he saw the flickering of a fire. When he got near enough, he could see Thane bending over it, cooking something hanging from two stout sticks. Relief surged through him. At his approach, Thane looked up and without any welcome, said,

"Walking by the river wasn't all that quick, was it? I've been waiting for you for ages. What kept you?"

"I fell in." Barry was exhausted and slumped to the ground, holding out his hands to the fire. Then he slowly took his shoes off and tipped out the water. Thane's face creased into a frown. From where he stood, Barry looked dry. He would not have put it past Barry to invent a story to make him feel bad for leaving him behind.

"Then how did you get out?" he asked, a cold edge touching his voice. "I should have thought the current was too strong for you."

"You don't care, do you? Because I'm not Sue," retorted Barry bitterly, looking up. "I called for help, but you didn't come." The censure in his voice was stronger than he realised. Thane could feel his temper rising. "Because I didn't hear you," he snapped, "and had you fallen into the river you would have been swept away. Suppose you tell me the truth."

"I am. I fell into the bog and a man got me out."

"Barry!" Thane was now exasperated. "There are no men along here and you're a fool. I thought you would have had enough sense to see where you were heading. It's well known people have been sucked down into that bog completely."

"You don't have to tell me that," Barry yelled back furiously, "the man has already told me."

"What man? I've had enough." Thane stood over him, his eyes like flints. "If we are going to travel together, I don't want any lies. Just how did you get out of that bog – if indeed you did fall into it in the first place?"

Struggling to his feet, Barry shouted, "I've told you already. I'm not in the habit of lying and I'm not going to start now for your gratification. I was stuck in the mud and the man pulled me out. Then he put me on the path and he rode off."

A pregnant silence fell over them both. Barry slumped back to the ground, having taken all that he could. Thane then smelt the bog odour coming from him. It suddenly occurred to him that he had heard a horse galloping – but he had put it down to someone on the other side of the river. He dropped down beside the boy and touched his shoulder with gentle pressure until he looked up.

"I'm sorry, Barry," he said contritely, "I should not have had a go at you. I'm so worried about your sister, I'm not thinking straight – but that is no excuse for my bad behaviour. Can we start over again? That is – after you've washed, of course."

"Only if you insist." Barry struggled to his feet. Then their eyes met. With a grin, Barry clasped Thane's hand. "You're right. We'll start again."

* * *

By morning there was no sign of last night's storm. An invigorating breeze brought with it the fresh smell of the countryside. Barry poked his head through the opening of a makeshift shelter Thane had constructed. The keen wind soon brushed away all traces of sleep. Because he was inadequately dressed, he did not venture any further. Thane had burnt his clothes last night to get rid of the smell of the bog. He was now wrapped in a blanket. Thane was preparing breakfast, or so he hoped, because the aroma of cooking smelt good. Thane glanced over his shoulder. He sensed Barry watching him, so lifted something from the ground and threw it in his direction.

"Here, take this. I picked them up earlier. They should fit because the lad they came from was about your size. I've also cleaned your shoes. They are here drying. Just a word of warning – don't you dare make a habit of falling in bogs."

Barry clasped the bundle and withdrew inside. Thane had acquired for him a tracker's outfit. The tunic top felt large, but by the time he had tightened the belt and made the jewelled dagger secure, he felt like an inhabitant of Therossa. As he emerged, Thane cast a critical eye over him and nodded in approval.

"That's better. You look more the part now. When we've eaten we shall pick up the horses."

"What horses?" Barry was astonished. He thought they were in the middle of nowhere.

"The ones waiting for us to collect."

"So you've got everything planned." Barry bit his lip. Thane had excluded him again. He eyed him thoughtfully, thinking how aggravating he could be when it suited him. "So where do we find these horses?"

Thane masked his expression again. In spite of his new resolutions, Barry's whole attitude hardened. How long was it going to be before he got treated as an equal? "Of course," he added flippantly, "if it's a secret, just put a blindfold on me when we move off."

Thane counted to ten. "You're getting very touchy, lad. If you knew what was happening, you'd understand."

"Then tell me," Barry exploded. "I want to help. If Sue's in danger I want to know. Don't treat me like a kid. I'm getting fed up with it."

"You're right." Thane sat beside him and took a bite from a dubious looking piece of meat. Barry didn't like to ask what sort of animal it came from because he didn't want to divert Thane's thoughts. He began to think after several minutes had elapsed that Thane had changed his mind. It came as a surprise when he inhaled deeply and said,

"I know you think of Sue as your sister, but she is Queen Ruth's daughter and therefore of royal blood. Amos can get very quick-tempered on this subject, as you have already found out. There's been hostility from one part of our kingdom about our bringing her here. But the Queen wanted her daughter and sent me to your land to fetch her. Now that she has returned for good, that hostility has increased tenfold. The enemies of the state used to have Raithe on their side so they were sitting pretty. They could persuade him to do anything and he was the sole heir to the throne. But now they've lost that luxury because when Sue came along, the twins forged a bond nothing will break. Should anything happen to King Tam, Raithe will be our King. Should anything happen to Raithe," Thane paused, "then the succession will pass to Sue." He had forgotten Barry was listening until the boy nudged him.

"Go on. Tell me something I don't know."

He took a deep breath. "King Tam is missing. He went on a mission and has not been heard of since. The band of men escorting him, my own father is one of them, have all vanished If he is not found in two years, the crown will automatically go to Raithe, his son. Should anything happen to Raithe, the succession, as I have already told you, will fall to Sue."

"Well he'll love being King so there's little chance of that happening," Barry exclaimed.

"This is not a joking matter," Thane said sharply. "Things are serious. Raithe is also missing. He was supposed to be here to meet Sue. This makes her position highly dangerous. She is the last heir. The enemy have only got to capture her, and the Queen will be forced to abdicate. That is what they're hoping for."

"Wait a minute." The jigsaw suddenly fell into place and Barry looked enlightened. "That fiasco you acted out in the boat last night. It was a planned manoeuvre and you threw Neela to the wolves, didn't you?"

"Sometimes such things have to be done." Thane showed no remorse. "We knew someone was giving out information about our movements to the enemy and we had to flush them out. Neela will not be hurt. No one harms an acolyte. Yes, we knew the ambush was going to happen, so I had already made plans to leave the boat and pick up Sue. It was planned that she would be waiting with the horses."

"Well, you really had me worried." Barry scrambled to his feet and wiped his greasy fingers in some grass. "I'll help you break camp. Then we can get going."

But Thane remained motionless and Barry sobered up. He realised something else was amiss. "OK. Tell me the worst."

"Tug, the acolyte escorting her, was attacked by a wild wolf. Someone unknown came along and killed the wolf before it could kill him, but – but that someone made off with Sue."

"Didn't Tug see who it was?"

"Did you see the man who pulled you out of the bog?"

Barry bit his lip. "I never saw his face."

"That's right. Neither did Tug see who took Sue and my horses. Let's hope some more have been left for me so that we can follow the tracks – although, after last night's rain, they may have been washed away."

* * *

"This is useless." Thane stared at the bleak landscape, clenching his fists. His frustration was at breaking point. Why was Lady Luck turning her back on them? From what the Shaman had said earlier, Lex Ansell had already discovered their subterfuge and a full-scale search was now on for Sonja. Everyone had different reasons for finding her first. It was not difficult for Barry to pick up on his mood. He gazed at the surrounding countryside which was bare and austere. Beyond a few groups of deformed trees, whose twisted trunks bent before the prevailing winds, the grasslands went on for miles without a break. Only here and there did one or two barren outcrops raise their heads to the elements. Sue could be anywhere.

Barry was at a loss for words. If there had been any tracks, last night's storm had obliterated them. Even Thane, whose sharp eyes picked up the smallest detail, found nothing to give him a glimmer of hope. Since early morning Thane and Barry had followed a faint trail. It was back-breaking work because they did not dare lift their eyes for one moment. Then suddenly, there were no tracks. There was nothing to explain why they ceased.

"Perhaps they weren't even Sue's tracks," Barry remarked gloomily, "we could have been following a rabbit all this time."

“Then where did the rabbit go?” asked Thane, irritably. “There are no burrows hereabouts.”

“A bird of prey had him for dinner,” Barry suggested.

In spite of the seriousness of their situation, Thane had to laugh. “I’ve got to hand it to you, Barry. When everything looks black, you’re the ideal person to have around. Come on, let’s head for that outcrop.”

They pushed their stallions towards the rocks. The grass sprang up behind them hiding their tracks almost immediately. If they had not been so worried, they would have enjoyed the feel of the wind in their hair.

“You can see for miles up here.” Barry took in a few deep breaths. “I’m going to climb up here for a better view.”

He made to move off his horse when Thane stopped him with a sharp “No!” Noticing the boy’s confusion, he added grimly, “I don’t want anyone to know we’re here. Standing on the top of that rock you would be seen for miles around. Just keep your eyes alert for any movement. When we reach the next rise, the mountains will be in sight. I think that is our best bet, to head in that direction.”

They picked their way through the waving grass. In parts it was high enough to reach the horses’ knees. At the top of the rise, the mountains loomed before them in all their glory. Seemingly they stretched for miles. For a moment they just stared, and then they noticed that between them and the foot of the mountains, there was a movement of some kind. Thane swore under his breath. Quickly they dismounted and pulled the horses out of sight. Then on hands and knees, they crept forward to peer through the grass. The wind blowing in their direction brought with it a foul smell. Occasionally a guttural voice could be heard and a whiff of smoke assailed their nostrils.

"Gypsies," growled Thane. "What rotten luck. Let's hope they didn't see us. We're stuck here until they move on."

"How long might that be?" Barry asked. "Couldn't we gallop past them? Our horses are fast."

"Two of us against a horde of Gypsies is best forgotten. They would overpower us in no time. No, son, we have to stay put. Let's try and have a bite while we're waiting. It could be a long time."

They slid down on their side of the rise to where the horses were cropping the grass. Barry stared back morosely in the direction from which they had just come. He tried to work out where they had walked through the long grass, but it had closed over their tracks leaving no visible sign to say they had come from that direction. Then his eyes opened wide. The grass was moving. Something or someone was making its way towards them. He turned to draw Thane's attention to it when, with raucous yells, three men burst over the ridge, brandishing knives.

The horses quickly shied away at their approach. On seeing Thane and Barry, the Gypsies halted. It allowed Thane time to draw his knife and Barry his dagger, and the Gypsies' eyes flashed with scorn. Their mouths stretched into evil grins. They saw just a boy and a man. It would be a bonus to capture them as well as the horses. There was no love lost between them and they had the advantage of surprise. But they hadn't reckoned on Thane's lithe movements. As they lunged at their victims,

Thane's blade cut deeply into someone's shoulder and Barry's dagger caught another Gypsy in the arm. Before any more damage could be done, Thane suffered a stunning blow to the back of his head, which sent him reeling to the ground.

Barry suddenly realised what a perilous position he was now in; then he heard a ferocious snarl. A whirlwind of white leapt past him going directly for the throat of the third Gypsy. With a shriek, the man fell backwards. One of the other Gypsies was turning to help him with a long curved blade in his hand, when an arrow pierced his chest. Amazement crossed his coarse features and he slid silently to the ground.

The screams from White Hawk's first victim ceased. With a snarl, the wolf turned to his next adversary. This man's eyes bulged in terror seeing the wolf tense up to spring. As the Gypsy raised his arm to throw his knife, a second arrow struck him in the throat. He made a terrible gurgling sound and fell to the ground.

Now that all three attackers were lifeless, Barry's whole body went rigid. He had never faced so much death before. At any moment he expected to feel another arrow pierce his body. He couldn't move.

"That was exhilarating. Are there any more?" The inquiring voice came from behind him. Barry turned slowly to eye the lad who stood there, a cocky grin on his face. He could not have been any older than Barry, but the boy recognised him. He was the renegade soldier called Zeno to whom Tansy had spoken when they escaped from the Drazuzi. Barry expected to see Lex Ansell and his men behind him, but the lad was alone. There was nothing to be seen except miles of grass.

"How the Devil did you get here?" Barry's voice was incredulous.

"I followed White Hawk," was the unexpected answer. "I knew the wolf would lead me to Thane eventually."

"Why did you want to find Thane?" Barry was at a loss." We're not even on the same side."

"Well I couldn't very well stand by and watch you get killed." Zeno looked put out, but then added resignedly, "I'm just obeying orders. I was told to watch Thane and see what he did, then report back."

That disgusted Barry. His attitude hardened. "So you're spying for Ansell."

"I suppose I am," he replied, but before Barry could cut in, he asked, "What are you doing out here in the wilds?"

Barry ignored that. "You're the one out in the wilds on your own, and without a horse. How daft can you get? Is Ansell trying to get rid of you?"

For the first time Zeno felt at a disadvantage. Alarm filled his youthful eyes when he realised his situation was not exactly good. He looked back at Thane's body on the ground and said as though inspired, "I've just saved your life."

"White Hawk had already done that," Barry returned sharply.

"But you're as good as on your own. He's not much use to you."

Barry glanced at Thane. "He'll come round soon. He was knocked out. So." He looked back at Zeno. "What are you going to do now?"

“I’ll leave you.” Zeno adjusted his bow over his shoulder. “Can you give me some food before I start off?”

“On foot?” asked Barry sarcastically. “Are you mad?”

At that moment Thane groaned and the two lads went up to him. Thane sat up, holding his head and wincing. His eyes took in the carnage around him and at last settled on the renegade. To Barry’s surprise, instead of rejecting the young soldier, he greeted him cordially.

“Thanks for your timely help, Zeno. When Barry’s finished cross-examining you, I think we had better rethink our plans.”

“But, Thane,” Barry objected, “he’s come here to spy on us.”

“Well he’s not going anywhere. He’s our prisoner and can be of some help to us.”

CHAPTER 10
ZENO

The three of them ate a cold meal, not wishing to risk lighting a fire. Thane was restless. For their own good he decided to inspect the Gypsy camp and made it perfectly clear to the two boys he wished to be alone. Barry and Zeno were left weighing each other up. Neither of them spoke until Thane was out of sight. It became apparent to Barry, who surreptitiously observed the newcomer, that Zeno was not a true soldier.

Zeno had no hang-ups about speaking of his life. It was a change for Barry to find someone so open and uncomplicated. Barry soon learnt more about him than Zeno ever learnt about Barry. Zeno had been driven from his mother's farm by a brutal stepfather who could not tolerate having him about the place. He was happy to leave, but unused to the ways of city life, and soon found himself in bad company. This was when he joined Lex Ansell's army. The lure of becoming a renegade had exciting expectations and he was happy with his lot.

However, it did not take long for the glamour to wear off. It was not the army he expected. The men were slapdash and loutish, and their values did not rise very high. His efforts to keep himself smart caused conflict amongst his fellow men. All of them vied for their leader's favours and took a dim view of Zeno being selected as officer material. He became the butt of all their ill humour. So he was given this assignment of following Thane. It did not take a lot of working out on his part to realise his fellow soldiers were trying to get rid of him. For his own personal esteem, he pretended this journey was of vital importance. The only reason he kept following the wolf was to kid himself no one else had the brains to do it. And so Zeno went on and on and Barry yawned. He jerked upright, realising that drowsiness was about to take over.

"Then why don't you join the proper army?" Thane had walked up on them, unnoticed. "They could do with you." He dumped a few blankets on the ground, and then turned his grave face to the two boys. "We've got to get moving. The Gypsies who attacked us were a reconnaissance group and will be missed when they don't return to their camp. We've now got extra blankets and a few more horses tethered up yonder. It will be good to have spare mounts. Zeno will want one and we shall definitely need another for Sue."

At the mention of Sue, Zeno immediately stopped what he was doing and frowned. "This Sue you mentioned. I have seen her before." He stared pointedly at Barry. "She was with you when we pulled you out of the ground. She is Sonja, isn't she?" The last statement was a shot in the dark.

"Do you want to make something of it?" Thane asked evenly, and Zeno flushed. "I want to help you."

"Look, son." Thane stared at him hard. "You can leave now if you want to and report back to Ansell and say you found me. One good turn deserves another as they say. You saved our lives with your timely appearance, so I will reciprocate and send you back to him – with a horse.

That is if you want to. You do know where he is, I take it."

Barry watched Zeno's face turn from red to white alternately. His whole demeanour gave the impression he had been insulted. Tilting his chin, he stared at Thane and retorted stiffly, "If that is your order, sir, then I'll go back to him, but I would much rather stay and help you."

Thane's expression remained grim. "Do I understand you want to change sides? Ansell will take a very dim view of that."

"He misled me at the beginning," retorted Zeno, "and I took a dim view of that."

When Thane next spoke his voice was ominous. "Understand this and understand it well. If you stay with us, there will be no going back. Any sign of subterfuge on your part and you're a dead man. I shall expect complete co-operation from you at all times. Well, lad – what's it to be?"

Far from being afraid, Zeno was jubilant. He almost grabbed hold of the older man but restrained himself in time and stood stiffly to attention. "Thank you, sir. I shall never let you down."

"See that you don't." Thane turned to Barry. "Now you get the saddles on these horses and Zeno and I will bring the others back here. I want to be gone from this spot and to reach the mountains by tonight."

Barry turned away before anyone saw his smile. For some reason he was pleased Zeno wanted to come along. They were about the same age, and these days Thane was always preoccupied. It gave him someone else to talk to. It was going to be great to have a mate.

* * *

The distance to the mountains was deceptive. They had been trekking for hours through a sea of grass and listening to the never-ending buzz of insects. Thane wanted to reach shelter before nightfall, but it had crept up on them surreptitiously.

Already, the nearly full moon was above them and they still had three or four miles to travel. Its light over the undulating plains made everything look ghostly. It was a bonus to the travellers to see where they were going, but it was also a disadvantage. Anyone looking for them would have no difficulty seeing where they were.

The buzz of insects had given way to the howling of wild wolves. The sound of their cries sent shivers up Barry's spine. He was pleased White Hawk was with them and he noticed how the wolf's ears twitched and his body tensed. White Hawk was on guard.

Suddenly something very large passed over their heads, momentarily blotting out the moon. It circled round them once before moving on. It was too large to be a bird and drew no interest from either Thane or Zeno. But excitement stirred within Barry who had such a lot to learn in this strange land. He wanted to ask what it was, but didn't want Zeno to think he was ignorant. He looked up when he felt Zeno's eyes trained in his direction and was sure the boy was secretly laughing at him.

"Have I got a smut on my nose?" he asked irritably, realising Thane was getting further ahead while he was lagging behind and gawking. Zeno moved his horse alongside.

"Where do you come from, Barry?" He couldn't hide his curiosity. "You have a strange name, speak strange words and seem to know so much about Sonja."

"I – " began Barry, when Thane looked over his shoulder. "Keep up, you two, or I'll leave you behind." His tone seemed unnecessarily curt, almost as though he was annoyed at their speaking together. Zeno quickly touched his lips in a warning gesture to Barry.

"Sound carries at night," he hissed, "the Gypsies may be following us."

Barry conceded to the wisdom of that remark and caught up with Thane. Beyond a grunt of approval, Thane never spoke again until they reached another rise in the grass. He stared around.

"We need a place to stop where the stallions can be hidden out of sight. There are often unexpected pockets in the ground where we can shelter in safety and not be seen. Zeno, you search that way and I'll go the other."

"What about me?" Barry was indignant at being left out. "What shall I do?"

"Stay and look after the horse."

"Right, sir." Zeno went off without a word. Once he was out of earshot, Thane turned angrily on Barry. "I would rather you didn't mention anything about where you come from or about your sister. That understood?" His words were snapped out, and Barry's jaw dropped. He couldn't stop himself from saying,

"Why – don't you trust Zeno?"

"Trust has nothing to do with it. He has to prove himself first." Upon which Thane swung his horse away and moved along the ridge. Barry was confused, and tried to make allowances for his attitude. He looked towards

Zeno who was doing exactly what he had been told, looking diligently for a pocket in the hills. Barry was tempted to poke around himself. It was boring just to stand here. He scanned the horizon for the want of something better to do and suddenly felt the hairs stand up on his neck. Even at this distance he could see something moving. There were several things, in fact. He wondered what they could be, and if they would hear him if he called out to Thane, especially since Zeno had said something about sound travelling at night. They might be the enemy and Thane was unaware of their being near.

Hearing a soft whine at his feet made him to glance down. White Hawk stared back, his golden eyes fixed intently on his face, almost as though he knew what was going on. Barry solved his dilemma by pointing towards Thane and hissing,

"Fetch him, boy," and had the surprise of his life when the wolf bounded off and with unerring precision nearly tripped up the horse Thane was riding. He cringed as Thane's oath reached his ears. Thane raised angry eyes in Barry's direction and the boy wondered why Thane always looked at him in that way when trouble was afoot. Swallowing his ire, he pointed towards the horizon. Thane followed his finger and stood rooted to the spot. He stared for a long time, trying to focus. The moon played strange tricks. One minute they could be seen, the next it had all faded away. Thane came back to Barry.

"That was good observation on your part, son. You handled the situation well."

"Zeno would have done the same had he seen them." Barry couldn't resist the dig.

"We'll never know, will we?" Thane retorted, ignoring it. "I can't quite make out what it is out there. It looks like rider-less horses – but that's impossible. Rider-less horses would be prey for anything out here in the wilds."

"Maybe someone is leading them," Barry suggested hopefully.

"It's still not a place for horses."

"Gypsies perhaps," he suggested.

Thane shook his head and squinted, still staring and trying to comprehend what he was seeing. He attracted Zeno who returned at once, hardly making a sound. He also followed the direction of Thane's finger and surveyed the moving spectacle for a while. He said casually, "I can see someone is riding the first horse."

"I can't see anyone," Barry said.

Zeno narrowed his eyes. "Whoever it is, is very small," he murmured, "looks like a child to me."

"Child?" Thane's voice rang with suppressed excitement. "Of course it is. Why didn't I think of it before? This would be the correct area." Then the light left his eyes and he sobered up. "But it can't be. The horses would not have been out in the open."

Barry and Zeno looked bewildered, and Barry said with a spark of determination, "I suppose it would be too much on my part to expect you to elucidate."

Thane showed no signs of having heard him – instead, a glow of animation lit up his face. He felt in his pocket and withdrew a tiny whistle. Raising it to his lips he blew, his companions heard nothing yet on the far horizon there was a sudden disturbance. The watchers clearly saw the line of horses break up. Someone was trying to check them, but one got away. The confusion was brought under control immediately. As the tiny speck of the runaway horse grew bigger, something large appeared in the clear sky, and zoomed unerringly towards it. The two lads went cold. This newcomer was five times the size of the horse. As it drew nearer, they saw its huge talons and were mesmerised by its enormous wingspan. The horse didn't stand a chance against so huge a monster.

Thane's eyes remained inscrutable; the whistle was still at his lips. The watching wolf set off in a flash to meet the unfortunate horse. Barry noticed Thane was blowing hard on the whistle and the horse suddenly fell. White Hawk howled and leapt into the air just as the monster's talons raked above the fallen stallion. The huge beast circled round it menacingly, raising a cloud of dust, then flew off into the night sky. The wolf howled after it, and Barry started to breathe again. The unharmed horse scrambled to its feet and with White Hawk beside it, cantered towards Thane. At close quarters Barry recognised Saturn.

"How did you know?" he asked.

Thane slid off the mount he was riding and gave his own horse an affectionate hug. With a soft whinny, Saturn blew on his face.

"Because of what Zeno said – about the child. I now know where Sue is. Whoever abducted her, took Saturn."

"You're joking." Zeno looked as though he was trying to steady his nerves. "The Princess would never come to this place. Only the snake people live out here."

"That's right," Thane grinned, "and that's where we are going – to visit them."

"You're mad. Count me out. I'm not going with you." Zeno made to move off but in one fluid movement

Thane had an arrow pointing to his heart. "One more step and you'll die," he said.

Zeno paused, trying to control his fear. "Alright, I've got no choice. You're in charge. But I'm still young and those women spell death to me. I don't want to die at their hands, I would much rather you shoot me."

Thane's eyebrows rose. "Don't be an idiot, lad. I'm not going to waste an arrow on you. Someone's got to stay outside and look after our horses. It might just as well be you because I know Barry won't be stopped from going in." He glanced obscurely at the boy who was wondering what he had let himself in for.

CHAPTER 11
THE CEREMONY

Sue was unaware how beautiful she looked in the gown they had dressed her in. It shimmered like gold dust and looked lustrous in the diffused light. Thin glittering straps held it over her shoulders. It fell to the ground looking like gossamer, its flimsy folds spread around her as she walked and gave the impression she was floating. Her entourage of girls propelled her along to the room she had first been brought to by the hooded man. She wondered how she could have missed seeing the little door tucked low in the cave wall. The girls paused beside it. They were concerned. So was Sue, but she was unable to speak. They expected her to go through it. The drug given to her had not diminished her mind. Her thinking powers were razor-sharp, but its effect took away all the control over her body. She was like putty in the girls' hands and could only move her limbs at the command of Deena. At least she could feel, but to speak would have been a bonus. She wondered what manner of drug they had given her, and why they felt they had to? They knew she couldn't escape.

Deena no longer spoke in a language she understood. Her voice was sharp and imperious. Never once did she touch Sue, but directed the girls as to what she wanted done, and while they used their superhuman strength, Sue was helpless to fend them off. The old lady watched them critically. With no bother, they had Sue on her knees in no time. The first three went through the door, and the others remained outside. They pulled her through from the front and shoved her from behind, and Sue felt like a sack of potatoes.

The task was accomplished with ease. She wondered if this was going to be her position for the length of the time the ceremony lasted. Once through the door though, she could see the ceiling was surprisingly high and the girls helped her to stand upright again. Deena walked past them majestically. Without looking at Sue, she ordered them to bring her to the temple.

This time Sue understood her words and dumbly watched as Deena vanished down the passageway in which she was now standing. The air smelt musty and the humidity was overpowering. In spite of the flimsy gown, perspiration ran down her back. There was nothing to show where the heat came from.

The girls gave her no time to take in her surroundings, but led the way down some steps and along a damp gloomy tunnel. Here the walls glistened with moisture. Hundreds of snakes slithered along the ground, perilously near her feet. If Sue had had her way, she would have screamed. But that was denied her. She didn't have the power to close her eyes either.

Step by step they proceeded along the rocky floor. Her ragged nerves calmed down a fraction when she realised the snakes did not divert from their course. There was little fear of her accidentally treading on them with her almost bare feet. The heat increased as they moved along. In the distance there was a dull red light.

It looked ominous because it flickered. By the time it was reached, her hair was plastered to her scalp and moisture covered all her exposed skin. She was completely unprepared for the bizarre sight before her. A smoke-filled underground temple, filled to capacity with hundreds of people. In the light thrown by flaring torches she could see several men, who were standing round the sides of the temple like guards, holding long thin spears.

Sue's eyes pierced the smoky atmosphere to take in the many rows of fluted pillars which arched towards the roof and were lost in the shadows. Each and every one was outlined by a red glow, which came from the fire roaring in the central pit. The flames licked greedily at what little air there was. Round the edge of the pit, a circle of rocks enclosed the furnace, and a ring of shallow water encircled these rocks. The water seemed to be moving, but a closer inspection revealed that what appeared to be water was a heaving mass of entwined snakes.

Her entrance caused all heads to turn in her direction. A murmur of appreciation came from their lips and a low chant filled the air; 'Sonja. Sonja. Sonja.' Sue wanted to gag when she saw they had live snakes in their hair. Outwardly, the impression she gave was of tranquillity. Inwardly, her stomach churned with terror, not knowing what they intended to do to her at this ceremony. A drumbeat vibrated through the air, filling the temple with noise.

It was the start of something because all eyes switched to the fire. It was only the power of the drug which kept Sue standing as the figure of Deena stepped from the flames, her red gown glowing as brightly as the fire. She seemed to be a part of it. Everyone, plus the girls beside her, fell to the ground in an act of homage. All Sue wanted to do was faint but the drug would not even allow her that refuge.

As the girls fell to the ground, so four dwarf-like men came and stood on either side of her. They did not share in the worship of the old woman. While Deena intoned to the crowd, two of them caught her arms and marched her forward to the very edge of the snake pit. Only then did the old lady leave the fire and step amongst the reptiles.

As though at random she bent, picked one up and held it aloft, where angrily it squirmed and wriggled, trying to escape. Sue was suffocating in the heat. Her body felt as though it was running with water. She was trying to tell everyone she hated snakes, but she couldn't make a sound and no movement passed across her impassive face. Deena shouted out something else to the crowd and a roar greeted her words. With unhurried actions she placed the reptile over Sue's shoulders. The snake thrashed in fury. The feel of its skin against her neck was repulsive. Her blood turned cold.

A second drumbeat vibrated round the temple and the old lady shouted out in an unemotional voice for the victims' benefit, "We now make her one of us."

A great cheer came from the crowd. One of the men caught the writhing snake behind its head and held it to Sue's arm. It hissed, its tongue flicked in and out. An incredible pain told Sue it had punctured her skin. The man threw the snake back into the pit and Sue felt the venom creeping down her arm and up to her shoulders. It was not only heat now that made her perspire. She thought she was dying. The women, young and old standing behind her, were rejoicing and chanting the same word all over again; 'Sonja. Sonja. Sonja'. The men lifted Deena from the snake pit, and from her gown she produced a small phial. She nodded to the men, who pushed Sue to the ground and held her down while Deena forced open her mouth and poured the liquid in.

This can't get any worse, Sue thought, unable to choke. Her mind was agonising at what was being done to her as the old lady chanted over her body. For the third time there came a drum beat and Deena lifted her arms yet again, and shouted, "Sonja is now one of us."

Sue's first thought was, *Thank goodness I'm still alive* and then she thought, *Thank goodness it is all over*, but in that she was wrong. The four little men with their amazing strength scooped Sue up from the ground and her worst nightmare came to life. They threw her bodily amongst the heaving reptiles. She lay where she fell. *Please let me die*. The thought was in her mind, as the snakes, annoyed at the obstruction in their path, slithered all over her, some even tasting her skin with their forked tongues. She knew she would never forget this experience, it would be with her for what life she had left, and that might not be for long. Death was hovering around her and she hoped it would come quickly.

The ceremony went on while they left her lying there. The chanting filled her ears. Then the men leapt into the pit and lifted her out. It was only then she realised nothing had bitten her. As she stood swaying on firm ground, supported by two men, the girls came up and rearranged her gown, then backed away. The men held out her two arms and Deena approached carrying a sharp instrument and small bottle, which she held up for all to see. Her voice rang out round the temple.

"We shall mark her with the serpent."

"Over my dead body," cut in a grim voice. "The Princess Sonja must not be marked. Now or ever." The words fell upon the congregation, bringing instant silence. The old lady looked towards the entrance of the temple and saw two men. Sue looked as well, and although inside she was deliriously happy, she showed no emotion. She watched Thane and Barry advance.

* * *

The torches spluttered as the draught of air circulated around the underground temple. The smell of smoke and so many bodies packed together in the enclosed space assailed the nostrils of the two newcomers. The silence, which had fallen at their entrance, now turned to hostility. All adulation ceased. Unfriendly eyes embraced their advance. The few men bunched together in front of the old lady and Sue, looking fiercely protective of their ruler. Although hardly half the size of the intruders, they showed they were a foe to be reckoned with. They stood aggressively, spears raised and pointing at them. Only a foolhardy person would try to push through them.

It was at this point Barry realised the gloomy place was inhabited by women of all ages. When he caught sight of the snakes writhing through their hair, he recoiled in horror and stopped in his tracks. Immediately he knew why Zeno had no wish to enter this place and sympathised with him. He was feeling extremely queasy himself. From out the corner of his mouth, Thane growled, "Keep on walking, lad," while his own eyes remained fixed firmly on Sue and the proud old woman.

Thane had heard of this place before and knew his being here meant his life was in danger. He had interrupted a ceremony, a special one, whereby they initiated women with the snakes. Whatever this entailed, it made them immune from any snakebite. Bile was at the back of his throat, especially when he noticed how Sue was dressed. He knew immediately she was part of this ceremony they were conducting. He hoped fervently they had not harmed her and they were not too late. Studying her face, he saw the plea for help in her eyes, which smote him hard. The King himself had told him of the diabolical drug they used to overcome willpower. With what was happening and the heat from the fire, sweat coursed freely down his body.

"Come no further, young man," Deena warned, "you trespass on forbidden ground. How you got in is of no consequence now, but you are not welcome." She drew herself up arrogantly, her dark eyes flashing with animosity. She made no attempt to move backwards. With the flames roaring behind her, she looked like an apparition from hell. "If you value your lives – leave at once. We are honouring Sonja in our own special ceremony at which only women are allowed to be present."

"You must be joking, they're not women," Barry shouted before Thane could stop him. The boy glared at the little men as they raised their spears and pointed them in his direction, waiting for the order to lunge. He looked directly at his sister, not registering how beautiful she looked, which on any other occasion would have made Thane smile and say, "Is this a fancy dress party?"

The old woman accorded Barry a contemptuous glance, letting him know she thought he was beneath her and not worthy of any answer. Then her eyes flicked back to Thane who was the true adversary. He watched her objectively, masking his face so that it was devoid of expression. He fought to keep his temper under control.

"You were not honouring Sonja," he said bitterly. "You were about to mark her skin for life. No one – I repeat, no one – marks Sonja, not even you."

Deena's face hardened, showing her displeasure. Ignoring the heat pulsating behind her, she asked disdainfully, "Who are you to say what Sonja can or cannot do? Do you see the Princess objecting?"

Thane swallowed his gall with an effort, itching to grab the old woman and throw her aside. It took all his willpower to remain calm. He knew the tips of those spears held by the men were lethal. They were smeared with venom from the snakes. One scratch on the skin and he would be dead.

"She's not likely to object all the time she's drugged," he answered angrily. "Look at her! She hasn't got the power to do anything. You're a fool if you think she is enjoying this ordeal. The Queen will take a very dim view of what's happening to her daughter."

His words were ignored. Deena issued a sharp order. There was no remorse in her for what she had done. And she didn't care what the Queen thought. She had been protecting the Princess's own interests. She was not going to allow these men to dictate to her. One of the dwarf men leant over the pit, and selected a snake at random. It hissed in anger, squirming and thrashing around. Its tongue flicked in and out and its red eyes gleamed balefully at everyone. Repulsion surged through Barry. He wished he were outside with Zeno.

Before his horrified eyes, the snake was placed around Sue's shoulders where it coiled up round her neck for leverage. She did not move or flinch away. Only her eyes showed her horror at its presence.

Thane's sinews tightened. He was helpless to do anything. Then it occurred to him that Barry might become hot-headed. His hand clamped warningly on the boy's arm to stop him from doing anything unwise. The old woman was playing a cat-and-mouse game with them. She wanted them to do something stupid so that she could order their destruction. Barry was astute enough to read the situation for himself, but all the same, his expression was pleading as he looked towards Thane. The older man gave him a tight smile and lifted his chin arrogantly.

"I am here on the Queen's business. We have come to collect the Princess, and, if you don't mind, without the snake."

"The Princess Sonja was put in my care by the Master." Now Deena's voice was dictatorial and she hid her chagrin that they had not fallen into the trap. "How do I know you are a delegate from the Queen of our land?"

Thane slowly withdrew his horn, looked to see if she was going to object, then deliberately blew on it. The gathering of women had not moved an inch during this discourse, but seconds after the sound of the horn vibrated round the temple, there were screams from the spectators. An enormous white wolf was suddenly in their midst. It towered above their heads. To them it was the size of a horse and it padded down the stone aisle to be with its master. Light from the torches reflected in its eyes and they shone like red beacons. White Hawk stopped at Thane's side, staring balefully at the old woman, and the little men – who could not decide whether to stay put or beat a hasty retreat. The wolf's upper lip twitched as if to snarl, and he bared his teeth. Then his eyes fixed on Sue and a curious whine escaped from his throat.

Sue had been standing transfixed all this time. Suddenly she felt strange stirrings in her blood and her muscles started to relax in her throat. The drug was beginning to wear off. A tingling sensation spread through her body and movement came back to her limbs. With a supreme effort she lifted her arms and grabbed the reptile from round her neck. She threw it towards the pit where it rejoined its companions.

"White Hawk," her voice croaked, as she tried to make contact with the wolf. He padded closer and sniffed her. The men hastily moved back a pace, looking towards Deena, but Sue's arms had already encircled White Hawk's neck and tears of joy poured from her eyes. Then she raised them to Thane and her brother, but they dared not make a move towards her yet. For the moment, Deena still had the upper hand.

The old lady begrudgingly turned to the assembly of women and raised her arms. "Peace go with you, ladies," she called. "The ceremony for today is over. Please return to your work." Then she motioned to Sue, looking askance at the wolf. "Come with me, Sonja. You will need clothes if you are leaving with your mother's delegate." Her enigmatic eyes rested on Thane. "You can leave by the way you came in – but wait outside for the

Princess. The Master will hear of this." She glanced distastefully at the wolf. "Take that animal with you, please."

Thane kept his jubilation under control with difficulty and remarked pleasantly, "I can't. He is Sonja's guard. You can tell that to the Master as well. Just mention White Hawk when you see him?"

* * *

"Are you ready to leave, Sonja?" It was more a demand than a question. The old lady, attired once again in her silver dress, stood watching from the entrance to the cave. Sue was still standing by what had been her bed. The acolyte clothing had vanished and in its place were furry leggings and a parka-type coat of the same material. White Hawk was sitting nearby, watching carefully as people walked by. He had no intention of moving from Sue's side, and Deena, feeling irritable, kept her distance. She had no love for the wolf. His size was off-putting.

"I shall miss having you here." Her gravel voice was low. "You look every inch a Princess, my child."

Sue flushed. In spite of what had happened, she had been well looked after. This remarkable old lady, whose age would always be an unsolved mystery, deliberated before saying her next words. She had no regrets at having initiated Sue into the Sacred Order of Serpents. Her own intuition told her that one day it would save her life. Maybe the timely intervention of Thane had been a good thing. No one would ever know her power now. She had not been marked to give it away.

"I have a gift for you, Sonja." Deena still did not enter, but held out in her hand a smallish package with scuffed corners, but otherwise well wrapped. Sue walked towards her with White Hawk shadowing her steps. She stared at the strange object. "Do not open it now," Deena said, making it sound like a warning. She stared deeply into her eyes. "One day," her rough voice continued, "you are going to be faced with death. That is the time when you will open it. Hide it now within the folds of your clothes and tell no-one it is there."

Sue shivered at the intensity of the words, but she placed it deep within a pocket and strangely forgot all about it. The old lady sighed in relief. Her voice returned to normal. "Before you leave, Sonja, someone waits for you in the large cave."

Sue's face lit up, anticipating Thane. With a radiant smile she shot out of the cave and down the tunnel, accompanied by White Hawk who paced her step for step. Bursting into the large cave with a welcoming cry on her lips, she pulled up short. Some of the pleasure left her when she saw the tall, cowled figure of a man. Deena followed her in, but stood well back.

He came towards her, swathed in his dark cloak, and just for one fleeting moment, Sue wished the hood would fall back and expose his face. Seeing him in the dark had not worried her, but in daylight it was off-putting to stare into shadows, and see nothing. White Hawk, however, had no such compunction. He left her, and squatted on his hindquarters at the man's feet. The man bent and ruffled the wolf's shaggy fur before he looked appreciatively at the way Sue was dressed.

"I see you are ready to leave, Sonja," he said. "Has Deena treated you well?"

Sue quickly composed herself, not realising how expressive her eyes were. She looked at Deena's enigmatic face behind her and said carefully, "It has certainly been an experience I shall never forget, staying here."

Although the man's eyes were hidden, she sensed he was studying her intently, and knew he was not completely happy with her answer. He paused before he said, "I blame myself for not coming back sooner. You must be missing your friends. Many things have needed my attention, but now I see I can cross you off my list. Thane has come to collect you. You will be safe by his side."

"You've seen him?" Sue did not realise how much she gave away when her whole face lit up at the mention of Thane. The man laughed softly.

"Well not exactly to speak to. I would rather he did not see me at this moment."

"Why?"

"He is not alone and my conversation with him would be private."

Sue frowned. "Then how did you get past Thane and Barry without being seen?"

Her companion lifted his hand, not bothering to hide the encircling snakes, and touched her forehead. He pressed away the lines with his fingers and his touch sent strange tremors through her body. "One day I shall tell you, but this isn't the time. I want you to promise me something instead, Sonja, otherwise I shall think twice about letting you go." Sue looked at him expectantly and heard his quick intake of breath as he said, “Tell Thane about the power of the ring you wear. It will help you in your quest to find your brother. I’m taking it that you’ve not used it since I was last with you?”

“I haven’t. I’ve been too scared.”

The man moved abruptly, whether by annoyance or concern, she had no idea. “I’m sorry that I frightened you with what I said. That was not my intention. Has the ring been trying to make you aware of it?”

Sue nodded dumbly, feeling miserable that Raithe had tried to make contact with her and she had ignored him. The man sighed, and he placed an arm round her shoulders. “Do not blame yourself. I’m sure when you tell Thane about it, everything, between you both you will work out. Go now, Sonja, with my blessing. I shall never be that far away from you.” He lifted her hand, and much to her discomfiture, kissed her lightly on the fingers. She made to pull her hand away, but he retained it with gentle pressure. “Just one last thing before you leave. Please don’t mention my being here when you join the others.”

He dropped her hand and she knew she was dismissed as he turned away in a billowing cloud of black material. Deena beckoned from the entrance to lead her outside. All she said was, “Thank you,” and without asking, Sue knew she was referring to her silence about the snake ceremony.

CHAPTER 12
THE LAKE

By the time the group had reached the lake it was late afternoon. They had spent a tedious few hours of travelling by hugging the mountains, but knowing at the same time they had to cross them to reach Therossa city. Sue was beginning to wonder when they would start to deviate. It wouldn't be long before the sun started to set over the vast expanse of water. Red reflections from the sky spread over the surface as far as the eye could see. The sight was breath-taking.

The four travellers slid from their horses to give their legs a stretch and, at the same time, allow the hard-working animals a brief respite. The water ahead had successfully checked their journey going onwards, so Sue looked to her left where the lake lapped against the mountains. The sheer rock face vanished beneath the murky water but also reared up to the sky starkly and inaccessible to climb, presenting a complete dead end. In the other direction, there was nothing to see.

The lake went on forever. It could easily be mistaken for a sea. Behind them, the way they had travelled, was desolate. The rolling grasslands had petered out long ago to give way to rough tundra over which the wind gusted with extraordinary ferocity.

Light was diminishing, and shadowy forms of different sizes hovered just beyond where they stood. Their intent left little to the imagination. Until this moment, Sue had not bothered about their presence. She thought the horses could outrun any predator, but now, seeing the way ahead was cut off, she became nervous. Even the stallions showed signs of unease. If only White Hawk had not abandoned them when they left the caves she would have felt safe.

Thane showed no outward sign of worry, so she tried to emulate him. But Barry was acutely aware of her anxiety and kept a close watch. From a distance, so did Zeno. Ever since Sonja joined them, he had lost his ability to speak freely. Something about her clove his tongue to the roof of his mouth and he acted like an immature youth, but all the time he desperately looked for an opportunity to help her. It stemmed from his upbringing. He had never spoken to royalty before.

Barry's light-hearted approach to her made him envious. Because of Thane, he did not realise the connection between them. Zeno was also having difficulty with the spare mount attached to a long rein. It was skittish and unpredictable and he had been pleased when the other Gypsy horse bolted earlier on. Coming from the Gypsy, it had not been so well trained as the others. He stared obliquely at Barry, who stood staring across the darkening water, then suddenly turned and fixed his eyes on Thane who was apparently lost in thought. He asked gruffly if horses could swim.

Thane grunted at what he thought was a frivolous question. Only Barry would ask a question like that. "They would – without us on their backs," he replied, "but I am not intending to get wet." He turned to chivvy up the others. "We can't stay here. It's not safe. We must find shelter before it gets too dark."Barry looked askance at the formidable rock face now tinged with red, and then behind them at the barren landscape. "Have you somewhere in mind?"

"Why is it I don't trust you when you come out with remarks like that," muttered Thane.

"Well you shouldn't ask silly questions. Why don't you look towards the right?" Barry retorted.

All eyes immediately switched along the edge of the water, following its line as far as they could see. Wisps of smoke made a hazy smudge on the evening sky. It wasn't necessary to comment; they all knew what faced them in that direction. Thane's 'Damn' was louder than he intended. Predators started to howl and screech in an unmusical chorus.

"Are we trapped?" Sue's voice was nervous.

Thane glanced at her because he knew she was frightened and he tried to give her some reassurance. "Not really. It's just bad luck that the Gypsies are there. It's a waterhole so we must expect them. All animals use it. I had intended walking round the lake, but it's out of the question now." He paused, turning to the young soldier. "Do you happen to know your way across the water?"

Being singled out made Zeno feel conspicuous, and he stammered. "Y - yes, sir."

"Well that's good to know. How many times have you crossed?"

"About f – four I think, sir."

"Excuse me for butting in, but we haven't got a boat," Barry interrupted.

"I'm glad you noticed." Thane was sarcastic, but he concentrated on Zeno. "For God's sake stop calling me 'sir' every time I speak to you. This is not the army. We are supposed to be friends. Try being a bit more like Barry – well – within moderation," he added hastily, seeing that boy grin. "Now I'm being serious. We are going over the water while we've got a chance. I'm going to lead Sue, and you, lad, will look after Barry. Can you manage that?"

While Barry was still trying to work out how they could cross a lake without a boat, Zeno was having troubles of his own. "I can," he answered, "but what about this horse?" Zeno flushed because he was now the centre of attention. He thought Sue was looking at him, and at times like this he wished he could sink through the ground.

The Gypsy horse now in question pawed the earth. His ears were flattened against his head and his eyes rolled, showing the whites. He was definitely going to be a liability when crossing the water. Thane assessed him. Zeno would need all his time to help Barry. He chewed thoughtfully on his lower lip, hating to make the decision, which was being forced on him. After a few minutes he said flatly, "There is nothing for it. We'll have to let him go."

"You can't!" Zeno looked appalled. His eyes strayed to the shadowy creatures edging nearer. "He's only one horse. Directly he's left on his own they'll kill him."

"And if we take him with us he'll have us in the water," Thane snapped angrily. "We've got to be practical."

"But we can ..." Zeno began, and Thane cut him short.

"There is no other choice." Barry was bewildered. "Why can't he swim? What's the problem?"

He received a glare for interrupting, but Zeno took his chance and said, "No one is swimming. There is a submerged pathway going through the lake known only to a few. It leads to a cave and a tunnel through those mountains. The only trouble is we must not miss our footing because the water either side is deep and dangerous. Horses have fallen in and never been seen again because monsters live in the depths. They drag them away."

"And," cut in Thane grimly, "that is not going to happen to any of you. If this horse had been docile I would have taken a chance by letting him follow behind us, but look at him." His voice cracked. "He's a responsibility I'm not prepared to accept."

They all looked at the horse in question. It had started to buck and its nostrils flared. It could sense the feral animals creeping closer, and tried to shake off the lead rein. Sue came alongside, concerned. She tried to stare into its fear-filled eyes.

"I think it can sense the presence of the Gypsies. Maybe they're calling to it."

"Then they can have it." Thane slashed the restraining rein with his knife before Sue realised his intention. The horse reared, and raced along the water's edge. Darkness converged on it from all sides, chasing its fleeing form. The horse stood no chance of survival; Zeno raised his bow, fixed an arrow, and sent it unerringly on its way to its target.

Another followed and the horse was dead before the predators reached it. It happened so fast, Sue felt sick.

Bile filled her throat and she stared mesmerized at the sight of the carnivores tearing the horse to shreds. Thane gripped her arms and shook her until she raised a white tearful face to him.

"Why couldn't you..." But her voice choked, she couldn't go on.

"Sue! It had to be done," he interrupted bleakly. "Either way, that horse was dead, but thanks to Zeno, it didn't suffer. It's bought us time and we must use it. Zeno," he looked at the lad with begrudging admiration – he admired the boy's quick thinking – "let's get going while we can. Barry!"

Barry roused himself from his stupor, trying to block out the savage howls. "Yes," he agreed. "I'm as ready as I'll ever be." But in his eyes was a horror he would never forget.

* * *

In a state of shock, Sue entered the water alongside Saturn. Thane led her with his hand on her rein. Revulsion still shook her body. Night was falling rapidly. Only a fraction of the sun now showed above the horizon. Elongated shadows swallowed up the red tinge, making the swirling water beneath the surface appear sinister. She was no longer thinking rationally after seeing the horrific sight of the predators attacking the horse, Thane became a monster in her eyes. She really believed he had deliberately allowed the carnage to happen.

She shuddered violently, unaware that her feelings made contact with the stallion she was riding. It sensed her agitation and became skittish. This was the last thing

Thane needed as he carefully followed the submerged causeway. At the horse's movement he uttered a curse. By now they were several yards from the shore, but for everyone's safety, he halted their progress. Zeno and Barry drew up behind him.

"Zeno!" Thane ordered curtly without turning his head, "is it possible for you to get off your horse and come and steady the one Sonja rides?"

"I can do it," Barry offered quickly, but Thane's voice was sharp. "Stay where you are, boy," Thane said, and that made him change his mind. The 'boy' part really rankled, and had Barry not been feeling so nervous, he would have glowered at the older man's back. As it was, he watched Zeno slide easily from his docile horse, and Barry realised he was not all that keen to put his feet in the murky water.

He wished Zeno had refrained from telling him what lived in its depths. The young soldier moved carefully up behind Sue. She closed her eyes to stop looking at the darkening lake in case she saw tentacles reach out for the horses' legs. Thane was so close beside her she drew comfort from his nearness.

Their horses could have been glued to each other. But that did not stop the nausea. Instead of receding, it became persistent. Her mind kept turning back to the savage gluttony she had just witnessed on the shore. She could not fend it off. A roaring sound started up in her ears; when it faded she felt as though she was falling into an abyss. Keeping one hand on the reins of Saturn, Thane put his other arm round Sue as she slumped against him and knocked him off balance. Saturn had himself under control in an instant, but from behind came a concerned voice from Zeno.

"Do you need any help, sir?"

Thane grunted, shifting his position slightly and said, "Just keep holding that horse steady while I lift Sue off and put her in front of me."

The changeover proved to be difficult. Without the young soldier's help they would have lost another horse. Zeno looped the rein from the now rider-less horse round Thane's wrist and moved back to where his own mount waited patiently. They were now ready to resume the journey. Thane's voice floated back to them, "Think you can manage this, Barry?"

"I'm bearing up," he retorted, with more bravado than he felt. "I just hope we don't have to come back this way. Once is enough."

Thane smiled grimly. The way he felt at the moment he endorsed Barry's feelings a hundred per cent. The journey to Therossa should have been made by river. The way they were going was the worst possible route, and they had been forced to go this way thanks to the activities of Lex Ansell. It was going to be a perilous time for them all. He urged his horse forward, concentrating on the job in hand.

A huge crowd of predators were now assembled on the shore, howling after the prey that was now escaping from them. The hairs stood up on Barry's neck when he realised they had nearly ended up as food for them. He badly wanted to see if they were going to follow across the submerged passage, but did not have the nerve to look. The clamour coming from them eventually died away. As soon as they were forgotten, the beasts started scrapping amongst themselves. Barry heaved a sigh of relief; extremely thankful his sister had fainted. It was taking all his willpower to remain sane.

Step by step the lead horses went further out into the lake. A breeze picked up energy and started to become troublesome. It made wavelets on the water, giving the impression it was alive with a multitude of creatures. Barry started to fidget, his confidence rapidly evaporating. Zeno surreptitiously took hold of Barry's reins and kept closely behind those in front. He recognised all the signs he saw in his companion. Barry was bemused, his eyes were fixed downwards, and he noticed that the water never reached higher than the stallion's knees, and rippled out in a half-circle as they walked.

It was when something unexpected jumped out of the lake, that Barry nearly lost his balance and recoiled. His chest muscles tightened. He tried to relax, but not successfully. It was the last straw when he heard a splashing behind him. What was causing it, he wondered? Was it amphibians? He tensed. Waves of panic shot through his limbs and he prepared himself for the worst. Sweat dampened his forehead. As far as he knew, Zeno was staring straight ahead, concentrating on Thane and apparently not noticing anything amiss. He felt he was completely alone. Another apparition rose from the depths near his horse's legs. In the dim light he saw a scaly claw and nose-less face with gaping maw. He lost control momentarily and retched. Then he felt thoroughly ashamed of himself. Whatever was behind them, growled ominously and pushed through the horses' legs, nearly making him fall off. His terror turned to relief as he realised it was White Hawk. Barry stealthily wiped his brow with his arm and Zeno grinned sympathetically, his bright eyes fixed on Barry's face.

"I felt the same way the first time I did this trip. By the time we reach the other end of the causeway you will be hardened."

"I feel ill," Barry mumbled in wretched confusion. "How many people have been lost on this path?"

"I've never seen any others," Zeno answered carefully. "Cheer up, Barry. White Hawk will keep any followers at bay. Look – go carefully now. Thane is turning."

Barry did not need to be told to go carefully. He was almost too petrified to move. He bit his lip to stop it quivering. "How will I know when to turn? I might go over the edge," he muttered.

Zeno drew closer to him and caught hold of his arm. "You will feel the horse mount a step. At that point we turn. Do not be afraid. I will not let you slip."

* * *

The turn was successfully negotiated with no one putting a foot wrong. They were now moving parallel with the shore. Daylight vanished and as far as Barry could make out, they were all floundering. Speed was reduced to such an extent, movement was almost non-existent. He was sure they were going to fall over the edge now that darkness enveloped them. He was full of doom and gloom, but wise enough not to voice it.

With an exasperated sigh, Thane pulled his horse to a halt, looking towards the distant peaks that were their destination. They showed up as a darker mass against the night sky. Clammy tendrils of mist swirled about them. He felt Sue's recumbent form stir and was pleased she was well wrapped up against the elements, but before long she would be aware of their predicament and he wondered how she would take it.

"How long do you think it will be before the moon appears, Zeno?" he asked grimly.

"An hour – maybe two," was Zeno's glum reply. A sudden surge of wind whipped their hair back and spray caressed their skin. He raised worried eyes to the sky, noticing the build-up of clouds. Drawing in a deep breath he felt compelled to add that there may not be a moon tonight.

Thane swore as their danger increased. They could not stand in the lake all night, and should a squall blow up, all would be lost. Standing still made them easy prey for the creatures living in the water. What they badly needed was light to help them forge ahead. He silently cursed himself for not having had the foresight to be better prepared.

"Do you think White Hawk could lead us?" enquired Barry, and as his subdued voice floated to Thane's ears, Thane wondered if the boy could see the wet bedraggled wolf looking expectantly at him for orders. "White Hawk cannot track in water," he replied. "What we need above everything else is light."

"The moon will be up soon and then you'll have light," murmured Sue contentedly, and she snuggled down against Thane as though what was happening about her had nothing to do with her.

"You could give us light," Barry retorted, and his fear made his voice sound accusing. The sound of it lingered on the night air. Thane's senses were immediately alerted. He thought that dig was for him.

"And where do you think I can get light from in the middle of the lake?" he enquired.

"Not you," Barry was getting reckless, "but Sue could. She managed it in the Drazuzi tunnels when we were escaping. She could use her ring."

"Never!" Sue's head came up with a jerk, and in spite of all its throbbing, she added quickly, "I'm never going to use it again – ever."

She heard the cowled man's words in her head. The ring would tell her enemies where she was. What on earth was Barry thinking of, telling everyone about her ring? When she used it the last time, it was for a matter of life and death. It wasn't like that now. They were just crossing the water. But she was wide awake after his remark and tried to peer into the darkness and assess where they were. It suddenly filtered through to her that everyone else had become silent, and the atmosphere felt strained. But this was typical of Thane. She wasn't going to be ordered to use the ring.

"Where are we, Thane?" she asked at last, just to break the unnatural silence. His answer was curiously flat. It sounded nothing like him at all.

"We're standing in the lake a long way out."

"Are we lost?"

"Not exactly. It's a little difficult to move because we can't see where we're going in the dark."

Sue detected frustration in his voice and felt confused. What had she said that was so wrong? What was it they were keeping from her? She tried to retrace her thoughts. Barry had been discussing her ring, and all she said was… Her thoughts trailed off. Although her hands were deeply embedded in her pockets, she could feel it burning on her finger with a terrible intensity. In consternation, she realised it was trying to tell her something and was no doubt flaring with light. It was light they needed and by her actions, she was deliberately denying it to them it. She was pleased it was dark and covered her embarrassment.

"I think I can help you." Slowly she withdrew her hand. As the chilly night air embraced her bare flesh, the facets of the stone shone out like a beacon, illuminating their surroundings. Water-life dived for cover and those creatures nearer and more daring, slowly submerged. Thane ignored Zeno's gasp of amazement. Automatically he steadied Saturn and the horse beside him, then shouted out,

"Quickly. Let's get moving. Hold tight, Sue."

His knees urged his stallion forward and the others followed, sensing his urgency. Some unknown power whipped up the lake into waves as though annoyed at them for getting away. They didn't worry at first, but then a strong current swept over the causeway and round the horses' legs, tugging and disrupting their gait. Impossible-looking creatures leapt over their path. This was more than natural causes. Some sinister motivation wished to destroy them. Thane understood and clenched his teeth, staring ahead through narrowed eyes.

"Watch your footing," he yelled out, although his voice was barely audible as the wind whipped it away. "Don't let fear take control. Nothing can touch us if we keep to the path."

Zeno pulled Barry closer. "You heard him," he hissed in his ear, "relax."

Barry hunched up and nodded. Making headway was not easy, even with the dazzling light to guide them. Inexplicably the lake turned into a sea. Waves started to roll towards them, getting higher and stronger as each one passed over them. White horses rode their crests and the volume of water hit them with a powerful undertow. Then the wind gusted with such ferocity they were nearly unbalanced. Sweat was pouring from Barry's brow and he could see no way of escaping this horror. Then above everything else, the night was shattered by a bloodcurdling roar.

Blood drained from Barry's face and he felt something hovering above him. It was as though the sky was falling in. The moving density overhead blotted out the cold and fierce wind, but Barry's blood froze when two huge talons clamped either side of his horse. The stallion squealed with terror, almost mimicking his own feelings. This was like the monstrosity he had seen flying over Saturn earlier. Its wings glistened green from Sue's light and as it plucked him from the lake, Barry forgot men and boys were not supposed to show fear, and screamed out.

He retched for the second time that day and as the air rushed past his face he was engulfed in darkness.

* * *

He still stood where he was on the plateau after the call of the ring had been answered. Sheeka would never let him forget he had asked for yet another favour. The use of the ring had come as a great surprise to the dark shrouded man. He had immediately raised his arms high and uttered a short incantation, waiting patiently for it to be answered. He knew help was on its way by the vibrations in the air. Before many moments passed they had appeared like a dark cloud overhead. One circled the area and alighted a few feet away from him, leaving his companions still circling up above.

Folding enormous wings and swishing his long barbed tail round for better balance, he fixed the motionless man with a challenging stare from heavily lidded eyes and said, "I hope you have a good reason for calling us out. One of these days your luck is going to dry up."

"It's a matter of great urgency, exalted one." The man had known the correct way to speak to this dragon. He lowered his arms and advanced to within arm's length of the noble head, which was snaking towards him. He showed no sign of fear at being near this magnificent creature.

"How many more favours are you expecting me to grant you?" The dragon had been cross.

"As many as it takes," retorted the man. "You are wise enough to know whatever you do will be to your advantage."

A rumbling roar came from his enormous armoured body, ending up with a puff of smoke, which was emitted from his nostrils. "Suppose we cut out all the platitudes and get down to business. You have disturbed my sleep."

A grim smile touched the man's face. "I am sorry about that, but you are right, Sheeka. However, out on the lake are some people and horses and they need rescuing before the Drazuzi Priest vanquishes them forever."

There had been a tense silence after his request and the wind swept over the plateau. “You called us out for that?” said the dragon, sounding almost querulous. His bright unblinking red eyes fiercely appraised the hooded man facing him before he raised his snout and emitted a sheet of flame that lit up the night sky. “That’s better,” he rumbled, and extending one leathery wing, asked, “Where do I take them? Do I bring them here?”

“No, Sheeka, take them to the beginning of the tunnel – and as a special favour to me – breathe on them so that they do not remember how they got there. I shall be deeply indebted to you.”

Sheeka roared again, “so you should be, I shall not let you forget this debt.”

He stood on taloned feet and stretched. Flexing his wings he surged off the plateau, circling once overhead and shot off in the direction of the lake with four other dragons following him. Sheeka would not let him down.

CHAPTER 13
THE SPIDERS

A Spartan fire, burning with occasional flurries, gave a touch of warmth and seclusion to the small oasis of greenery where Thane and Sue were sitting. Their horses were cropping what little grass was available and Barry and Zeno were doing their best to find food in the inhospitable area around them. Deep lines of anxiety were etched on Thane's face because there was no sign of White Hawk. He would not entertain the possibility of the wolf perishing in the lake. The others were distressed and did their best to refrain from mentioning his name.

Sue was hunched up and brooding. Her thoughts were about the previous night, remembering how against her will she had used the ring for light. It had created an atmosphere. Idly twisting it round her finger now, she wondered how a piece of glass could have this effect. Looking up, she saw Thane watching her. Immediately she felt awkward. She pushed her hair back with the pretence of smoothing it down and tried unsuccessfully to blot out hearing the hooded man's voice telling her, "Tell Thane about the ring." Sue cleared her throat, realising there could be no better time than this when they were alone together, yet the words stuck in her throat. Her voice squeaked when she made the attempt, and Thane raised his eyebrows.

"Do you want a drink?"

She shook her head. "No thank you. It's about last night. Was the light from my ring any help? Because I'm sorry to say, I must have passed out again. I don't remember anything after that or how I got here."

Thane chewed thoughtfully on his lower lip. He didn't think it wise to let her know he couldn't remember either. He was puzzled. They had been facing certain death. The waves were pushing them from the passageway, and the next thing he remembered was waking up in this place, surrounded by mountains and greenery. He suspected the presence of magical powers, and all he could come up with was the ring on Sue's finger. He threw a piece of wood into the flames and said carelessly,

"Stop worrying about it. The light enabled us to reach this place, which is all that matters. Without it ..." he paused. "I don't like to think what might have happened."

"Thane...the ring Raithe gave me," Sue began, then halted, not knowing how to explain. He smiled at her encouragingly. "Yes. It's beautiful. Mind you don't lose it. I'm still surprised he gave it to you. His father gave it to him years ago."

That was unexpected and Sue digested the information in silence. She stared down at the ring and the green facets that were reflecting the sun. "He said it was supposed to keep us in touch with each other."

"And has it?" he prompted. His question sounded casual but his eyes and mind were alert as they surveyed her face.

"Yes. Oh yes," she whispered, trying to control the quiver in her voice. "Thane, he has spoken to me through this ring. I know it sounds daft. It surprised me the first time it happened. I didn't have any memory at that time, but it was through him I became aware that the Drazuzi Priest was evil."

Her voice faded away, Thane moved closer to her and he lifted the hand wearing the ring. "Why did you never say anything to us? Tell me – why hasn't he come to greet you like he was supposed to?"

"Because – because he can't." Sue choked. "He's a prisoner. I saw it all in the stone, and the men who captured him. Thane," her eyes became stricken as she looked at him, "I've got to find him."

Thane pressed her fingers reassuringly, not enlightening her that Therossa was a huge continent. "I suppose you didn't see what the place looked like where he was captured?" he asked cautiously.

"Not really. I saw only the long thin waterfall behind which they dragged him."

"Shark's Tail!" Thane shouted excitedly. He gave her a hug. "Sue, I know where that is. Why on earth didn't you tell me before? We could have done something about it."

Now Sue looked miserable. "I couldn't," she mumbled, and wouldn't meet his eyes. "I promised I wouldn't say anything or use the ring again. Every… every time it flares out with light, the enemy knows where I am."

"Who the Hell told you that?" Thane exploded with suppressed fury. "Don't you realise how vital it is to get Raithe back? We've already lost his father. We must not lose him as well."

Sue's emotions were warring within her. Thane gripped her shoulders and gave her a gentle shake to make her look at him. "Sue! Who has been telling you this?" he demanded. "You've got to tell me before we go any further."

"I… I…I can't. I promised," she answered unhappily.

"Then for me. Break that promise." Thane saw the expression on her face. "Or don't you trust me?" he added. He could not keep the bitterness from his voice. She felt as though she were drowning. She looked at him, her eyes imploring him to understand. Then it suddenly struck her she didn't know who the man was who had told her about the ring, and thought it funny. A hysterical laugh escaped through her lips.

"I can't. I don't know his name," she said.

"Describe him then."

This is ludicrous, Sue thought, and she smiled as she said, "I've never even seen his face."

"Sue!" Thane was exasperated, and she could no longer suppress her laughter. Tears rolled down her cheeks and as she wiped her eyes with the back of her hand, she muttered, "I only know that he has a serpent tattooed on each wrist," and she missed the stunned expression on Thane's face because she was not looking at him.

*   *   *

Having flushed out an overgrown rabbit and two plump birds from the sparse greenery, the travellers spent the morning cooking them and packing what was left over for their forthcoming journey. Thane tried to make sure everyone understood that the journey they were about to undertake was going to be underground. He explained that the spectacular mountains rising high above their heads were a no-go area because the horses would not be able to manage the steep passes. This was digested in silence and they stared ahead at the tunnel in front of them. Barry studied the massive shoulder of rock that partially blocked the entrance, and knew that he would have plumped for the overland route any day. The tunnel looked dark and uninviting. Not many things got under his skin and he certainly did not suffer from claustrophobia, but he had a horrible feeling in the pit of his stomach that this was not the way to go. Sue would be unnerved by their underground venture. Barry deliberated for a while before asking Thane how he expected them to see once in the tunnel. They were not worms. Where was the light going to come from? His eyes instinctively went to Sue's hand, and both he and Thane saw the horror leap into her eyes. Before she could protest, Thane said quietly,

"You can forget the ring. It will not be needed. Zeno!" he called to the young soldier. "Go and find the torches, then we can start."

Zeno went into the tunnel and was soon lost from view. Barry wondered if he should have volunteered to go with him – not that he knew what to do. A cloud of dust and a few swearwords came from the cave, and Zeno returned with his arms full of prepared torches. Seeing Sue's surprised look, he grinned and said,

"It's an unwritten law that travellers using this method of crossing the mountains must always replenish the stock for other people's use. We are lucky. We are not going to be using many."

Thane relieved him of his burden and handed the torches out, giving three to each of the travellers. Under his eagle eye, each one strapped two to the horse he would be leading – and kept one in his hand. Now they were all grouped together, Thane called their attention to one more thing. "Only one torch will be alight at any given time," he ordered. "This way we shall have enough light to see us to the other end of the tunnel." His voice was crisp and full of authority. "Animals and other different things also live in these tunnels. If you ignore them, they will ignore you. So I want no panic from any of you… understood?"

He did not expect an answer, but Barry fixed him with an owlish stare. "What sort of animals."

"The usual ones," Thane retorted pedantically, "that have four legs, fur coats and sharp teeth, all right?"

But Barry was not in the least bit put out and then asked if they were dangerous. He looked at his sister, which Thane could not help but see.

He took a deep breath "Only if you provoke them, and before you ask – yes, some are large and others small." He saw Barry clamp his teeth together and let out a sigh of relief, but decided on saying one more thing. "I must warn you that it's going to be very cold. If you have spare clothes with you – put them on. Otherwise you must make do with what blankets we have. The only person I do not have to worry about is Sue. She is dressed sensibly."

Sue felt herself glow in her fur leggings and parka. Deena had prepared her well. Her second sight must have shown her which way she would be travelling when she left the snake people. Before he stamped out their fire, Thane lit the first torch and led them into the tunnel. At the beginning it was wide and they could easily walk four abreast. The roof gave plenty of space above and a strong current of air kept everything at a reasonable temperature. Only one horse baulked at the beginning, but after he settled down progress was reasonably fast. Conversation became sparse because the conditions in which they were walking tended to give everything an echo.

Before long, the torch Thane held started to splutter. Sue, walking next to him, held out her torch to be ignited. It flared up, blinding them all, and their shadows were thrown on the walls looking like grotesque giants. They felt a subtle change in the atmosphere. It became chilly and the cave walls started to narrow in. They were now forced to walk in single file. Thane took the torch from Sue and asked Zeno to move up front with him. At the same time, he spoke over his shoulder and called to Barry to keep his eyes open, because he was now the rear guard. That made Barry feel important, as Thane hoped it would.

The path became uneven with unexpected pitfalls. They felt the pull on their leg muscles. Stalactites formed above them. The deposits of calcium carbonate made them look beautiful as the light from the torch reflected off their glistening sides. The deeper the party penetrated into the mountain, the larger these stalactites became. Soon they were ducking their heads. Then the nightmare got worse because they stumbled over the stalagmites growing up the other way. This was bad for the horses. Barry was compelled to shout out to Thane to stop.

"We need more light back here before one of the horses goes lame."

His voice echoed back to him, reverberating like thunder as it sped along the tunnel. But his question got the desired effect. A second torch was lit and Zeno passed it to Sue. They continued carefully on their way as though the incident had not happened. Conditions slowed their speed down to a crawl. Coldness infiltrate through their clothes. Barry shivered. "This is worse than the Drazuzi tunnels." Sue picked up his words and agreed with him. "But at least we haven't met any animals yet."

Barry stared morosely at her back; silhouetted against the light from the torch she held. He caught his breath and his blood froze. Up until then he hadn't thought it could get any colder. Something was moving along Sue's shoulder. A grotesque object that had a fat hairy body and eight thick shell-covered legs, each with a pincer at its end. This monstrosity filled his vision. It was the size of a saucer. It was crawling on Sue's shoulders with deadly intent, attracted by the warm air coming from her mouth.

As his horrified eyes swept over her body, he saw more of these creatures, even larger, making their way up her leggings. It's a wonder she never felt them. Tightness gripped his throat. He wondered if any were on him. He stamped his feet, even though it was a futile action, to dislodge them. What on earth were they? Were they dangerous? They looked as though they came from somebody's nightmare.

Thane's instructions had been to ignore them, but he couldn't. They looked deadly. Lifting his unlit torch with the idea of swiping them off his sister's back, he nearly dropped it as one of them fell from the roof and balanced on the end of his torch. The weight of its body pushed the torch back towards the ground. The wicked eyes were large and malevolent, and it fixed them unerringly on Barry as it moved down towards his hand. Miniature needle-sharp teeth overlapped its lower jaw and Barry's imagination ran riot. He felt those teeth sinking into his flesh.

Then he looked up at the roof, which was a bad mistake. It was a heaving moving mass. Eyes glowed in the light of the torch. Several of the creatures dropped away at once, two landing on his horse. The stallion shied and neighed in fear. The sound in the tunnel was deafening. Thane halted in alarm. Sue spun round to look at her brother. She saw the massive repulsive creatures immediately. Strangely, they did not terrify her, but their colossal numbers did. There were so many falling from the roof. This could not be ignored. The horse was ready to bolt. She did not wait for Thane's reaction or think about herself. Lifting her hand into the air and exposing the ring, she cried out, "Get rid of them."

Thane was beside her as the ring burst into a green brilliance. The dazzling light flooded every part of the tunnel. The creatures quickly reduced in size and scuttled away with a soft shuffling sound, until nothing but bare glistening walls could be seen. Only then did reaction creep up on Sue.

"Turn round, Sue," Barry managed to choke out. "I want to check there's nothing on your back."

Barry was trying hard not to shake. Zeno held his torch high which helped with the examination. Thane's breath rasped in his throat as he enquired, "Are you two harmed in any way?" He tried to defuse their panic.

Sue shook her head and added firmly, "I'm staying with Barry."

"We're staying together," retorted Thane, his voice grimmer than he intended. "Sue, how long will your ring sustain that light?"

"I don't know."

"Well, we'll have to see. Push on to the cavern, Zeno. There will not be any wildlife there. We can't afford to be held up in the tunnel. Those deadly crusted insects will return if the light goes out."

He pushed Barry towards the young soldier and said in a voice he hoped sounded casual, "I think I will guard the rear for a while. Can't let you have all the excitement."

* * *

The journey went on. It was almost impossible to hurry because the horses needed help going through many difficult patches. The tunnel twisted and turned and there were minor rock falls. Sue and Barry became keyed up, waiting for the unexpected to happen again. At last they reached a large cavern, which Thane had declared as a safety zone. He called for a halt. Tired and dispirited, Sue leant against the shoulder of her mount and closed her eyes trying to blot everything out. Although she wasn't cold, she was thankful for the rest. Her lips were parched and her throat unbelievably dry.

Never had she imagined that walking through a tunnel could be so arduous. The others noticed her fatigue, which made them all the more determined to hide their own anxieties. Zeno was the only one to approach her with any help. It took some time before he worked up enough courage to speak to her. He wished he didn't feel as though he was taking liberties, but as far as he was concerned, he did not think she was looking at all well. He offered her his water bottle. "You must drink and moisten your mouth, Sonja."

Sue's eyes flew open with surprise and she looked into his face. Immediately he was flustered and wished the ground would open up and swallow him. Gulping nervously, he pressed on. "You must not worry. Your condition – I – I mean – the way you feel is not serious. It all stems from the cold in this tunnel."

Sue thanked him and took a sip of water. With a shudder she passed it on to Barry and Thane because it did not taste like water to her. Something hot and fiery burnt her throat causing her whole body to glow. It was the perfect beverage to drink in the freezing temperature. The cavern walls were partially covered with ice and the coldness in the atmosphere misted their breath. It was like fog floating through the air.

The stalactites and stalagmites had fused together in this large cavern and made a system of columns stretching the whole length of the cave to where the tunnel continued at the other end. However, the beauty of the place was lost on the travellers.

Thane offered Sue a piece of meat, and as she stretched out her hand to take it, she realised with dismay her ring was no longer glowing. A feeling of guilt assailed her because she had used the ring for her own ends. Perhaps it would never light up for her again. She had been warned and foolishly ignored it. Thane rebuked her sharply.

"Don't get obsessed with that ring, Sue. Take my word for it, there is no way it will ever let you down. Anyway, thanks to its performance a little way back, we are all right and we've got plenty of torches for the remainder of the journey."

"But what if those..." she began, only to be cut short by Thane with unnecessary haste. "There will not be any," he said, and then he could have kicked himself.

Barry immediately backed his sister up. "How can you be so sure?" he asked annoyingly. "I seem to remember your saying last time, ignore them, and look what happened. We were swamped with them and..."

"Thank you, Barry," Thane snapped, adding sarcastically, "You're a great asset to have on this journey."

"I'm only trying..."

"Then don't. Have a piece of meat and stop upsetting your sister."

Sue prudently moved away, wondering why those two drew sparks off each other. She blew air onto her numb hands and realised Zeno had moved with her. It could have been coincidence, so she took a few more steps and he followed a few paces behind her. When she stopped, he stopped, but still maintaining the same distance. Annoyance flooded over her, and she spun round, saying testily,

"I won't bite if you get too close," and instantly regretted it as he turned a bright red. Sue felt remorse at uttering the sharp words she could not take back. She tried to make amends by saying, "I'm sorry. Forget it, Zeno."

"No. Do not apologise, Sonja. It is not your fault." Her apology made him even more embarrassed. "I should have known better than to follow you."

"Follow me!" echoed Sue in amazement. "How is it possible not to follow anyone in a small cave?"

Zeno was swamped with confusion. He had difficulty acting normally in her presence at the best of times. It became worse now, because he realised all heads had turned in their direction. "I'm sorry, Sonja," he mumbled.

"Stop calling me Sonja," Sue flared, anger mounting more swiftly than it should have done. "My name is Sue. Please remember and get it into your head that I'm no one special. If you can't treat me the same way as you treat Barry, then – then –" She was lost for words and Thane was suddenly between them.

"For goodness sake calm down, you two," he glared at both of them. "We need to be united on this journey and to look after each other's backs. I think it's time we were moving on. The sooner we get out of here the better. We are halfway through the mountain."

"Is the second half as interesting as the first half?" asked Barry innocently.

Thane stared at him suspiciously and decided to ignore the remark. "Zeno," he called, and his voice brought the young soldier to attention. "I want you to lead with Barry." He returned his gaze to Barry with an expression carved out of flint. "You will do everything Zeno asks. If he wants silence – make sure he gets it. Your life could depend on it."

Barry hunched his shoulders. "I might have guessed it would be just as interesting as the first half, since you said there are no more of those legged creatures – what is it to be this time?"

"Worms," replied Thane.

"Worms." Barry's mouth fell open and he hastily shut it. Looking at the two men, he realised they were not joking. He looked at Sue, but she just shrugged. "Let's move," was all she said, and turned to collect her horse, wanting nothing more than to get out of this underground nightmare.

The continuation of the tunnel was totally different from that they had just negotiated. The freezing air was worse than stepping into a walk-in refrigerator. The only thing in its favour was that the walls fell back giving them extra room. They were smooth and covered in fluorescent lichen. One torch was more than enough as its reflection was thrown back to them from the walls' and magnified tenfold. Before long, this strange phenomenon of lichen turned to ice, which encased everything. Now the going was slippery and they moved ahead with care.

"We are passing underneath a glacier," Thane informed Sue softly. "It will not take long, but it's best not to speak until we are at the other side."

That remark was enough to stop Sue asking questions. She appreciated the subtlety of it. She watched Barry draw his thick blanket about himself and sympathised with him. She could feel the chill herself with what she was wearing. Breath from the horses condensed on the air and they walked through a permanent haze. Light shimmered on mirror-like surfaces. At times it glowed with a luminous rich blue tone. The air was brittle and the ice gave the impression of being alive as it crackled and pinged as they slowly walked by.

Barry started to shiver. He clenched his teeth tightly and turned to Thane. As he opened his mouth to say something, the older man shook his head and clamped a hand over his own mouth to warn him to be silent. Perplexed, he turned to Zeno who mimicked the same action. Barry gave up and stared gloomily ahead, wondering how many minutes he had left before he was frozen solid.

All the time, Thane and Zeno were watchful, especially when they passed part of the ice tunnel, which was riddled with catacombs, tunnels led off in all directions. For no apparent reason, Zeno halted, causing the others to stop automatically. Sue was fascinated as she stared down the blue shimmering tunnels, intrigued at their beauty, until a movement in one of them drained all the blood from her face. Before she could utter a sound, Thane's hand was held tightly over her mouth and she had to watch, with mesmerised eyes, the huge slug-like creature slide along one of the tunnels towards them. Its body took up all the space and two long flexible antennae sprouted from what she thought was its head, though she could not see any eyes.

A sinister squelching sound resounded off the icy walls as it slithered and pushed its limbless body along. Was this the worm that Thane had so casually mentioned? Sue felt her insides knot. He had said worms – were there more? It was nearly on top of them when it stopped. It seemed to be sensing the air. Just two more yards and it bunched up, and suddenly turned down an opening they could not see. The length of its body, made up of segments, made her feel sick.

Thane removed his hand and started to breathe heavily. "Move quickly, all of you, in case it returns," he ordered.

They had no need to be told twice. Sue and Barry did not wait to get an explanation. They urged their horses forward and followed Zeno. By the time the ground started to descend, they were weary with exhaustion.

Although the glacier had been passed without any more mishaps, Thane would not stop. He pressed them onwards.

CHAPTER 14
THE WATERFALL

A glimmer of light in the distance was a welcome sight for the weary travellers. Through bleary eyes Sue stared at it, hardly comprehending what she saw. At first she thought she was hallucinating, but hope made her ask, "Is that the end of the tunnel?"

"Yes." Thane's relief was obvious. The pent-up tension left his body. "In a little while this tunnel will widen into a cave and I hope there is no one in it. It's a well-known resting place for travellers. The cave should be well stocked up and we can get some sleep before venturing into the outside world."

They took him at his word and pushed slowly onwards without bothering to answer. But the horses, which they were now able to ride in the broader tunnel, became lively and no longer dragged their feet over the ground. The cave when they reached it was exactly as Thane had said, large, dry and big enough to accommodate them all. The temperature had not altered much, but the frigid edge was missing. Thane swiftly dismounted and helped Sue down to the sandy floor before she fell. It took a minute or two to make her legs support her weight. Barry slid off his mount and rubbed his limbs vigorously to get the circulation going.

He made no bones about his feelings, declaring, "All I can say is, it's going to be great to be out of these freezing tunnels. Fresh air can't come quickly enough. How many hours have we been cooped up in here?"

"Well over a day," Thane retorted.

"A day?" Barry was surprised. He straightened his back. "Are you trying to tell me we have been walking all night?"

"You'd better believe it." Zeno gave his horse a pat of appreciation for bringing him through the tunnel. "I for one am ready for some shuteye. Journeys are not usually as eventful as our one has been."

"I can't think why we don't go outside right now," Sue said as she wistfully looked towards the opening. The light drew her like a magnet but Thane was adamant. "You think it's cold in here," he said, "outside is a mountain pass and high enough to make the environment hostile. You've just been battling against the temperature, whereas now you will have the wind factor to take into consideration as well. We need food and sleep before venturing out there. I would not be surprised if a blizzard isn't blowing."

He drew himself up and stared around critically, calling out, "Zeno, can you prepare the kindling for a fire, and you, Barry, lay out the blankets and make up some beds. You'll find some dry bracken over by the wall. And Sue, don't think you're getting out of it. Suppose you see to the food, while I feed the horses."

Barry had the sense not to argue. He felt Thane's eyes on him. Shrugging his shoulders, he set about his allotted task, consoling himself with the thought that someone had to give the orders. For once in his life he accepted making the beds as a normal occurrence instead of starting a lengthy debate on how did he know the bracken was dry, and how was it possible to find firewood in a bare and barren cave high up in a mountain pass.

Sue knelt in the sand, too weary to argue, opening the packets of cooked meat which she herself had packed what seemed like days ago. Before long, a fire crackled merrily behind her. She sat back on her heels and watched the smoke drift up to the roof where it disappeared amongst the hidden fissures. Their tasks completed, they sat around in comforting warmth, and relaxed. Zeno passed round his water bottle again but Sue hastily declined until Thane insisted she had at least a couple of mouthfuls.

That was the last thing she remembered until she opened her eyes again and found Barry lying one side of her and Zeno the other. She lay for a while collecting her thoughts. Since no one else was moving, she gingerly sat up, careful not to wake the sleeping lads. The horses whickered a friendly greeting, but of Thane there was no sign. Sue got to her feet and stepped over Barry, then made her way to the cave entrance, guided by a waft of tobacco smoke. There he was, leaning nonchalantly against the rocky wall. Some inner sense warned him of her approach and he quickly put out whatever it was he was smoking. Turning to her with a smile, and looking more like the relaxed Thane she used to know, he asked easily, "Have you come for some fresh air, Sue? Make sure you're wrapped up well. I think we're in for a bit of snow."

Sue stood beside him and caught her breath, surprised that the cold wind could be so fierce. It stung her face and whipped colour into her cheeks as it roared between two mountains. Snow packed the crevices and other little hollows, but only a smattering lay on the ground. The sky was leaden, promising there was plenty more snow to come. She peered over the rocky wall, down into the gully some thirty feet below. Tufts of reed-like grass bent before the wind. Her hood blew back and the wind made contact with her face. She quickly withdrew into the shelter of the tunnel. Where they stood, they were partially hidden from anyone in the gully below, but could easily be seen should anyone passing below look up.

Having told Thane the others were still asleep, Sue stood with him in companionable silence, letting her mind drift. For the first time in ages, she thought about her mother, and thinking of her mother brought Raithe to mind. She must find Raithe. There was no way she could go to her mother until she had found her brother. Thane had said he knew where he was.

She was turning to him to speak when he said, "Yes, I know what you're thinking. We're going to search for Raithe. That is our next task. I'm only sorry it means delaying your reunion with the Queen."

"How much further have we got to go?" she asked, and shivered. The towering mountains overwhelmed her as they pressed down from high above. Everywhere was so desolate.

"Go to where?" Thane demanded. "To your mother's palace, or to the waterfall?"

"Both."

"For Therossa it is quite a long way. You have to remember the journey is longer now that the sky bridge is broken. But for us to reach the waterfall you must listen carefully, Sue."

Sue listened, straining her ears against the howl of the wind. Then she heard the thunderous fall of water. Her blood tingled, realising it had to be the waterfall. They were near to her brother. Excitement leapt into her eyes and Thane took hold of her arm and drew her back into the shadow of the tunnel. "We shall wake the others up and get moving while the weather remains reasonable. A snowfall could hamper the horses. I should think…" Then he stopped abruptly as a coarse laugh floated up to them from the gully below. Sue made to move back and look below but Thane held her anchored to his side. The sound of voices and horses' hooves clattering on the rocky path, immobilized her anyway. They had moved from sight just in time. The men below passed by without looking upwards. Thane let his breath out in relief. This cave was well known and they could have decided to come in.

"That sounded like Ansell's men," Thane said, grimly, "and if I may hazard a guess, they are guarding Raithe. It would be a great benefit if we knew just how many men there might be with him. I shouldn't think it's a job they're falling over backwards to do."

"So how do we find out?" Sue automatically whispered, although the men had long since passed by.

"You are going to – not me," answered Thane.

"Me!" Astonishment made her voice rise, "but I don't know..."

"Sue – your ring," cut in Thane tersely. "You said you've spoken to Raithe through it. Try speaking to him now."

Sue lifted her hand and for a few seconds looked at the ring, dull and lifeless on her finger. Something told her this was not the correct time. Yet for Thane's sake she rubbed it. The facets remained like dull green glass. There was not a flicker of life within the ring. She became agitated. Despair filled her. She was almost in tears. "I can't do it," she said, her voice breaking as Thane covered her hand with his.

"It's nothing to do with you, Sue," he said gently. "Raithe may be asleep. Don't look so downhearted – it's not changed anything. We're still going. Let's wake the others."

Sue relaxed. "Why didn't I think of that? The passing of those men may just be a coincidence."

"Of course," Thane agreed as he pushed her towards Barry and Zeno, but inwardly he was worried. This wasn't the place to meet casual people passing by. Those men had a purpose here – and that purpose must be Raithe.

* * *

Sue dug her hands deep into her parka pocket, trying to find a little warmth, and turned her back to the ferocious wind. It cut through her garments like a knife. She stood rigidly, staring ahead. She was aware of her companions standing behind her. They were there because of her. Her glazed eyes stared through the breach in the rock to where a moving curtain of water hurtled down from high above. It surged out from an inaccessible dark hole above her and fell hundreds of feet past where she stood, and continued on its thunderous descent to the lake far below. It was the run-off of melting snow from the high peaks that looked impregnable. There was no way she, or anyone else, could climb up there and get behind the water.

Spray formed a moving mist as droplets of water were carried on the wind. It made the dark lichen-covered rock wet and glistening, and in places it was covered with a thin layer of ice. It was obvious to anyone looking that it would be impossible to get any closer to the surging water than they already were, unless of course one wanted to lose one's life. Desperation shone from Sue's eyes. She could feel what everyone was thinking, but was too polite to say to her face. She knew if she went one step closer, they would forcibly restrain her. It was almost the last straw when she heard Thane's voice ask,

"Are you sure this is the correct place, Sue?"

He stood beside her, his calculating eyes watching the water thunder by. There was no way round it as far as he could see. He was unable to see through the curtain of water. Anything could lie on the other side, and he was willing to bet there was nothing but the rock face there, no cave. The spray on Sue's face hid the tears of frustration, which were pouring down her cheeks. She bit her lip, nearly drawing blood, so clearly in her mind's eye could she see the men dragging Raithe through the water. She stared at the scene despondently; common sense telling her no one could drag anyone through this. The ferocity of the water would dash them to pieces before they were halfway through. Surely the ring did not lie.

Barry remained unnaturally silent. He was feeling sorry for his sister. He wasn't sceptical about her story. He believed she had seen it all in the ring. If only he could do something to help her. Moving back a little way, he stood with Zeno and the horses that were getting skittish in the unfavourable elements. His eyes watched the rainbow colours and texture of the falling water. Zeno beside him grew restless – then coughed to get some attention.

"May I say something?" he ventured hesitantly.

"If it has any bearing on this, you can." Thane swung round to look at him, but kept a firm hold on Sue. She was liable to do something silly.

"Well," said Zeno, "the last time I came this way – I never reached this height, but I did see the Shark's Tail," he ended lamely.

"You just said you never reached this height," Thane exploded in exasperation. "Get on with it, man."

"Did you know you can see this self-same waterfall a lot lower down the mountainside?" Zeno hardly dared to look at Thane. He felt he was telling him how to do his job, but Thane was thunderstruck. This was news to him. He gave Zeno his whole attention. "Go on," he urged.

"It can't be seen from the path," continued Zeno, "but there is a narrow gully leading away, almost hidden. You cannot take horses along it, and there is just room for one person to walk. It leads to another part of the Shark's Tail – well concealed – and it's almost identical to this."

"How did you find it?" asked Thane.

"I was in a patrol of men with Captain Ansell," Zeno replied.

"That figures." Thane turned to Sue, his expression buoyant. "Did you hear that? Zeno said there is another place from which to view this waterfall. I'm sorry to say I didn't even know it existed."

Sue nodded, feeling a lot happier. She rubbed her hand over her eyes like a child and tried to smile. "Then I'm not going mad. Can we go and see it?"

"You bet we can. Zeno – will you lead the way? We're in your hands now."

The world seemed a much brighter place for the young soldier. His shoulders went back and he started leading the party downwards. They led the horses because of the uneven ground. Little hard bits of what felt like grit hit their faces, but it was no more than frozen snow. Thane kept close to Sue's side, rarely moving away, and seeing that she was being safely looked after, Barry walked ahead with Zeno. The intense cold and sharp winds made the journey exhausting, even though they were travelling downwards.

With the exception of Sue, all eyes were on the lookout for other men on the path. As the weather closed in, Thane thought the likelihood of meeting anyone was very remote. No one would be foolish enough to be out in weather like this. They picked their way over the slippery surfaces, bracing themselves against the blizzard-like conditions that were trying to take over. It was pointless to talk because words were borne away on the air. Sue felt her hand burning in her pocket. It was almost unbearable. The pain made her gasp. Thane looked at her sharply. "What's the matter?"

"The ring," she gasped. "It's calling me. May we stop?"

Thane quickly looked around then drew her into the lee of some jutting rocks. It was not ideal, but better than nothing. Sheltering her with his body and the huge mass of Saturn, he lifted her hand from the parka pocket and sucked in his breath at the sight of her hand. The green light from the ring dazzled them as it lit up the murky gloom. Although her hand was swollen, Sue ran a finger over the brilliant facets of the ring and Raithe's face materialised in several of them.

"Sue." His voice sounded weak and was hard to hear. "Can you hear me? Please come. I need you. I'll – I'll tell you – you how – " But his voice trailed away. The roaring wind made it difficult to catch his words. Sue and Thane both lowered their heads and Sue called huskily. "Raithe, are you alone?"

"Yes – no – I – " His voice faded again and the image wavered. When it returned, Sue remembered to ask, "Are you guarded?"

"Yes – two – but that's not the problem, – I – I," he whispered and this time the ring went dead and Sue choked down her disappointment. The pain receded from her hand and they both stared at a piece of dull green glass, exchanging puzzled looks. Thane smiled at her reassuringly.

"Don't worry, Sue," he said. "We'll find him. We're getting very near." But she was worried. Raithe didn't sound like his normal self. Sue relayed her thoughts to Thane.

"That's not surprising after being a prisoner for all this time. Silence could mean anything." Thane tried to answer encouragingly. "He wouldn't want to be heard by his jailors. Come on – let's catch the others up."

Slightly appeased, Sue followed Thane back to the path. Barry and Zeno had made little progress and not missed them. It was beginning to snow heavily, making the ground treacherous. It would be easy to miss the path.

Even though she was clad warmly, Sue felt cold. By the time Zeno halted, her legs were moving automatically through the swirling snow. She hardly cared where she was. The stallions were having difficulties. It was only when Zeno pointed it out that she saw the narrow fissure for which they were looking, and thought how easily they could have missed it.

Thane decided he would take Sue to the waterfall and the other two would wait with the horses beneath an overhang until they came back. It might possibly shelter them from the worst of the weather. Once they were safely installed, Thane and Sue moved carefully along the hidden track. Sue's languor vanished. Her excitement grew because she knew in her bones this was where she had last seen Raithe. Very soon she would be reunited with him.

* * *

Directly they stepped into the narrow cutting it was like entering another world. They were sheltered from the unfriendly elements raging outside the pass. The closeness of the rock face cut out the ferocious wind still screaming through the inhospitable mountains. The way was narrow and treacherous. Not only because it was icy, but rocks still fell from above, accumulating in unstable piles. The slightest touch was liable to start off a miniature landslide. Sue was the first to acknowledge it was not a place to bring horses, yet she felt guilty when she thought of Barry and Zeno huddling together under the overhang. It took ten minutes before she saw and heard the thunderous roar of water falling from above. So anxious was she to reach the waterfall, she became careless and nearly fell when a boulder moved beneath her feet. Thane caught her in the nick of time before she sustained an injury, and gave her a little shake.

"Take care, Sue. If you break a leg we shall be unable to proceed. I want to save Raithe just as much as you do."

Sue nodded, anxious to forge ahead. They moved on, but now held on to each other for mutual support and their progress became faster. When the curtain of water came in sight, Sue knew it was the right place. She almost expected the ring to flare out in agreement. Thane did not wait for her to say anything. Her eyes glowed. Her face was so full of expectation he knew their search was successful. They moved off the path and pressed against the rocky wall of the mountain. They found a ledge, partially covered with weeds, which went straight through the thick spray and disappeared into the darkness beyond. The way in had been found.

"Right." Thane gave her a poke. "I'm going to lead. Are you ready?"

Sue grinned. "Aye aye, sir," she said, and followed carefully behind him. After a few steps she asked in a suppressed whisper, "Do you think we need a light?"

"Possibly, but we must try and do without it," Thane returned grimly. "Raithe is not going to be alone and we don't want to advertise our coming."

She did not contradict him. Stealthily as she could, she moved along, hugging the wall. It was a strange sensation to walk through the water. They did not get as wet as she thought they would. It was thick spray, projected from the main source of water surging downwards and disappearing into the ground. Once behind the waterfall, they felt very small and insignificant. She had the eerie sensation of floating. The noise made it impossible to talk.

Thane touched her arm and motioned to her to follow him. She was reluctant to leave the waterfall, it mesmerised her, but she quickly turned her eyes away and followed as Thane went deeper into the tunnel. No way was she going to be left behind. Their eyes slowly adjusted to the darkness, and once they turned a bend in the tunnel, the roar of the water was muted. Thane paused to get his bearings, but held a finger to his lips to stop her from talking. She jumped suddenly when she thought something slithered by her feet, but Thane gave no sign that he had noticed anything. Holding her hand tightly so that they did not lose one another, he penetrated further into the mountain. The sound of the water disappeared completely, but another unexplained sound caught their attention. Still pressing forward, they saw a faint glow in the far distance.

"Be careful now. Keep your eyes alert," Thane hissed in her ear and he withdrew an arrow from his quiver.

The light ahead was of enormous help. It showed the ground was smooth and they crept along without mishap. At times they heard the dripping of water, and in these parts, the walls glistened. As they approached nearer the glow, they slowed down. The noise they had heard earlier turned out to be the sound of muted voices. They approached the end of the tunnel where it widened out into a large cave. Here, torches were wedged into crevices of its walls, giving plenty of light. The cave was empty. Sue stared around curiously; disappointed that no one was here. They walked in a little way – and then saw the deep cleft in the ground that split the cave in two. The fracture in the rock was too wide to leap across, but a very narrow bridge with no guardrails spanned the chasm. The chasm seemed to be bottomless. Beyond it drifted the sound of voices. The bridge had to be crossed. Sue's knees turned to jelly at the thought of this.

"You can do it, Sue," Thane whispered encouragingly, looking at her doubtful face. "You did the sky bridge. Think of Raithe."

Sue took in a deep breath. Thinking of Raithe did help. She steadied herself. When Thane stepped onto the bridge, he held out his hand to her. She caught hold of it tightly as though it were a lifeline and slowly moved across. Not until they were safely over the bridge did she start to breathe again. Then a peculiar smell invaded her nostrils. It brought up the hairs on the back of her neck. She knew something lived here which was not human, and Thane seemed to sense it as well. With dilated pupils she looked around, and noticed that nearer to the cave roof, above some tumbled shelves of rock, was a dark cavity, and the smell seemed to issue from there.

Thane jerked at Sue's arm to make her move on. This was not the place to linger. The cave was left behind and they found themselves in another winding tunnel. Torches still lit the way, which was just as well, because another yawning chasm cut across their path. It was even wider than the first one. The only way across it was another bridge, but this bridge was made of rope. To Sue it appeared to be frayed, and not very substantial. Somewhere in the distance, the voices now sounded louder. She expected to see the men who were speaking at any moment, but wherever they were, somewhere on the other side of this abyss, they could not to be seen. The way ahead was still illuminated with torches. Thane pondered for a moment, not liking the odds this bridge presented: it was in poor condition, he was sceptical of it taking his weight, and the roar of water rising from below the ground sounded off-putting. Yet the bridge was obviously well used and he could not see any other means of getting across it. Deep down, he was full of foreboding. Sue would never tackle something that swayed from side to side. He turned to her, but before he could say a word, she had read his mind and said doggedly,

"I'm going across. I can hang onto the rope."

From previous experience Thane knew better than to argue with her. "In that case, I'm going first," he retorted firmly, "and for good measure, I'm tying this rope about your waist in case of accidents." From his body he uncurled a strong rope, which he knotted tightly round her waist. At her raised eyebrows, he added, "If you should fall, I can still haul you up."

"Proper Boy Scout, aren't you," she mocked.

"I like to be prepared if that's what you mean," he replied. "Now – I want you to watch me carefully so that you can do the same thing. Remember – take your time. The idea is to keep a perfect balance. Move one limb at a time. Before we start – are you sure about this, Sue? You could wait here until I come back if you wished to do so."

Sue's answer to that was a glare so he shrugged resignedly and gave up. With bated breath she watched him catch hold of the two top guide ropes, which went all the way across the yawning chasm. It looked easy. Then he put his feet gently onto the lower ropes, which crisscrossed each other for strength and safety. It swayed alarmingly and for a moment she thought he would fall. Her heart felt to be in her mouth. Thane waited until it steadied, then started to move forward again. It was not until he was on the other side and turned to look at her, that she realised the pain in her chest was because she had stopped breathing. She felt sick, but now it was her turn and she fought off the nausea. She shut her eyes to blot everything out. Then she heard Thane calling to her softly.

She took a deep breath to steady her nerves. She thought of Raithe, and put her trust in Thane and the rope tied round her middle. Her hands were hot and sticky. She was sweating profusely as she stood on the edge of the drop. *Don't look down*, her mind kept telling her; *just pretend you're caged in and can't fall.* Like a dying man she grasped the two guide ropes and thought how thin and unstable they were. There was no support in them to take her weight. Her fear immediately came to the surface. It was a long time before she placed one foot on the rope and felt herself pitching forwards. Then as she put down the other one, the swaying took her by surprise, knocking her off balance. But the jerky movement gathered momentum and at that moment she did not realise she had screamed in fear. Her legs became rigid and she was incapable of further movement. As the bridge moved up and down with no help from her, her terror of falling was worse than anything she had ever experienced.

Thane's face was bathed in sweat as he watched helplessly on the other side, unable to do anything. It crossed his mind to pull the rope that was attached to her, but if she fell, she would hurt herself against the jagged sides of the gorge. Something clicked inside Sue's mind and for no reason she thought of the ring and Raithe. Before she knew it, the ring flared a brilliant green. From out of nowhere appeared a tall dark shrouded man; he enfolded Sue in his arms and leapt the abyss with her and left her in a shaking heap at Thane's feet, disappearing as quickly as he had come.

Thane was stunned, even though he knew who the man was and exactly what had happened. He wondered why the stranger had not waited to make himself known to Sue. Bending over her, he started to untie the rope. She clung to him, tears running down her face, but they were not tears of fear – but of joy.

"I did it, Thane," she choked, "I did it," and then Thane realised she had no idea of how she had got to this side. She thought it was because she had crossed the bridge herself. There was no way he was going to enlighten her about what had happened.

CHAPTER 15
FINDING RAITHE

Sue was soon on her feet, impatient to continue. Thane could only wonder at her stamina. She had blotted out successfully the crossing of the rope bridge and he did not like to remind her it still had to be crossed again on their way back. Then he realised the voices they had heard previously had stopped. It could only mean they had heard Sue's scream. The tunnel ended at the foot of rising steps leading to another cave. This one was spacious, but had many smaller caves leading out from it. An army could hide out in here. Thane knew he had to be careful, especially with Sue at his side. At the moment, the place seemed to be deserted. The enemy must be a lot further in the mountain.

They examined the cave and saw what remained of a meagre fire. Pots were strewn around and one was still on the spit. No mouth-watering odours came from it. It held a carcass already burnt to a cinder. Where were the talking people? Unease filled him. This was too easy. Where was Raithe? Where were the guards who were supposed to be looking after him? How much further in would they have to go before they met trouble? He took out an arrow from his quiver to be on the safe side.

After a cursory glance, the caves around them seemed to be empty, so Thane moved further into the cavern. Sue bent to investigate the burnt offering, and that action saved her life. An arrow flew over her head, so close her stifled gasp made Thane spin round. It was too late to avoid the second arrow completely, but the fact that he had moved saved him from its full impact. It pierced his upper arm, which spurted blood. With an oath, he dropped his own arrow and pulled out the one in his arm. He was rendered helpless to defend Sue.

She cried out in alarm and ran to his side, picking the arrow up. Two scruffy unkempt renegades, with several days' growth of hair covering their harsh faces, approached them menacingly. Thane's search had not been thorough enough. They burst out from their hiding place in one of the smaller caves.

"How did you find this place?" snarled the bigger of the two. His clothes were stained with food. His eyes, which were no more than slits, glittered evilly. "Who told you how to get in here?"

Sue reached for Thane's bow. "I'll shoot them," she jerked out, but Thane pushed her back with his good hand. "You don't shoot scum, that's too good for them," he snapped. "Keep out of the way. They're nothing but animals and parasites. Why else would they be lurking here?"

The wiry looking outlaw affixed another arrow, and with deadly calm advanced closer. The look on his sallow face was vicious. He was not cowed by Thane's words. He knew exactly whom he was dealing with. "That's right," he sneered. "You act the big strong man in front of the lady for all the good it's going to do you. You two are not leaving this place alive. Once we've made you tell us why you're here, we're going to kill you."

An unpleasant smirk touched his thin lips, especially when he saw Sue's expression of horror. "Nosey people pay with their lives," he added. "So answer my question?"

"I didn't realise this place was private," Thane growled, grinding his teeth against the searing pain in his arm. "What are you hiding?"

The big man stiffened and looked evil. "What's that supposed to mean?" he snarled, then licked his lips as he appraised Sue. "Keep him covered, Henti," he ordered, "while I see what this woman's made of."

Sue shrank back in alarm and Thane drew out a knife to defend her. The renegade laughed. "Don't start playing the hero, sonny," he admonished, "put that toy away. You'll be dead if you throw it, then there will be no one to protect the lady."

The hopelessness of their situation hit them both. There was no escape and no back-up. Barry and Zeno would not leave the horses to come looking for them. Thane cursed himself for being lulled into thinking this place was not adequately guarded. Originally he had thought the voices indicated the presence of Raithe – but Raithe was nowhere to be seen. They had walked like flies into the spider's web because of his stupidity. Hoping she was unobserved, Sue edged backwards to pick up a torch and use it as a weapon, while Thane held the men's attention. But Henti was aware of her movement and sprang at her. His wiry arms tried to grip her through the thick furry parka. At the same time Thane spun round and felt a blow on the side of his head. He keeled over and fell to the ground.

Sue struggled against her adversary, fury giving her added strength. Unexpectedly, it was Deena's words that rang through her head 'One day you will be faced with death. That is the time to open it.' She had forgotten the package. Now she acted on those words and put her hand deep down into the pocket of her coat. Her fingers curled round the package. Praying that Deena knew what she was doing, she withdrew it. Thane attempted to raise himself up and saw her twisting from Henti's grasp. Sue feverishly tore the package open, which almost fell apart at her touch; and just in time because Henti thought she was easy prey.

He suddenly froze. Apprehension crossed both the men's coarse faces because Henti yelled out in fear and backed away. In disbelief, both renegades stared at the unexpected horror in Sue's hands. Two black serpents, rearing up in sinuous coils, their unblinking red eyes fixed on the men. Taking advantage of the men's hesitation, Sue moved towards them, knowing she was perfectly safe. The snakes swayed to and fro. The men backed away. Everyone knew their bite was deadly. Just one bite, that's all it needed to kill them. How come this chit of a girl could handle them – unless …? Henti relaxed. These snakes had no venom?

"Shoot her, Henti," bellowed the big man, but Henti moved towards her. He intended to call her bluff. He came too close and Sue threw the snakes at them both, with all the force she could muster. Horrific screams filled the cavern. The snakes were hungry and annoyed at being in captivity for so long, so they attacked the men who did not stand a chance. At the sound of the mayhem, Thane managed to sit up. But by then it was all over. The men were dead, and he looked around, bemused.

He watched as Sue collected the snakes, which lovingly slid up her arms to her neck. He felt sick. Her father was never going to forgive him. He hadn't got her away from Deena in time. She turned to him and knelt down. "Let me bind something round your arm," she said.

"Sue! Where did they come from?" he asked weakly, looking askance at the snakes coiled near her face. Sue grinned and said,

"You mean these snakes in my pocket? I've had them ever since I left Deena." But she did not add she had no idea that the packet contained snakes.

* * *

"Do me a favour, Sue," entreated Thane, who had managed to struggle as far as the cave wall and use it as support for his back. His head was aching dully from the blow he had received and he clasped his wounded arm with his good hand. Sue tied a bandana she had found on Henti's companion round Thane's wound.. Under normal circumstances she would never had touched the bandana, but in the empty cave there was nothing else to use – and it did stop the bleeding. She stood beside Thane, concern in her eyes as she noticed the beads of perspiration on his forehead and the ominous flush spreading over his tightly drawn face. She bit her lips and looked at the water bottle in her hand, which she had also removed from Henti's pocket. She let Thane drink from it, and then wondered anxiously whether it contained something different from water. He was cringing away from her.

"What do you want me to do, Thane?" Sue showed no ill effects from the drink.

"Just get rid of those snakes, will you. They give me the jitters."

Sue jerked back at once. His request came as a complete surprise. Her hand rose and unconsciously touched the snakes which were coiled round her neck. She tried to think of a reason for Thane's aversion, forgetting that not so long ago the sight of them would have filled her with revulsion. Thane flinched, so she said, "they won't hurt you all the time I'm in charge of them – and I can't leave them here after they saved our lives."

He drew in a deep breath and shouted in exasperation, "Snakes will live almost anywhere. Reptiles are cold-blooded creatures. They cling to you only because of something Deena did at that ceremony. Just get rid of them Sue. Barry and Zeno will have fits if they see them crawling all over you and, I dare say, the horses, will bolt." He paused to draw in another breath, and thankfully saw she was wavering, so made his voice sound cajoling. "Deena never expected you to make pets of them."

She saw the funny side of the situation, and to his relief, laughed. "You're right as usual." She dusted down her clothes. "You rest here while I go and see if I can find something to put them in."

"No! I'm coming with you." Thane attempted to walk, but groaned, furious at his inability to help her. "Just give me a moment…" His voice trailed off.

Sue studied him thoughtfully. "You need to conserve your strength for getting out of here. I promise I shall not be long."

Thane slid down to the ground, but grunted irritably, "then be careful. There may be some more guards around."

"If there are – they will wish they had never met me. I've still got the snakes," Sue retorted rather unwisely, and with those words, moved off. Thane watched her go, frustration overwhelming him. When she vanished from sight, he clenched his teeth and struggled to get himself back on his feet. Meanwhile, Sue wandered deeper into the caves, following another tunnel which was still lit with torches, though there were not so many of them. Their flickering light did not dispel the shadows. *There must be something important down here*, she thought, why else was the place illuminated? A subtle change came over the atmosphere. There was a dank smell in the air. Sue's curiosity made her temporarily forget she was looking for somewhere to put the snakes. She noticed the walls were now damp and thick with lichen. The whole area was repellent and she wished Thane were with her, especially when a noise reached her ears. It sounded like rasping that came from the cave ahead of her.

A weak shaft of light touched the floor. The rasping continued and Sue concluded it must be another guard, sleeping, although why he should choose such a dismal place for repose was beyond her. Moving stealthily forward she reached the cave and peered in. A choking cry escaped her lips.

Raithe was slumped in an unnatural position on a bed of straw and she thought he was dead. He looked nothing like his former self. A vivid bruise stood out in sharp relief on one side of his white, pinched face. His golden hair was matted with blood and fell, half covering his closed eyes. Round one of his ankles was a heavy, rusty manacle and its chain disappeared into the darkness. The smell of this place made her feel nauseous. She didn't check that it was empty, but moved into the cell and fell to her knees beside Raithe. Emotion choked her. She could not control the tears that filled her eyes. She thought this was all because she had taken so long getting here through not trusting Thane. Then she saw the faint movement of his chest.

Disregarding the fetid smell coming from the filthy straw, she leant over to gently touch his face and was alarmed as her fingers came into contact with a feverish, clammy skin. He mustn't die. She lay down and embraced him, before fury overwhelmed her. Raithe was ill. They had not reached him a moment too soon. Listening to his harsh breathing, she was at a loss what to do next.

"Raithe! Wake up," she choked. "I'm here. This is Sue. I've come to get you away from this disgusting place. Raithe...Raithe, please speak to me. Open your eyes."

She pressed her cheek to his. Her hood fell back allowing her golden hair to escape. The snakes were irritated at their exposure to cold air and quickly uncoiled from her neck. Sue hardly registered their going as they slithered away to hide in the straw. She only knew her brother made no sign of hearing her. A sob caught in her throat. She could not control her crying. Then a voice coming from the direction of the cave's entrance said,

"Do not spoil the illusion. Angels never cry."

Sue jumped up and turned round to see who had spoken. She had thought she and Raithe were alone. It was not a guard, but a tall gaunt man who leant against the rocky wall. From what she could see in the flickering light, his face was thin and covered in several months' growth. His tattered clothing was dishevelled and one bare leg was tightly gripped by a manacle in exactly the same manner as Raithe. Sue's fear that she was being accosted by a guard disappeared. He was another prisoner.

"Who are you?" she asked, not caring what she looked like.

"Me! I am of no consequence, my dear," he answered in a well-educated voice. He was elderly and stood there at the entrance, studying her thoughtfully. "You, on the other hand, should not be here. How did you get this far without the guards killing you?"

"I – I – I came to get Raithe."

"That's very commendable of you." He paused, fighting for breath, and coughing. She knew where the rasping noise came from. He suddenly slipped down the wall just as Thane had done earlier and rubbed his face awkwardly with dirty fingers. Sue noticed his hand was trembling. In fact, his whole body shook. He became aware of her scrutiny.

"I'm sorry, my dear," he apologized. Perspiration made his face damp, even though the air in the cave was cold. "I do not have a lot of strength left. I've been here too long I suppose – and Henti does not like cooking. Where is he, by the way?"

Sue swallowed nervously. "He's dead," she whispered.

His eyebrows raised a fraction and he seemed to comprehend everything about her. "I think I understand," he said. "I saw your two friends slither into hiding."

Sue's hands flew to her throat and with a gasp of dismay, she suddenly realised the snakes had gone. "It's not quite what you think. He – "

"Do not apologise, Sonja," he interrupted, "ah yes – I know who you are. I am sorry about your brother. He is very ill. I've tried to help him since he's been here, but our jailors keep us apart."

"Can you help me lift him to make his breathing easier?" she asked, turning back to Raithe, still willing him to open his eyes. She was not strong enough to move him on her own. Thane would have helped but Thane was hurt. The other prisoner made no attempt to come to her aid. In her desperation, Sue almost glared at him. He noticed her reproachful eyes and shook his head sadly.

"I'm sorry. It's not that I don't want to help the Prince. My – my chain does not allow me to come any further into this cave. This is the nearest I can get."

"Isn't there a key to that manacle?" Sue was clutching at straws, and then she wished she hadn't asked. She saw the bitterness in his eyes as he said, "If there is, then it has been well and truly hidden. You, my dear, must get away from here before the next shift of guards arrive. They will not take kindly to the demise of Henti."

"I'm not going to leave Raithe, and anyway, they'll have to get past Thane first," she replied."

"Who?" The prisoner was no longer slumping. He straightened his back. The action brought on a spasm of coughing which wracked his body. It was several minutes before it passed and left him exhausted. Although Sue was loath to leave Raithe, the condition of the other man upset her. He needed help also. She scrambled to her feet.

"I shall get you some water. Don't go away."

He laughed humourlessly at her choice of words. "Be careful, Sonja," he warned. "There is – is – is." And another fit of coughing made him gasp for breath.

Sue did not wait for him to recover. Quickly, she made her way back to the large cavern and met Thane walking unsteadily towards her. Lines of strain etched his face, but he noticed at once the absence of the reptiles; and felt a surge of relief pass through him. Before he could thank her, Sue grabbed hold of him and hugged him ecstatically.

"Hey – hold on. What's this for?" he asked in mock alarm. "Is it because I can't hug you in return?"

"Thane – I've found Raithe."

"You have?" Thane brightened at once. This news gave him just the right incentive to overcome his own injuries. "That's great. Where is he then?"

He looked around, expecting to see Raithe following – but Sue was so excited, she tried to pull Thane along. "He's ill way back in the caves. I think he's unconscious."

"Show me." Thane quickly took command. Suddenly, all that had recently happened was forgotten on hearing this news. He knew their position in these caves was dangerous; other soldiers would come along at any moment. They must pick up Raithe and get out. He would feel a lot safer once he was with Zeno. Sue did not find it easy to get back to the cell-like cave, because Thane stumbled a lot and needed her support. Then she heard the other prisoner coughing in the distance.

"Oh dear," she cried contritely, "I forgot the water."

"I shouldn't worry. If Raithe's got a cough and he's unconscious – you can't give him water."

"No." She was flustered. "The water's for the other prisoner. Not Raithe."

Thane stopped in his tracks. "What do you mean by the other prisoner? Is there someone else with Raithe?"

"Yes – I intended to get him some water."

Thane thrust a bottle into her hands. "Then give him some of this. It's what you took off of Henti. I don't know what's in it, but it's certainly got a kick," and he proceeded along the tunnel to find Raithe.

Things were exactly as Sue had left them. Raithe had not moved, and the other man was still sitting on the ground, but he looked up at their approach. She heard Thane suck in his breath and he stood rooted to the spot. He forgot Raithe and fell at once beside the older man and gripped him round his shoulders. "Father, I can't believe this. Is it really you?"

CHAPTER 16
THE COWLED MAN'S IDENTITY

Thane's temper knew no bounds when he saw the rusty old manacle fixed round his father's ankle. There was nothing he could do to get it unlocked. It was made from iron, and mere human hands were never going to do the job. Desperately he tried to think of something that would spring the locks. In the end his father, watching him, said dejectedly,

"Give up, Thane. The best thing you can do is to get Sonja away from this place before another batch of guards arrives to replace the ones you've disposed of. When you're out there in the open…blow your horn for help."

This sounded too much like an order and Thane was incensed. Anger flared in his eyes. "I've spent months searching for your whereabouts, and now that I've found you, I'm not leaving you behind," he retorted grimly, to which his father returned dourly,

"I'm not going anywhere, son. A few more days are not going to make any difference to me. But if the Princess is captured, you above all people know that everything will be lost. I shall have been imprisoned all this time for nothing."

Thane ignored him and looked towards Sue, who knelt beside her brother with one hand on his feverish brow. She studiously avoided meeting his eye. He turned back to his father propped up against the cave wall. "When I leave this place, we're all going together."

"Be sensible, man," his father said fiercely. "Look at us. The Prince is unconscious, I cannot walk and you are wounded in the arm. It's going to take all your strength to get Sonja out of here."

"We're not leaving," Thane spat back heatedly, "I shall get you out of here somehow."

"You're not a magician, lad. You can't do it," his father shouted back.

He had barely got the words out when a babble of angry voices floated up the tunnel in their direction. There was no possible place to hide. They had not realised the new guards had arrived already. There was nothing to be done for the shackled prisoners. Sue, however, was another matter. Thane went swiftly to her.

"Get in that corner," he hissed urgently, "and I'll throw some straw over you. The soldiers will be here in a minute and mustn't find you."

Sue reluctantly moved away from Raithe, and under the watchful eye of his father, Thane covered her liberally with fetid straw, nearly gagging on the stench that came from it. He mentally sent his apologies to Sue. Then with a sudden intake of breath, he jerked his hands away as two black serpents slithered to where she lay.

"Sue," he choked. "What are the snakes doing here?"

"Don't worry about them." Sue's voice was muffled. "They're under control." She felt them as they sought the warmth of her parka, and a surge of joy went through her. If anyone tried to harm Thane, she was confident she could save him, or anyone else. Thane backed away from her and spun round as three guards charged into the cave, anger bristling on their brutal faces. They were filled with a blood lust to kill, having just found their two dead comrades in the other cave. The sight of Thane, standing there brazenly by the Prince's body and making no attempt whatsoever to defend himself, threw them off balance. Thane was well known and immediately recognised by the Captain of this little group. He was a favourite of the Queen. There was no love lost between the two men. The Captain also noticed, much to his satisfaction, the wound on Thane's arm, which was just starting to bleed again. That injury could be used to their advantage.

"Seize him, men," he snarled in a hard voice. "He's bluffing you, standing there. He can't defend himself. Let's teach him what we do to people who kill our mates in cold blood."

"I didn't kill them," Thane answered calmly, not even moving. "If you had taken the trouble to examine their bodies, you would have seen the snake bites which did it."

That made the guards dither. They were extremely superstitious about bites of any kind. One licked his lips nervously, having seen the snake bite on Henti, and with Thane standing there, daring them to touch him, he lost his confidence. Then it occurred to him they were three against one, and there was no way Thane was going to win, so he sneered,

"How come you weren't bitten also?"

"Do we really want to know?" interrupted the Captain coldly. He stared at Thane vindictively. "I don't know how you managed to get in here, but I'll tell you something you might not like. You will not be finding your way out. I've changed my mind about killing you. You'll make a much better hostage. You can join these pathetic morons living at our pleasure. Meecha – stop gawking and get another manacle. You, Ruddo, make sure you keep this one under constant surveillance. Shoot him if he moves. He's likely to do something sneaky."

The renegade named Meecha ambled out the cave while his mate kept a wary eye on the motionless Thane. He was almost willing him to make a run for it so that he had a good excuse to shoot. Thc Captain viciously kicked at the man slumped on the ground at the cave entrance, to move him out of the way and Thane felt rage surge through his body. His father remained stubbornly silent but his eyes held a warning for his son when he realised Thane's intentions. Meecha at last returned with a manacle, letting the chain rattle over the uneven ground. The Captain ordered it to be fixed round Thane's leg. "If he kicks up a fuss or moves…shoot him, Ruddo."

Feeling decidedly uncomfortable and nauseated by the overpowering smell, Sue decided it was time to make her appearance. Whether it was right or wrong, she did not care, because she could not imagine Thane allowing the men to get near enough to fix the manacle. To prevent him from getting shot, she grasped a snake in each hand and rose up out of the straw, keeping them well out of sight behind her. To the gawking men she looked like an apparition from hell, with straw sticking out of her white parka, but in her haste to protect Thane, she had forgotten to cover her head. The Captain recognised her at once. She was the spitting image of the Prince. His small eyes gleamed with triumph. Excitement coursed through his veins at his unexpected success of having her in his power as well. His voice was almost incoherent as he ordered,

"We don't need him now – shoot him. We've got Sonja."

As Ruddo raised his bow to take deadly aim, and Thane spun round to see what Sue was up to, she moved swiftly forward and threw one snake at the luckless archer. With an ear-splitting scream, he dropped his bow and attempted to dodge away from the deadly serpent.

"Help me, Captain," he howled. "Stamp on it."

The Captain's triumph turned to bemused horror. He could do nothing to help Ruddo. He himself was held in a hypnotic trance as Sue approached him with the second snake wriggling in her hand. He knew it was trying to get at him. Its red eyes looked voracious as it stared at him.

"Spare me, Sonja," he blustered. "I wasn't going to harm you. Keep away from me. You're going to regret this."

Sue heard his pleas as though in the distance. She felt empty of all emotion. She was no longer in control of her body. She stared at the captain, as did the snakes held in her hand. Her eyes became distant and glazed. Another power held her in its grasp. She had no knowledge of how close she came to the Captain. Her voice was expressionless as she said, "this is for my brother – lying ill in the straw, for Thane's father, living in degradation; for Thane, whom you thought to shackle like an animal; for you." She threw the second snake at him.

His face was frozen in terror. Meecha dropped the manacle and fled down the tunnel. They could hear his voice screaming to other people.

"Cut the rope and stop them from getting out."

Then all was silent in the tunnel and in the cave were a young man and his father, rooted to the spot. Sue started to shiver violently, her eyes coming back into focus. She saw the dead soldiers, and remorse swamped her. The tears would not stop flowing when she realised what she had done. Thane came up to her and put his good arm round her.

"Sue – it wasn't you this time," he whispered in her ear. "It was some power of Deena's."

"I meant only to scare them," she cried piteously.

Thane glanced at his father above her head and knew he would never speak of this matter to anyone. He tried to chivvy Sue up, saying, "Well, something good has come out of it. We have got the key to the manacles. Now we can open them."

She followed his glance to where Meecha had dropped the manacles before he fled down the tunnel and indeed, a key protruded from the lock.

* * *

Thane supported his father with his good arm, masking the injured one that hurt like hell. They stared in frustration at the wide chasm ahead where the destruction was obvious. When the soldiers had fled, they had made it impossible for the prisoners to escape by slashing the rope bridge. It hung uselessly over the edge of each side of the fissure. They now found themselves faced with a dilemma. The torches were burning low and the prospect of starvation was rearing its ugly head. As far as Thane was concerned, it had been nothing but a catalogue of disasters ever since they entered these caves.

"Don't put yourself down," Thane's father said, "even if Raithe were conscious and the rope bridge intact, we should never have managed to get across the gorge. Still, you never know. Maybe the two men you left outside will come looking for you."

Thane's expression did little to inspire hope. "Zeno and Barry would not leave the horses in these blizzard-like conditions and it's ten to one the soldiers have seen them, whisked them away, and stolen the horses as well."

His father answered curtly, "for goodness sake snap out of it, Thane. It doesn't suit you to be so defeatist. We are the only people left to help the Prince and Princess. Think of it as a challenge, a battle of wits. We have no food, and before long, unless something unforeseen happens, we'll have no light either. What does that make you think?"

"Not a lot," replied Thane glumly.

"Then try a bit harder. Without light we are lost."

"Light – that's it – light," as he repeated the words, Thane was galvanised into action. He turned his father face about. "You've given me the answer. Come on – let's get back to Sue."

The older man was very reluctant. "What's the rush? Can't it wait a moment?"

"No – every minute is precious."

His father waved him on. "If it's that important – you go ahead. I'll stumble along in my own time. To be perfectly honest, son – I am not at my best when snakes are on the loose. Especially since I've seen Sue in action."

"Between you and me," answered Thane with a grin, "neither am I – but you can't judge Sue on that. She was being influenced. Actually, we'll be very safe with her. Hang on to me. I'm not leaving you here."

It took a considerable time for them to negotiate their way back to the smaller cave. Thane's father had only small spurts of energy; he was so emaciated after his long spell of imprisonment. Although Thane was eager to get back to Sue, knowing exactly what had to be done, he was also patient and caring with his father. By the time they both stumbled back to the evil smelling cave; with just one torch manfully spluttering to give light, they noticed immediately that Raithe was sitting up, with Sue supporting him.

"He's feeling better," she told them happily before they had a chance to remark on their good fortune. It was painfully obvious she had not noticed the feverish cast to his face and the dark smudges under his eyes. Raithe was entirely reliant on the strength of her arms. "I've given him some water out of Henti's bottle as we still had a little left, but I'm afraid it's all gone now."

"Oh my God," groaned Thane, allowing his father to sink to the ground. "That was not water, Sue."

Sue's happiness turned to dismay. "Don't scold her, Thane," Raithe cut in weakly, his voice sounding harsh because he had not talked for a long time, "I enjoyed it while it lasted." He moved his head slowly, suddenly aware his fellow prisoner was almost beside him. "Hello, Vance. How did you get free?"

"We're both free," grunted Thane's father, "and the guards have gone." He turned away from the ailing Prince to his son. "Now what is all this excitement we have raced back for?"

Thane knelt in the straw beside Sue and tried to veil the concern he felt for Raithe, but for the moment, everything rested on Sue. He took her hand in his and exposed the ring. "You must use this ring to get us out of here. With its help we can escape," he said earnestly.

Sue stared at the ring blankly. She did not see the connection. It had done its job by leading her to her brother. It was not likely to help anymore. Yet Thane's eyes were pleading with her to use it. She raised her other hand slowly to rub it, and when Raithe lost the support of her arm, he swayed alarmingly.

"Don't do that, Sue," he whispered hoarsely, on seeing what she was about to do. He struggled to cover her hand with his. "Between us we can make great magic." His breathing was becoming shallow, but he struggled to continue, and put out his other hand on which he wore the ring with the wolf's head. It was the one his father had given him. "We must hold these two rings together," he panted painfully, "and that will bring the master of these rings to us." He swayed almost drunkenly.

"What do you mean?" Sue gasped.

"Trust me." Raithe shivered violently and almost toppled over. Thane caught hold of his hand and turned to Sue. "Come on," he said, "I'll hold your hands together. Quickly, before your brother passes out again."

With Thane's assistance the two rings met and a shock like electricity ran up Sue's arm. A sudden flare of light filled the cave, not like the brilliant green of her ring. It lit up every sordid detail. The occupants of the cave flinched in the radiance. Raithe was losing his balance, unable to sustain sitting up, but his bright feverish eyes saw the cowled man and he managed to murmur to his sister,

"Sue – meet your father," and with that he slumped back into unconsciousness.

It was almost too much for Sue. She was shaking at the dramatic revelation. Thane still had a grip on her; otherwise she might possibly have done something silly. Astonishment immobilized her actions and she just stared dazedly at the cowled man who had appeared, and watched in fascination as his cowl slipped back and for the first time she saw the face of the man who had protected her from all kinds of danger. There was no mistaking whom he was, an older edition of Raithe, with a lean generous face and keen blue eyes that were now fixed on her. His head was topped by a mass of golden hair and he had a neatly trimmed beard. No wonder Deena had found it amusing that she did not know the man who had brought her to the snake people. Sue rose awkwardly to her feet, tongue-tied and suddenly overcome by shyness now that she knew who he was.

Tam stepped towards her and held out his arms with one word: 'Daughter'. She was caught in a bear hug and Thane smiled in relief. His one concern had been she would be annoyed when she found out who he was because he had not revealed his identity sooner. But Sue was overcome with joy that at last she had met the man who stood by her mother all those years ago when her grandfather banished her from the family. At length Tam pushed her back gently to Thane and turned to that young man's father. Bending low, he grasped the hand of his old friend and said,

"Vance, old man, it's good to see you again at last. I knew you had not perished with our companions, but I was unable to do anything to help. Oran put a spell on me after I fled the ambush. He might just as well have killed me because the chances of breaking it were a thousand to one. But miracles do happen and thanks to my children – the spell has been broken."

Vance coughed, and his grip on Tam tightened. He was about to speak, but the newcomer silenced him swiftly.

"Explanations can wait until we are safe. It is essential we get away from this place. At least one of the soldiers who escaped, knows Sonja is here and he will come back with an army. Did you want to say something, Thane?"

Thane nodded grimly. "Yes, I'm afraid we're trapped here. The bridge has been smashed."

Tam was unimpressed. "They wouldn't be soldiers if they hadn't done that. There happens to be another way out."

"Then don't you think they would have blocked that up as well?" retorted Thane dryly.

The King smiled at him almost indulgently. "I shouldn't think they ever went near it, knowing what it contains. Now let's stop wasting time and get moving. You help your father, Thane, and I will carry Raithe. I need you by my side, Sue."

Tam did not need any help in scooping up his son in strong arms. Sue was a little apprehensive as she followed him, mulling over his remark, 'knowing what it contains', but she hid her feelings under a forced smile. He led them in the opposite direction from the large cavern, going deeper into the mountains. The tunnel narrowed alarmingly and the roof came down so low they had to bend. The strategically placed torches had petered out a long time ago, and the only light they had, seemed to be following them. It had not dimmed ever since the rings had fused together. Sue thought it prudent not to ask where the light came from but then the roof became higher again and Tam waited for everyone to catch up. A peculiar smell hung in the air. Sue remembered it from when she crossed the stone bridge, a long time ago with Thane. It had the stench of something that was not human and already the hairs on her arms were raised.

The light showed the opening to another cave, a dark yawning cavity. Tam paused on the threshold and they all clustered round him, immediately hearing a continuous rasping sound coming from ahead. Then they saw a heaving mass of black bodies, which made Sue's stomach muscles contract. They covered every inch of the floor. Sue was reminded of the underground temple, but there was a subtle difference, at that time she had been drugged. Thane schooled himself to mask his emotions, and deliberately averted his face from his father. Tam's eyes probed the faces of everyone, seeking their reaction. They did not have to speak. He knew what they were thinking by picking up on their vibrations.

"Through here is the way to freedom," he stated bluntly.

Vance hunched his shoulders and said pessimistically, "You have a different way of saying 'death' from what I do."

The King smiled at his friend's ill humour. "I did not go through the snake ceremony for pleasure. But that is another story. Between Sue and me, we shall lead you through this pit of reptiles. We have the power to keep you safe from harm, providing you show no signs of fear." His eyes were inscrutable as he studied them. "You are grown men. Surely you can put your faith in Sonja."

A stunned silence greeted his words. Sue swallowed a lump in her throat the size of a golf ball, and she looked up at her father, trying to read his expression.

"How did you know about me?" she asked tentatively. Tam looked stern and said, "Deena takes too many liberties, but at heart she is a good woman with an unusual gift for seeing into the future. She did what she thought she must when she saw what was ahead of you, and then informed me when the deed was done. I forgave her when I found out you were not marked, and I have you to thank for that, Thane. So, gentlemen, my daughter is just as capable of walking through those snakes as I am. Whoever holds on to her will remain unscathed. I cannot help you because I am carrying Raithe. So do we go forward?"

Thane noticed Sue's eyes on him and immediately he stepped up to her and caught one of her hands, giving her a reassuring smile. "I would entrust my life to you."

"So would I," Vance added gallantly, and he grasped her other hand. "Just please remember I cannot move quickly. I don't want you to leave me behind." He glanced at Tam quizzically. "What are we waiting for?" he asked.

CHAPTER 17
SHEEKA TO THE RESCUE

Although Sue knew she would not come to any harm, it took all her courage to step down into the pit of squirming reptiles. Her every sense was aware of their deadly bite. How could Deena's magic calm hundreds of snakes so that the travellers could walk through them? She sympathised completely with Thane and his father, both of whom were reluctant to take this way out. Once Tam, with Raithe in his arms, had started on his way, Sue saw the uncertainty flicker in their eyes.

He was already halfway across, having every confidence in his daughter to lead the others to safety. She held on to their hands and Thane stepped beside her first, then came Vance, stumbling slightly, clinging onto her other hand. They neither of them looked down at their feet. They were both convinced they would step on the wriggling snakes. How could they possibly avoid them – there were so many. The snakes slithered over each other aimlessly. Sue, who was watching the reptiles intently, noticed they miraculously slid away from the travellers' feet. There was always a patch of bare rock ahead.

Vance was having difficulty from the onset. He floundered continuously. His stamina had been drained during his enforced captivity. He was a big man and Sue was finding it hard to support him and she dared not let go of his hand. He was covered in a sheen of perspiration, which made his fingers keep slipping. The odour in the enclosed space was overpowering. There seemed to be little or no ventilation. Thane, completely unaware of Sue's dilemma, watched Tam ahead with fixed eyes, trying to adjust to the slow pace at which they were moving. He wanted to get out of this place. His hand grasped Sue's with almost maniacal strength.

Having reached the other end of the pit, Tam realised his daughter was having trouble. He placed Raithe on a ledge beyond the cave and went back to help her. He took the situation in at a glance and without a word, caught hold of Vance and relieved her of the pressure. With a choking gasp, Sue then concentrated on Thane, and with great determination, dragged him through the heaving pit. Once the nightmare was over, she gagged, and leant weakly back against the wall of the tunnel. The other two were doing exactly the same. Tam touched her arm gently.

"You did well, Sue. In a little while we shall be out of here and with luck, you should see your mother tonight. Do you see that patch of light near the roof? That is where we are heading. Once through there you will be in the cave with the stone bridge. All your worries will be over then, because I shall fetch help for us from a higher source."

"What if the enemy is waiting for us?" Sue asked anxiously.

Tam laughed grimly. "I hardly think they will be. Right, everyone," he said as he turned to Thane and Vance, "let's get going while we are able."

* * *

What at first had seemed like a good spot for Barry and Zeno to wait for the others, deteriorated as time went by. The overhang was not much of a shelter; it was all right for a short rest, but not for long stays. Gale force winds whipped up the snow and piled it in drifts. Before long, there was as much snow under the overhang as there was outside. The horses were miserable and huddled together. Their coats were white and their heads hung down. Their breath made a cloud of mist form in the air above them.

Barry stamped his feet and hugged his body to keep the circulation going and to try and get some warmth. Zeno, who was a little more acclimatised to conditions, kept a careful eye on the stallions. Standing around was not good for them. If there was a medal given for perseverance, Barry thought, it should be given to them.

As swift as it had come, the blizzard petered out and the wind dropped, but with it, the temperature plummeted. The world around them was now covered with an unbroken mantle of snow. It was very beautiful to look at, but decidedly unpleasant to be out in. Barry blinked a few snowflakes from his eyelashes and the horses shook their heads, pawing restlessly at the ground. Zeno was worried.

"This is not good for them," he stated anxiously. "They need exercise before the cold sets into their limbs and does damage. Something must have happened to Thane and Sonja to delay them this long."

Barry was filled with apprehension. "Do you think they've had an accident? I'm going to look for them."

Zeno wished he had never spoken, but when Barry attempted to put his words into action by trying to launch himself through a snowdrift, Zeno grabbed his arm roughly and showed a spark of authority for the first time. "Don't be so stupid, man. They wouldn't thank you for interfering and you could kill yourself by not knowing where you were going."

Barry shook free of Zeno's detaining hand and glared at him. "You just said there was an accident."

Zeno did his best to remain calm. "They were your words, Barry – not mine," he retorted, unperturbed. "I said delayed."

"That's the same thing," Barry exploded. "She's my sister and I'm worried." Then he shut his mouth because he saw Zeno's face change to incredulous surprise. He remembered too late what he had said in the heat of the moment. Thane would kill him, but Barry was beyond caring. If anything, he was relieved Zeno now knew of the relationship. He could not understand Thane's reason for keeping it a secret. All the same, he did show remorse for his betrayal of Thane's confidence.

"Zeno," he began awkwardly, and the young soldier raised his eyebrows.

"Forget it, Barry. I'm more worried about the horses than your status in life. They can't stay out in the open any longer. Before long it will be night and the air becomes freezing. We've got to get them back to the tunnel where I can light a fire."

"But we're supposed to stay here," Barry objected, even though the thought of a fire made him want to return to the tunnel.

"We're supposed to use common sense," replied Zeno abruptly. "Come on. You take two of the horses and I'll take two. It will be hard work but I can guarantee you'll soon feel warm."

Barry cast one more worried glance towards the spot where he last saw his sister, then reluctantly followed Zeno. The way back was uphill, but surprisingly the wind had kept the rocky track free of drifting snow. By the time they reached the steep pathway, which led up to the tunnel entrance, the light was going and both lads were exhausted. Zeno would not allow Barry the pleasure of stopping, but chivvied him on to climb upwards. Just as the last stallion disappeared from sight, a dull thudding sound reached their ears. Both lads crouched out of sight and watched to see what was coming. They were not held in suspense for long because six renegade soldiers marched along the track. The two boys started violently. This was serious. Were they going to the waterfall, which would be disastrous for Thane, or just passing by? Zeno dragged a protesting Barry into the tunnel.

"A fire first," he snapped, trying to defuse the younger boy's panic. "And then we'll rub down the horses. After we've eaten something, we shall leave the horses here and investigate."

After the hostile environment outside, the cave felt almost like home. Barry attended to the horses, rubbing them down and feeding them, while Zeno busied himself with the fire and looking for food. They had not realised how ravenous they were. There was no dispute about who had the best job, they worked together in harmony until everything had been done. Only then did they sit down before the cheerful fire and watched the flames lick around the wood. They pondered on their next move, while the firelight played over their drawn faces. They felt relaxed and it lulled their reasoning; until they were no longer able to think straight. Before long, because of their fatigue, the fire weaved its magic spell and they fell asleep.

The wood crackling and the soft snuffling from the contented horses were the only sounds to be heard. The slumbering lads were dead to the world. Time passed by unnoticed. Only the stallions pricked up their ears as sound emerged from the tunnel. Saturn whinnied to draw attention to the fact someone was approaching, but still the boys slept. It was someone shouting out rudely that shattered the peaceful atmosphere. "Don't move or try to escape. We've got you covered."

The sharp voice brought Barry awake in an instant, and Zeno's hand froze in mid-air, as he was about to draw on his bow. It was infuriating to have been caught unawares. He glanced warningly at Barry who had his back to the new arrivals. Barry always acted before he thought.

"You can forget that," the newcomer said, indicating Zeno's bow. "If you're stupid enough not to post a sentry, you take what's coming to you. Move away from those horses, the pair of you. Come on – move quickly."

They scrambled awkwardly to their feet, in the shadow-filled cave. Zeno was furious at not foreseeing this happening. Barry was equally angry at being caught asleep. These people had approached silently from the ice caves, and with their horses' hooves muffled, had managed to creep up and capture them. The two lads stood motionless, not seeing more than an outline of the intruders, but the arrows pointing at their hearts were visible. Now was not the time to argue who was right or wrong. Thane had led them to believe this cave was a safe resting place for all travellers.

Barry unwillingly moved with Zeno to the far side of the fire. As he turned to face the enemy, the glow from the fire lit up his features and immediately there was a startled gasp.

"Barry! What on earth are you doing here?" It was a voice he knew so well. "Come to us quickly and we'll help you get away from that renegade before the rest of his men come back."

Barry gasped. "Tansy! How did you get here?" Amazement kept him rooted to the spot, but Tansy's companion was wary.

"Get over here at once, you fool." That was Annalee's voice. "We've still got your jailor covered. If that renegade harms you I'll shoot him. It seems we've got here just in time to rescue you."

"But I don't need rescuing," Barry blurted out. "This is not a renegade. This is Zeno."

Zeno had not moved. He respected a bow and arrow and Annalee still had hers pointing at him with a steady hand. Tansy, however, lowered hers and stepped forward, but still her expression was grim. "We don't care what his name is. He is Lex Ansell's man, or he was."

Barry did not like the way things were going. "What do you mean by 'he was'?" Barry deliberately stood in front of Zeno. "He's my friend. So if you intend to shoot him you can shoot me as well. Why don't you put your arrows away and come and have something to eat? We've got plenty of food."

The two girls looked at each other, but their intended victims had obviously decided to ignore them. Zeno may have felt uneasy, but he camouflaged it well and deliberately bent down to put more kindling on the fire.

From what he knew of the two trackers they were both good shots and at any moment he expected to feel an arrow pierce his flesh. Barry gave the girls a grin, and tried to mollify them. Annalee lowered her bow and nodded towards the stallions, where Saturn looked at her with his soft brown eyes. "How come you have four horses?"

"Because we need them," retorted Barry.

"Stop being annoying. Saturn belongs to Thane."

"So that's why he's here."

"Then where is he? And where's Sue?" Annalee stared around in bewilderment, and Barry retorted aggravatingly, "Let's eat and we'll tell you – providing you reciprocate and tell us how you happened to be here."

* * *

As dawn broke it was obvious that the storms and blizzards had gone. The inclement weather was replaced with hot sunshine, which quickly warmed the surrounding area. Only a light breeze blew through the pass and Tansy stood on top of the slope, enjoying the fresh air. It was a welcome change after their tedious journey through the mountain.

All differences had been resolved between the trackers and Zeno. They now accepted him as one of their own, especially after Barry had related everything that had happened to him since the river ambush. When Barry heard how uneventful the girls' trip through the mountains had been, he quickly related all the horrors that they had faced. Annalee thought this had happened because of something connected with Sue. She attracted these bizarre happenings. Some higher authority was doing its level best to prevent her from reaching the Queen – which made it imperative for them to find her and Thane right away. The loss of White Hawk was a terrible blow. They felt it badly and realised Thane must feel quite vulnerable without his bodyguard.

Annalee was soon joined by the other three and they led their horses down to the mountain track. The path, being clear of snow and ice, made it possible for them to ride the horses, which was a real advantage because they could make up for lost time. In high spirits they headed back for the waterfall feeling confident they could overcome any soldiers they met. The mountains loomed high above their heads with no cloud to hide the snow-capped peaks. Zeno once again pointed out the cleft in the rock face because the two trackers were unaware of its existence. The question as to who was going through it started up an argument. Each one of them had reasons of their own for being the one to go. It would have reached a stalemate had not something suddenly blotted out the sun.

Incredulously they stared up into the cloudless sky. In disbelief they twisted round, seeking whatever it was that had eclipsed the sun. Zeno's sharp eyes caught the tail end of a shadow as it disappeared behind a mountain, but before he could utter a word, it was over their heads. They automatically cringed, as a winged, armoured monster flew above them with a roar. It vibrated through the mountains. It was followed almost immediately by another monster, and they both vanished from sight.

"Try and get the horses under that overhang," Zeno yelled. "It will at least be some cover for them."

The horses were already uneasy, and the ones without riders tried to break free. Tansy acknowledged his words as sensible and quickly dismounted to help him, but Barry hadn't moved. His eyes were enormous as he watched the predators disappear. "What are they?"

"Dragons," snapped Annalee, "and no friend of ours. Stop staring and give us a hand."

Her words were drowned as with a roar the dragons were back again, spiralling above them and getting lower. Barry couldn't help it. He was transfixed. The beautiful green scaly bodies that shimmered in the sun mesmerised him. Their huge wingspan was so beautiful. He had never seen anything like this in his life before. The sight was awesome.

"Barry." Annalee pushed him angrily. "We're in danger. Help us." But Tansy managed to exclaim, "They're going to land, thank goodness."

"What's good about that?" Barry stuttered in astonishment.

"It means they are not hunting. Our horses are not the attraction." An extraordinary thought hit Tansy. "But possibly someone has summoned them here. It has to be something very important to make a dragon move."

The deafening roars from the two dragons were causing miniature landslides. They also warned other travellers to be wary of their presence. The foremost one swooped to the ground, his huge talons acting as brakes on the rocky track. His massive body was too near the little group for their comfort. When the second dragon landed, the pair completely blocked the trail. The first to land stretched his long neck, and with his mouth gaping wide, aimed a jet of flame at the nearby mountain. Then, folding his leathery wings to the side of his scaly armoured-body, he swept his heavily lidded eyes over the cringing group of people before him.

"Who had the audacity to call me?" he roared imperiously, and smoke issued from his nostrils. Barry was bemused now, trying to get over the fact that the monster could speak. Before Tansy could summon up enough nerve to answer, a commanding voice spoke from the cleft in the rock face behind her, saying, "I did, Sheeka."

The dragon's great head swivelled in that direction. A gasp of astonishment came from everyone except Barry, who knew no better, and Tansy blurted out, "It's the King."

If the others were impressed, the dragon was not. "You dared to call me out again so soon?" Sheeka thundered aggressively. "The little gift I took from you the last time did not deter you? What is it this time you disturb me for? I have more than paid my debt to you."

Tam stumbled forward under the weight of his son in his arms, followed by a dishevelled Sue. Then next was Thane, supporting his father, while blood stained the sleeve of his tunic. Annalee's throat was choked with emotion at seeing her brother injured and her father alive. She rushed towards them. Tansy's cry of 'no' came too late. Sheeka's barbed tail swung round and knocked her off her feet. Rather stunned, she picked herself up and Barry was beside her. He knew exactly how she felt because he wanted to go to Sue, and had not got the nerve to pass by this majestic animal.

"I ask only one favour of you, great Sheeka," said Tam, stopping before him and holding out his unmoving burden. “I need swift travel to Therossa for my son who is very ill – and my best friend Vance who cannot travel unaided. May I presume on our friendship and ask you to convey us there?”

“What do you think I am – a caravan?” Sheeka asked querulously. “We dragons are the true nobility of this continent and you wish to use me like a puny horse.” The dragon’s eyes were half-closed, almost as though he were going to sleep, but nothing eluded him. His big head looked round the group, swivelling back to the King again, “You are a presumptuous man. I am not your servant.” His voice became bored. “This is the last time I shall answer your call, and this time – mark it well – I shall expect payment,” he added.

Tam bowed to him, saying, “thank you, exalted one,” and for the moment Sheeka was mollified. The King looked past him towards the speechless travellers, taking in the skittish horses. His voice was full of gratitude when he spoke to them.

“I know you have travelled a long way searching for my son and protecting my daughter. I’m sorry to be whisking her away, but it is important to keep her with me. Head back to the city, all of you, and I shall meet you there again.” He turned back to the watchful dragon, enquiring, “Sheeka, have I your permission to climb on your back?”

“No you have not,” the dragon boomed with a show of temper. “Shoona will carry you. I shall carry the other three,” and his calculating eyes were fixed on Thane, Sue and Vance. Tam bit back the retort he was about to make, but his look was guarded. “Make sure you bring them to my palace safely,” he requested.

A throaty laugh rumbled from the dragon and a small jet of flame and smoke came from his nostrils. He waited passively while Tam and Thane settled the Prince on Shoona and the King clambered up beside him. As they were about to move away, Tam leant over and said in Sue's ear, "Travel with me now, Sonja."

Sheeka, for all his size, had acute hearing. His head swung round violently and with baleful eyes, which had the power to shrivel anything, thundered, "She stays here. If you want my help, you, and your son go with Shoona."

The dragon took to the sky and Tam shouted out desperately, "Look after her, Thane."

CHAPTER 18
THE PLATEAU

The path became little more than a ribbon as it wound its way between white speckled humps far below. The panorama spread out in all directions, disappearing into a bluish haze. Sue sat comfortably above the wings on the massive shoulders of Sheeka. She could feel his muscles working as his wings beat rhythmically in the air. Her hood had fallen back and the golden curls on her head streamed out unhindered behind her, looking like a halo in the brilliant sunshine. She clung to a ridge in Sheeka's scaly body and received no objections from the dragon. Sue felt perfectly safe.

Seated just behind her was Thane, keeping a wary eye on her. Beside him was his father, roped to him for safety against unforeseen accidents. In his weakened state, he was not able to help himself much, but his mind was as sharp as a razorblade and his eyes were alert. The other dragon followed close behind, carrying Sue's father and Raithe. They were almost within hailing distance, but the wind would have carried their voices away. Thane's good arm held on to Sue, and tightened instinctively when Sheeka took a dive.

"How are you feeling, Sue?" asked Thane, his husky voice barely audible, but she heard him, and could hardly restrain her cry of delight. "It's marvellous. I have never felt so excited in all my life. How much further have we got to go?"

"Quite a way," Thane shouted against the wind. "You're not getting scared – are you?"

"Not at all – in fact," she replied, "I'm thrilled. I never thought anything could be so exhilarating. Barry must be green with envy. Sheeka is being very careful the way he flies."

Thane grunted, secretly wondering what ulterior motive the dragon had for giving such a pleasant flight. "You don't want to say that and give him a swollen head," he snapped rather grimly.

He heard Sue's tinkling laugh. In her excitement, she saw no wrong in the dragon, and to his dismay she added, "Sheeka is not like that. He's wonderful. I've never seen anything so beautiful in all my life."

The dragon turned his big head and looked at her. Thane felt his heart plummet into his boots. Sheeka had heard her words. Dragons were known to be unpredictable – but they were also vain and conceited. Sue did not realise it, but she was making a rod for her own back.

Before long, Sue's attention was taken up by the huge expanse of green below them and Thane said quietly in her ear, "That is the Royal Forest of Redwoods."

"Then we're getting near to Therossa," Sue breathed ecstatically.

"Yes. Before long you will see the spires," said Thane with a happy smile on his face.

"Thane." Vance's voice cut in sharply, and his son looked at him enquiringly. "What is it?" he asked.

"The other dragon," replied the older man. At his words they both looked. Sue twisted round to see what it was doing and dismay flooded her face. The other dragon was heading in a different direction, getting smaller even as she watched. "Thane!" she choked. "What's happening?"

Thane's mouth was set into a grim line. "I think Sheeka's playing a game with us. He obviously has other ideas. Hang on, Sue. I'll not leave you whatever happens."

At his words, Sheeka gave an enormous roar and fire belched out of his mouth and nostrils. He started diving steeply and with a shriek Sue clung on for dear life.

* * *

Thane's worst fears were realised and he held Sue tightly as Sheeka plummeted to the ground with blatant disregard for their safety. The forest seemed to come up to meet them at an alarming speed, but at the last moment Sheeka levelled out before swooping to the ground. He lifted his head and with a great roar accompanied with smoke and fire announced his arrival to the other dragons basking in the hot sun. Then, swivelling his long neck round, he glared fiercely at his passengers, shouting, "Remove yourselves from my back." His voice was intimidating.

Sue looked around, completely confused with the sudden turn of events. After the last twenty minutes of invigorating wind playing on her face, its sudden withdrawal left her overcome with heat. Unsteadily, she moved herself off the dragon's shoulders; her limbs were shaking and she nearly fell. Thane said something quickly to his father, and aided her to the ground. Sue could do no more than sink to her knees, unable to sustain her balance. She took in deep gulping breaths and heard

Thane say, "Rest – while I get my father down," and she saw him clamber back onto the dragon to release Vance.

With an almighty roar, Sheeka was off immediately, lifting his body off the ground. Terrible anger engulfed Thane as he fell against his father. By the time he had righted himself the dragon had flexed his wings and was soaring into the air, carrying Thane and Vance to an unknown destination. Thane caught one brief glimpse of Sue standing alone on the ground. She was almost paralytic with the fear which engulfed her as she watched Sheeka getting smaller and smaller until he was blotted out by the dazzling sun. She was standing on dangerous ground, hardly daring to move and surrounded by fire-belching monsters. The sky was full of them, their wings glistening in the light from the sun. They circled overhead in lazy spirals and after a while she had to admit to herself how beautiful they looked, all shapes and sizes and all colours of the rainbow.

Unable to stand the heat, especially in this area, Sue cast off her thick parka and trousers and let them stay where they fell. Feeling the cooler air about her skin made her less sluggish, and her brain became active. Somehow or the other, Sheeka had contrived to get her here alone, so she knew it was imperative for her to escape before he returned. Without moving her position, she took in her surroundings. The most hopeful factor was the nearness of the Redwoods. They were only about two hundred yards away – but for the moment they were completely inaccessible because of the presence of so many dragons. No way was she prepared to walk amongst them, their very size was a deterrent. Mountains were to her left and in the other direction was a plateau, a vast expanse of land with little variation except for the number of dragons. Sue never knew so many existed. Up until now they had been only a figment of fairy tales, yet here they were, dotted all over the place. Many were slumbering on the hot rock with their long necks laid out like snakes, others were feeding, at which she did not look too closely – and one or two enormous ones fixed her with an unblinking stare from calculating eyes.

It was asking for trouble to stay where she was. With a supreme effort she put one foot forward in the direction of the forest, when an imperious voice spoke from behind her, saying,

"I am Silver, mortal woman. Do you wish me to show you where to go?"

Startled, Sue spun round, expecting to see a human person, only to find herself face to face with a white dragon, about the size of a horse. Her wings and scale-covered body were shot with red – for a dragon she was an exotic creature. But Sue was finding it hard to show friendliness after being forced here. Without giving much thought to her answer, she said, "Only if it's the way out of this place."

"That is a very unwise remark to make." Silver drew herself up haughtily. "Mortals are not welcome here. You should count yourself lucky to be invited."

"Invited?" Sue exploded. "I was forced here. Sheeka was supposed to take me to Therossa City and instead dumped me here."

"You sound disapproving." Silver raised one of her talons and fastidiously started cleaning it out with her teeth. For a moment Sue thought she had been forgotten, but the dragon held out her talon for inspection and added regally, “No one criticizes our King. Please remember that.”

“Except my King,” Sue returned bluntly. “He struck a bargain with Sheeka, and Sheeka broke it by bringing me here.”

Faint wisps of smoke issued from Silver’s nostrils and her heavily lidded eyes studied Sue more thoroughly. “So you are this Sonja I have heard so much about,” she remarked. There was a lot more power in her voice now, and a rumbling came from her throat as she continued. “To think we are both daughters of a king. I find that quite amusing. You are nothing like I expected. You have no power that I can see. Still, mortal – what shall we do to celebrate the occasion?”

Sue swallowed the angry retort on her lips. Who did Silver think she was, being so condescending? It suddenly struck her that maybe she could lure the dragon into helping her escape, so as sweetly as she could, she said, “I am very hot. Maybe you could take me to those trees where it is shady.”

The young dragon looked at Sue through inscrutable eyes. Then she lifted her noble head and flexed her wings. “Climb on my back,” she ordered abruptly.

Sue needed no second bidding. She clambered up very easily and sat herself on Silver’s shoulders, thinking things were going her way. With luck, once she was amongst the trees she could escape. With slow rhythmic movements, the young dragon took off. She did not fly very high – but neither did she head for the forest. Her rasping voice reached Sue’s ears clearly.

“Know this, mortal girl – and remember it well so that you do not make the same mistake twice. Thoughts can never be hidden from us. We are a supreme race. My father would banish me if I allowed you to escape into the forest. But do not despair. I am going to show you something that will make you so happy you will want to stay."

Nothing will make me happy to stay here, Sue fumed to herself, and she did not care if the dragon picked up on her thoughts, at the moment she felt too humiliated. Slowly the excitement she had felt earlier evaporated. It was sickening to be on the verge of meeting her mother again and then finding herself here. Maybe she could reason with Sheeka when he returned. She had not done anything to displease him. Then she wondered if it was possible to reason with a dragon – or was he as intractable as Thane suggested? Silver picked up on that.

She roared ferociously for so young a dragon and Sue desperately tried to mask her thoughts. They skimmed over the plateau of basking elder dragons, who watched proceedings through one eye. It was a waste of time to have two eyes open. Without any hint of its nearness, they came to the edge of the plateau where the ground dropped suddenly away. Sheer rocky cliffs fell down to placid blue water – a long, long way below. The stark cliffs seemingly spread for miles in either direction, with no sign of a break or way down in their formation.

Silver landed on the very edge, deliberately, Sue surmised, and she felt a sensation of vertigo. It crossed her mind how easy it would be to tumble downwards, if the dragon so wished. Looking ahead, she gazed over the sea or lake, which disappeared into infinity. But before that her eyes rested on a miniature plateau. The grey vertical rock rose from the water, its sides so smooth there was no possibility of anyone ever climbing up its sides. Its top was bare and flat. There was nothing on it except for one small white rock in the middle.

"Hold tightly, Sonja," came Silver's arrogant voice, "I'm taking you out there, and leaving you there until my father returns."

Without waiting for Sue's agreement, which she would have ignored anyway, Silver gracefully took off from the top of the precipice. After a few strong flaps of her leathery wings, she landed effortlessly on the isolated pinnacle of rock.

"Get off quickly, mortal," she roared. "I cannot stay here."

"But I don't..." Sue began, then her voice ended in a shriek as Silver raised herself onto her back legs and Sue fell with a thud to the ground. Another roar filled the air, coinciding with Silver's, but the dragon was already airborne and heading back to the main plateau. Sue immediately realised an animal was bearing down on her. A blur of white knocked her over and two huge paws held her down. A tongue rasped over her face and a soft whine filled her ears.

Incredulously, Sue was looking at White Hawk. He was not dead after all. He had not perished on the lake. She could forgive Sheeka anything at that moment. Thanks to his devious actions, she had found a long-lost friend. With an articulate cry, she buried her face in his fur. Now she didn't care how long she stayed here.

* * *

Sitting closely beside White Hawk, Sue stared out to the horizon, and realised that the sun, that was slowly disappearing from sight, was the same sun that Thane and all her friends were watching as well. In a roundabout way, thinking that made her feel closer to them. Every time a dragon flew near the rock, the wolf bristled and bared his teeth. He meant to protect Sue at all costs. Her elation at having found him alive was slowly diminishing. She was despondent and unhappy at being a prisoner. Sheeka had not returned, which showed her he was in no hurry to see her again. What was his reason for keeping her here?

She wondered how White Hawk had survived in the past, spending so much time living on a bare rock; but every day a dragon swooped low over the barren plateau and dropped a dead animal for him to tear to pieces. No one seemed to be bothering about her wanting any food. Maybe they did not know what humans liked. Did they expect her to gnaw at the carcass as well as White Hawk? Looking at the revolting pile of ripped fur and crushed bones, she automatically retched.

The last rays of sun vanished below the horizon and darkness spread rapidly over the water. A chill breeze swept round the pinnacle of rock. Sue was missing her parka. Shivering, she moved closer to the wolf for warmth and sat there, staring out into nothingness. What else was there for her to do? White Hawk, sensitive to her predicament, remained close by her side, motionless and on guard. Eventually the moon rose and a thousand stars studded the black velvet sky. The quietness of the night was shattered. From the main plateau a huge green dragon appeared, the moon making his scaly body iridescent. He circled round them, massive leathery wings creating a draught, before he levelled out and swooped to the ground, standing a few feet from Sue. She steeled herself to ignore his presence. White Hawk's hackles rose, his upper lip lifted to reveal bared teeth and he growled deep in his throat. A smaller animal would have taken the hint and slunk away, but the dragon disregarded all his threatening actions. He knew he was safe. Because of Sue's restraining arm, the wolf made no attempt to launch himself at the enemy, but his golden eyes glowed and dared the dragon to come any closer. Sheeka looked at Sue and the wolf disdainfully, and said sourly,

"So you two are friends. What a pity. Silver should never have brought you here. I get far better results by keeping my enemies apart."

"Why am I here?" Sue's eyes blazed and she hoped it hid her fear. "What have I done to upset you?"

The dragon settled himself more comfortably, taking his time and noting with satisfaction that she was a bag of nerves. "Nothing, Princess," he replied. "You are just a pawn in a bigger game, like the wolf is. You are payment for services rendered."

"What payment? I haven't asked you for anything." Sue's husky voice was incredulous.

Sheeka's tail thrashed the ground and fire spurted out from his long snout. It hit patches of coarse dry grass and shrivelled it up. From the corner of his eye he watched to see if his exhibition of power impressed Sue. "For continually doing your father's bidding, I claimed the wolf when I lifted you all from the lake." Sue could not control her start of surprise. "I have claimed you for taking his son and friends to Therossa city. I shall show him I am not his servant."

"So you think capturing me will hurt him?" Sue drew in a ragged breath and wondered what ploy she could use against this omnipotent dragon. Thane was right. Already she was learning how vindictive he was. He had not expected her answer.

"Of course it has hurt him." Sheeka voice was scornful, but his eyes were watchful. She should have shown hysteria by now, he thought, but instead she remained calm, so he continued aggressively. "You are his daughter – are you not? And he wants you back."

Sue began to take his measure, and was driven to say, "He's only interested in the Prince. If you really want to know, I'm the only person you have hurt. I was on my way to see my mother. I was looking forward to seeing her again, and, and," in sheer desperation she managed to produce a sob in her voice, "now it is all lost because I'm here. I am unhappy. She is unhappy, and, and I hope you are *very* happy."

A thunderous roar came from the dragon. His head snaked close to her and she could feel his hot breath on her face. "Do you take me for a fool, mortal girl?" he said angrily.

"A fool." As Sue repeated his words she crossed her fingers and stared the dragon straight in the eye. "Do not put yourself down. How could anyone as magnificent as you ever be called a fool, you, who are so wise and king of this entire domain and have a beautiful daughter, you, who can ride the skies and overcome any foe? Did you know how much I enjoyed flying with you? I thought you were wonderful and…"

"Stop!" Sheeka roared, and smoke belched from his nostrils. "You try too hard, woman. You think you are clever. I could stamp you out with one foot," and he lifted one up just to see the fear in her eyes and that made him feel better. "In the morning I shall decide on your fate, yours and that wolf." Another belch of smoke issued from him before he added, "though why I'm bothering about the wolf, I do not know. We could eat him."

He turned his head away contemptuously and flexed his wings. The interview with her was over. "Don't run away, Sonja." Then he laughed harshly at what he thought was a witty remark. It was like thunder rumbling in his throat as he lifted his hulking body off the ground and took to the sky. Breathing fire that lit up the sky, he headed back to the plateau.

Sue shivered, and huddled closer to the wolf. Even playing on the dragon's vanity hadn't got her anywhere, in fact, she seemed to have annoyed him. Her eyes listlessly scanned the water down below, watching as it hit the rocks and broke into what looked like a thousand diamonds. She wondered about the possibility of jumping to escape. It was daunting to see how far down the water was. Could she manage it?

Sue stared at her hands. The ring looked lifeless; why should it sparkle, it had done its job and found Raithe. There was no point in rubbing it now. It was not light she needed, but a miracle. It was useless to contact Raithe while he was ill. Out of sheer boredom, her fingers caressed the facets, and much to her amazement they flooded the area with a brilliant green glow. White Hawk turned his head away and with a sinking heart, Sue knew Sheeka would see the light and fly back.

She was aware of the cowled man standing nearby, but he made no move to come too close, and his usual greeting did not come readily to his lips. For all she knew, it might not be her father. His voice was indistinct when he said roughly,

"I wondered how long it was going to be before you used the ring. I've come to take you away from here."

Sue rose to her feet, but White Hawk whined and backed away. Sue was immediately disturbed. There was something wrong. "How can you get us both away when this place is inaccessible?" she asked dubiously.

"Both!" The hooded man was clearly startled. "I'm not taking you both. I've just enough power to carry you away."

Sue stepped back to be nearer the wolf. The feeling of something wrong was strong. If it was her father why didn't he greet her? Why had he completely covered himself up again? The prescience of danger was overwhelming. "If you can carry only one person, take White Hawk. I shall be safe with Sheeka."

The cowled man stiffened. "Don't be stupid, girl," he admonished, "This is not a time for sentiment. Come with me now. Sheeka will kill you."

"No." Sue knelt beside White Hawk and hugged him. "He will not kill me. He has a code of honour, but he will kill the wolf. Please take him back to Thane with my love. Come back for me later if you have the time."

"Don't be such a foolish person. Your mind is addled. Come to me at once. We must be away," he insisted.

"No," she retorted, "you go away. We're staying here."

A roar filled the air, so violent the ground shook beneath their feet. The cowled man vanished and Sheeka stood in his place. The changeover was too quick to be an illusion. It was the dragon being devious and trying to bend her will to his by using a shape-shifting magic. Somewhere deep within her, Sue knew these dragons were magical creatures that wanted dominance over everything, but instead of being cowed after the trick played on her, she was furious.

"Why did you pretend to be my father?" she asked. "What were you expecting to gain? To think I thought you were honourable! Instead you're nothing better than a conceited…"

"Silence," the dragon roared, and his forked tail thrashed the ground. It missed Sue and White Hawk by inches. "I had to test you and find out if your love for your friends was sincere. I have no wish to hold you here." His booming voice broke off because Silver landed lightly beside him. "I shall take you and dump you in the forest."

"And you'll take White Hawk as well?" Sue asked quickly.

Smoke issued from his nostrils. "Only because you passed my test, mortal woman," he said. "Climb on my back and Silver will bring the wolf."

Sue turned to White Hawk, and at the same time Silver moved towards him. His ears went back and he howled; before anyone knew what he intended, he leapt off the plateau. Sue screamed out in horror. Silver flew after him and her talons caught his body before he hit the rocks and water below. She banked round and flew back over the plateau. Only then did Sue start breathing again.

Her limbs were shaking, and in a deceptive tone, Sheeka said regally, “Hurry up and sit on my shoulders. There is no telling where my daughter will drop the wolf.”

CHAPTER 19
THE HOMECOMING

Shivering as the cold night air caressed her bare skin, Sue clung on to Sheeka. If she turned her head, she could make out the other dragon trailing in their wake. Once Silver found Sheeka following her, she abandoned the lead to him since he knew where he was going. Sue thought they were lucky to have such a bright moonlit night, but in actual fact, it made no difference to the dragons, they could see under any conditions. Below them was the dark mass of trees, which spread out for miles in all directions. Moonlight could not pierce the thick foliage, but at one point, Sue was sure she saw lights beneath her. Obviously it was nothing of importance, because Sheeka still flew on. The Redwood forest was vast.

Sue tried to relax, wishing that she were riding on Silver, and allowed herself the luxury of thinking about her mother. She must be getting near her home. Their last meeting had been in this forest below them.

After endless flying, the forest thinned and a fire became visible amongst the trees. Sheeka circled around unnoticed by those below. Screwing up her eyes, Sue tried to see who was gathered round the flames. Disappointingly, she saw only dark movements. However, Sheeka's eyes were keener than hers because after two circuits, he headed onwards. Silver still kept following their trail with a squirming wolf, which kept up an incessant howling as he was held in her talons. Sometime later, a streak of light was seen in the sky, and beyond it the evidence that dawn was on the verge of breaking. The trees ended abruptly and now sea spread out below them. The first signs of habitation appeared, as little lights bobbed up and down on the waves. Sue drank in the scenery as the dragons followed the coastline. Then etched against the lightening sky, were spires, towers, minarets and slender turrets. She caught her breath in wonder. Rivers looked like silver snakes and lakes shone out like glittering gems. Sheeka banked sharply and spiralling down landed in the Royal Park. Silver landed beside him and let the demented wolf escape.

Sue slithered off the dragon, her feet touching soft grass. Sheeka was impatient to be away, having no love for cities. He did not even ask how she felt. With a muted roar he said, "Goodbye, mortal girl. You are on your own. Come, daughter – we must go."

But his great voice booming out drew attention as he took off. Silver waited for a brief moment, her unreadable eyes fixed on Sue. The girl walked unsteadily towards her, not realising that from the shadows, eyes were watching her every movement. Without fear, she reached up and touched the dragon's long beautiful neck – for some reason, not wanting her to go.

"Thank you for your help, Silver," she whispered huskily, "and for saving White Hawk's life. He could have died. I should never have been able to face Thane again."

Silver moved her wings slightly and her tail twitched, the only sign she gave that Sue's words moved her. There were sounds coming from the nearby shadows. The arrival of two dragons had not gone unnoticed, even though it was barely light. Her throat made a rumbling sound.

"I shall always be on hand to help you. You and I will stay together. After all, we are both kings' daughters."

A feeling of gratitude swamped Sue and for a moment she could not speak. She managed to ask gruffly, "How could I ever get in touch with you?"

"Just call out my name, Sonja, and if it's from your heart, I will come," she replied.

Then with a roar and display of fire, she soared into the air to join her father. Sue watched her silhouette getting smaller and smaller, until the tiny speck merged into the receding shadows. The feeling of being alone did not last very long, because at this point Sue became aware of several indistinct human forms standing a little way off. She was in Therossa and would very soon be with her mother. They would know where she should go. She turned to face them and saw an assortment of people who had hastily dressed because they had been lured to this spot by the dragons.

Their curiosity was not veiled. They were suspicious. A portly man with a bald head and apron over his breeches seemed to be the one in charge. He stepped forward to speak, his actions tentative. He asked who she was and where she came from. The others clustered closer, eager to hear her answer. Sue stared at them, stunned, and while they waited, the silence grew longer. A muttering came from the people there.

"Witch! Witch! Witch!"

Sue felt stupid, unable to understand their language. Some were becoming angry and they pointed to the sky, then to her. They were fearful and uneasy at what they did not comprehend. They thought she was a human dragon sent to destroy them. A small bare-footed girl pulled at her mother's skirt for attention, and when she eventually got it, jabbered away excitedly. Sue caught only one word, which she understood, and that was Sonja. The mother pushed her away with an exclamation of annoyance and Sue took the opportunity of pointing to herself and saying.

"I am Sonja," and she repeated the name. "Sonja."

Agitation rose amongst the crowd. The hum of their voices was like an angry swarm of bees. Someone hastily tried to light his tinderbox and the little girl dashed back into the shadows. The man who had first spoken held a light and moved carefully towards her, almost as though he was afraid she would bite. Sue tried not to flinch as he shone the light under her face. She could feel the heat from the naked flame, which threw grotesque shadows and highlighted only one part of her face.

A gasp of horror came from the watching people. Not because they recognised her, but because she looked like something spawned from the devil – and she had arrived riding a fire-spewing monster. She must not be allowed to escape. They were now furtively egging on the bald man to make a citizen's arrest and take her to the guardhouse. Sue had no conception of what was in their minds. She had no idea she presented the appearance of a tramp. The terrible let-down at the way she had arrived in Therossa made her feel faint.

It was still dark because the moon had vanished and the sun had not yet shown itself. Most people were still in bed. She moved away from the people, distraught, not realising they thought she was trying to escape. As one, they surged forward with the idea there was safety in numbers. Sue looked frantically for the wolf. She could not face this on her own.

"White Hawk!" she screamed.

The men in the group were about to lay their hands on her when White Hawk hurtled from the shadows. He would have launched himself on the luckless men had she not shrieked, "Come to me, White Hawk."

Much against his own instincts, the wolf stood close by her side, defying anyone to step nearer. He had no need to bare his teeth; the group of people were already intimidated and had backed away uncertainly. The little girl could be heard shouting excitedly to someone and from the cover of the trees came three soldiers and an older man. The little girl kept pace with them, keeping up a running commentary.

As the villagers melted away, the soldiers stood at a respectful distance, allowing the old man to walk straight up to Sue and the wolf. The relief at seeing them both alive and well rendered him speechless for the first time in his life. There was relief in Sue as well at seeing him, and she was delirious with happiness. It was Amos.

"Amos!" she cried, flinging her arms round the astonished man and hugging him without reservation. "I'm so pleased to see you."

Amos was touched and gratified at her welcome. He had to clear his throat and gently disentangle himself from her arms. "Not so much as your father and Thane will be to see you. Come on, the pair of you. Let me take you to the Palace."

* * *

Rowdy songs floating out from the guardhouse filled the night air. The constant chink of mugs told everyone ale was flowing freely within. They did not need a celebration to enjoy themselves. The Therossian soldiers were a happy bunch, although those who were patrolling the walls may have felt a little down at not being with the happy gathering. But in the end, they had been the lucky ones who had seen the two dragons flying over the city. Dragons were tolerated because of their power and size. There was no way anyone could win in a battle against them. They rarely came over the city, but when they did, people opened their eyes in wonder at their beauty.

As Amos approached the gates and saw the dragons disappearing up into the sky, his expression was sour. He did not hold with the King's collusion with the magical creatures. They were a proud and omnipotent race – not to be trusted. From experience he knew they were devious, cunning and did little for love. What they expected in repayment was more than anyone could pay.

He stood by the gates and paused, pleased that the long night was nearly over and the passing of the dragons had meant nothing at all. It had been a very exacting day with Thane and the Prince trying to rally the people to form a posse so that they could get Sue back from the dragons' stronghold. He felt too old to get involved. His hot-headed days were over, and he knew they were on to a losing battle. For a while he intended to relax in the cool night air.

He was speaking with the young officer in charge of the watch and at first did not notice the poorly clad girl approaching the gates, but when she was within shouting distance he became suddenly alert, because her shrill voice yelled out, "The big dragon has brought Sonja to us, but the people think she is a witch and are going to harm her."

Amos swore, and swung round to the startled officer. It never crossed his mind that the girl might be lying. "I want a few men," he snapped, "just in case there is trouble," and he got it immediately. He followed the girl with no thought to his own safety. Amos was a man who asked for and got respect without even trying. It crossed Amos's mind that he should send someone for Thane, but he dismissed the idea at once. He strode out into the night, the little girl keeping up a running commentary as she led the way.

They reached the gathering of people, and at a glance Amos could see the situation was getting ugly. His heart plummeted. He knew exactly how unexpected events acted on superstitious people, and the dragons must have triggered off this situation. Then he noticed with satisfaction that White Hawk was having no difficulty in keeping them at bay. His old heart leapt for joy at seeing Sue standing there with the wolf. Rumour had it that he had perished a while back. Before he could even utter a word, Sue looked up and saw him, and flung herself in his arms unreservedly, scattering people right and left. Amos was touched, much more than he would let on. He knew that as long as he lived, he would always be fiercely protective of Sue. Her arms hugged him and he wished she were his daughter. Against his will, he slowly disentangled himself from her embrace.

"Come on, Sonja," he said gruffly, and coughed to cover his embarrassment, "let me take you to Thane who is driving everyone mad because he wants to form a posse to find you."

"Thane is doing that?" Sue's eye sparkled, and Amos grunted. "Yes – and that brother of yours," he added dryly.

"Barry?" she queried. Amos scowled, just like she knew he would and said predictably, "he's not your brother," then realising Sue was grinning at him mischievously, smiled dourly. "You knew I meant the Prince, didn't you?"

"Of course," she agreed, "but you asked for it. You are so serious over something that is not all that important, whatever you think; I'm still related to Barry. He is, after all, Raithe's cousin."

Amos prudently ignored what he did not want to hear. He turned abruptly to the gawking people and glowered at them beneath his bushy brows, wondering how it was they never recognised the Princess. Most of them had been unable to follow the conversation, but in their own language he told them to go away as everything had been resolved. They obeyed him, drifting back to their humble homes. The little girl was being chastised by her mother for not telling her that the girl brought by the dragons was the Princess Sonja.

White Hawk padded alongside Sue, and Amos led the way back to the gates where many soldiers were waiting with undisguised interest. At their approach, they sprang to attention but to Amos's regimental mind, Sue spoilt it all by saying, "I'm sorry if I've kept you all up. I didn't mean to arrive this late – or is it early?"

Smiles appeared on the soldiers' faces, but vanished as Amos growled, "the Princess Sonja is tired and confused.

You will find things will be different in the morning. Get back to your posts." With that, he took Sue firmly by the arm and led her through the gates. She had the distinct feeling he was treating her like a child. They passed the guardhouse, where the singing was louder than ever, and her escort fell out and waited for Amos to disappear from sight so that they could nip in and tell their mates they had met the Princess.

Amos apologised about the noise, but Sue had not even noticed it. She was too happy in the realisation that at last she had come home. For weeks she had thought of this moment, and now that it was here, felt a touch of nervousness. Would her mother be pleased to see her after the way she had broken her heart the last time?

The cobbles beneath her feet felt uncomfortable after walking over grass and rock for so long. The awareness of buildings was overpowering. She chafed there was not enough light for her to see things properly. But her prayers were answered when a shaft of sunlight spread across the sky. Dawn soon vanquish the shadows. They crossed what she thought was a courtyard to a flight of stone steps leading up to great wooden doors. On either side were glowing stones, which reminded her of Deena and the snake people. At the top of the steps, Amos paused, and said simply.

"Welcome home, Sonja."

He flung open the door with a flourish. As the light poured out, so did the sound of many voices. She braced herself, expecting something momentous to happen, but the opening of the door went unnoticed, the people in the room being engrossed in their own affairs. Feeling reprieved, Sue studied her surroundings. Before her was a large hall with a raftered ceiling from which hung many lanterns. She got the impression it was a place to eat. The benches had been pushed back against stone walls and the centre was left clear for people to congregate. It was full of an assortment of soldiers, hunters and trackers. At the far end, on a raised dais, stood Raithe and Thane. From what she could see of them this far back, they both looked the picture of health. She doubted she would ever get used to the Shaman's healing. Thane was still in his tracker's outfit, and a spruced-up Raithe looked resplendent in a long-sleeved white shirt with dark fitting trousers and a white cloak hanging nonchalantly from his shoulders. In spite of his princely appearance, there was nothing pompous in his actions. Thane and he looked like a couple of good mates, standing there and speaking to the crowd. Sue felt she was an interloper and turned to Amos, uncertain. He gave her a gentle push.

"Go in and let them see you. Those two are trying to rouse up enthusiasm to get a search party organised to find you. You can save them a lot of time and bother by appearing amongst them."

Sue went forward, doubtfully at first and then with growing confidence. The wolf remained by the door with the old man, but his golden eyes followed her every movement. The noise and uproar was just as bad, if not worse, than the guardhouse. Everyone was standing up and shouting out their opinions. Thane and Raithe were making a good job at cajoling support for their cause. Even though men and women liked Thane, and would follow him anywhere, everyone knew it was tradition to argue. It made the cause sound better and much more worthwhile. The outcome would still be the same.

No one had noticed the newcomer. Their eyes were fixed on the men before them. Sue pushed her way through the crowd without anyone giving her a second glance. Everyone was pushing and shoving. It was taken good-naturedly. She was one of the crowd and they accepted her actions. No one realised who she was until she had reached about halfway down the hall. Then the light from a lantern directly above shone on her hair and made it shine exactly the same as Raithe's. This drew the eye of several trackers. Their attention was now focused on her. Astonished, they moved slightly to give her a path. The silence from them began to spread and this in turn drew the attention of the two on the dais, to their direction. They saw Sue immediately.

"Sue!" They both shouted her name simultaneously and leapt from the platform scattering the crowd. For Raithe they parted ranks and made a passageway, which Thane took advantage of. Brother and sister clasped each other, not noticing the old man at the back who wiped a tear furtively from his eye, oblivious of the many other eyes watching them because they looked so alike. Their clothes were the only means of telling them apart. Raithe's face was full of emotion, and Sue's shining with happiness, After all these weeks of travelling, she was at last with her brother. Eventually, pulling away from him and studying his face, she murmured in amazement, "You're better. Not ill anymore. I was so worried about you."

"I know you were," answered Raithe, but his lips twitched. "It was something you gave me to drink that did the trick." She knew he was laughing at her, so grinned and hugged him again. This time it was Raithe who broke the embrace. "Sue – I don't quite know how to say this – but thank you for saving my life. You came just in time, I was told."

"It was not just me," Sue countered quickly. "I can't have you thinking that. There were lots of us working together. Mostly thanks are due to Thane."

"Well, I know that," said Raithe, smiling broadly, "but put yourself in my shoes. I can't hug him – can I?" Then Thane was beside her and gripped her hands. He did not need to tell her how he felt. Sue read it in his eyes. The pressure of his hand increased as he said, "I don't think anyone can feel happier than I am at this moment."

Raithe cocked an eyebrow at him. "Then in that case it's up to you to make sure she stays." He turned to the assembly of people, his whole attitude amiable. "Thank you, my friends, for rallying to our call. As you can see, we no longer need your help. Don't go away. Stay here and celebrate the return of Sonja. I am going to take my sister to her mother now – and I suppose I had better take Thane because he will only follow if I don't."

There was a general good-humoured laugh. As brother and sister left the room, Thane walked behind them. At the door Thane stared incredulously at the white wolf, choked to see him still alive. White Hawk threw himself on his master and Thane's day was made complete.

CHAPTER 20
LEX ANSELL'S BROTHER

The group of people, led by Raithe, made their way from the noisy hall to where the actual Palace showed up like a white ghost in the shadowed dawn. Sue's mind was in turmoil as dormant memories of Tamsworth Forest reawakened. How long ago was it since she had left those peaceful woods and the forest retreat of the Queen? For the first time she started to experience doubts. What sort of a life was she going to have here now that all the adventures had finished? She looked up at Thane's happy face as he walked buoyantly by her side with the wolf following. Maybe her thoughts were reflected on her face because he gave her hand a reassuring squeeze. Walking on her other side, Raithe was eager to show off his home. He would be devastated if he knew of her doubts. He was gaining a sister, she was losing a lot. Thank goodness Barry was somewhere around.

The palace was not the huge grandiose building she had been expecting, but a one-storey house that sprawled out with a tower built on each end. The pointed roofs of each tower supported a slender spire. Although she looked hard, there was not enough light for her to distinguish the exterior of the building, except to know it was white. They did not pause. She was led through a bevelled glass door, and before she knew it, they were stripped of friends because Amos and White Hawk had been left outside.

She had no time to query why, because her brother urged her to walk forward along a wide corridor. The beauty of her surroundings held her enthralled. The walls were panelled with mirrors reaching from floor to ceiling. Torches, which gave off heat and light combined, were shaped stones whose lights were reflected back a thousand times in the mirrors. Marble columns, with a vein of gold running through them, interspaced the mirrors and arched to the ceiling. Although the floor was marble, a beautiful red carpet ran the length of the corridor, and up the stairs at either end.

Several rooms led off on either side, all with double doors and edged with gold. They were spacious and furnished to suit the person to whom they belonged. Thane pointed out his room as they passed. He often stayed here. Raithe explained that his apartment was in the tower behind them. His mother and father occupied the other tower, which was where they were heading.

The corridor ended and three arches reared before them. The middle one led into a domed winter garden where an array of beautiful flowers and tall graceful palms were set out to perfection. Someone obviously took great pride in this garden. The outer archways curved round on either side, to join further up and spiral to the top of the tower. Halfway, just before they joined, there was a room on either side, but the doors to them were closed.

At the base of the elaborate staircase, Sue paused with a gasp of dismay. She had seen her reflection in one of the mirrors. Until this moment she had not thought of her appearance, but she looked no better than an unkempt wanderer seeking refuge. How could she burst in on the

Queen? Typical of her companions, because they were men, they wanted to know why there was a hold-up.

"Because I look like something the dog dragged in. I can't see my mother in this disgusting state. I need a wash."

"What on earth for?" Her brother stared at her. "You look fine. You didn't show this concern the last time you met her. What's different now?"

"You didn't see the way Annalee and Tansy scrubbed me down. That's not happened this time. I've got all the filth and smell of caves on me. I feel terrible."

Raithe dismissed her fears with a laugh. "I came home looking very similar but it didn't worry our mother then, so snap out of it."

"You were ill and could do nothing about it," began Sue, "but I'm…"

"That's enough. Stop it right now," Raithe cut in, his voice not far short of commanding, "Our mother will not care how you look so long as you're here. She loves you, Sue, now come on and stop wasting time." He turned his back on her and started walking up the stairs. Thane's voice halted him.

"I'll stay here," he said quietly. "It is, after all, a family reunion."

"You will not," Raithe objected, allowing these interruptions to get at him. "If it hadn't been for you there is no telling where my sister would be now." Almost as though he sensed a rebellion, he scowled at them both and added petulantly, "Now that's settled, we'll have no more arguing. Let's go." He acted so like his former self that it made Sue grin. She said to Thane, "The Prince has spoken, so jump to it, man."

Raithe glared at her and she glared back, equally fierce. Thane laughed. He forgot his former objection. "If you two are going to act like this all the time, I think I shall ask the King to send me on a mission."

"Sorry," apologised Raithe trying to look contrite, but failing miserably. "Just kick me when I get high-handed."

Sue tucked her hand in his arm. "Are you going to lead the way up or am I going on my own?" she asked.

Harmony restored, they proceeded upwards, feet sinking into the thick pile of the carpet. They passed the two closed doors on the way up the twisting staircase and did not stop until they reached the top landing. Here the door was open and a cheerful glow of light fell onto the floor. From within, a soft murmur of voices could be heard. Sue was suddenly nervous, and had Raithe not got a firm hold on her arm, she would have fled back down and out of the building.

A tall man filled the doorway while she was deliberating on what action to take. He was dressed in an embroidered waistcoat which covered his long-sleeved shirt, and dark trousers piped with gold. So different from the black cloak and cowl which Sue was used to seeing on him. Sue was confused until she saw the smile of welcome on his face and flung herself into his arms. They tightened round her, and she was drawn into a room where her mother, clothed in a green-sheathed dress, was pulling back heavy curtains to let in the early morning sun. Her long dark hair fell loosely to her waist.

With an incoherent cry, her mother sped across the room, and Sue met her halfway. In a tight embrace, they stared at each other with tears in their eyes. The moment was too poignant for words so that for a few seconds,

Tam just stared at them. Then realising he also had other guests, he ushered his son and Thane into the room, sat them in chairs and placed drinks at their elbows. He looked tired – there were lines of strain about his eyes.

"I haven't slept," was his answer to a query by Thane. "We have the upper hand at the moment, but the revolutionaries are still out there and getting stronger. The Queen is worried about her daughter's safety. We are sure they are biding their time before they attempt to kidnap her again. She is an easier target than Raithe. If Sue gets wind of it, her mother fears she will want to return to her old world."

Raithe and Thane exchanged glances and Thane said reassuringly, "I think you will find she is here to stay providing you don't lock her up in the palace, away from all the friends she has made. She is like a bird, sir, and needs to be free."

Tam remained unconvinced. "I understand she will never be a model daughter like her mother is hoping for – but what about her brother and sister she has left behind? She will miss them one day and become bitter."

Thane swallowed a mouthful of liquid before he said, "there is only one she cares about – Barry, and he has followed her here. He means to stay. Actually, he will make a good tracker."

"Barry," the King mused. "I met him once some time ago. He fell into a bog if I remember correctly. Said he was following you after I had pulled him out. Didn't he tell you about me?"

"Not exactly," Thane answered wryly, remembering the incident. "He didn't seem to remember much about you."

Tam sighed. “It was that damn curse,” he said, but he did not enlighten them any further. He turned his head towards his wife and daughter. “I thought this was supposed to be a happy moment, not a crying contest. When you two women have finished crying over each other, do you think you could join us?”

Guiltily Sue wiped her eyes, but they were tears of happiness because everything was exactly as it had been on her last visit. They walked across the room hand in hand, to sit with the men. Tam’s eyebrows rose on seeing Ruth’s detaining hand and asked dryly, “Aren’t you going to let go of her?”

Ruth sighed, “I’m so afraid she is going to vanish again,” but she removed her hand obediently and Sue gave her another hug. “I’m not going away again – well, not voluntarily. Therossa is now my home and I want to be with you all, for always.”

There was no denying her sincerity, but Tam needed more convincing. “What about Moira and Gaynor, and your grandmother?” His voice was hard as he asked, “Surely the pull of them is going to drag you back to your old world?”

Sue shook her head, slightly embarrassed at having four pairs of eyes upon her. “I resolved all my ties before I left,” she said. “My grandmother…” She paused, for the first time feeling a pull on her emotions, but she swallowed and continued steadily, “She has been misguided by events. Although if there was a way I could occasionally see her, I should be grateful. There is only one stipulation I bring with me, I want Barry to live here with me.”

"Barry is welcome," Ruth retorted with enormous relief showing on her face, "although I did not realise he was with you this time. He is a great lad and I like him very much. I am sure Raithe will love taking his cousin around." She saw Raithe give a nod. Then she looked earnestly at her daughter, "Why is he not here with you now?"

It was Thane who answered. "Because he is travelling through the mountains with Annalee and Tansy, bringing the horses home. The dragons could carry only so many people, so they carried those needing medical help."

Ruth was immediately alarmed. "Will they be safe on their own?"

"Of course they will. They've got Zeno with them."

"Zeno." Ruth looked startled. "That bounder is a renegade."

"Not anymore. He threw his lot in with us long ago and has proved his worth time and time again. Without his help we should never have found Raithe." Thane blinked, trying to keep his voice steady and eyes open. Tam yawned, stumbling to his feet.

"This is ridiculous. I am far too tired to get into arguments now. The main thing is, we have welcomed Sue home. When the others arrive, we shall have a party. There are many things you have not heard. That will be the time for storytelling. Now – I know you all think it is morning, but I am going to bed. I have been up all night. Ruth! Look at Sue. She's just about to fall asleep. Suppose you show your daughter where to go," and he yawned pointedly at his son and Thane. "That applies to both of you as well."

* * *

"From the top of this hill, Barry, you will see the city of Therossa for the first time." Annalee cantered alongside the lad and she looked immaculate. He wondered what secret the two girls shared because he was hot and dishevelled, with perspiration in his hair. He didn't like the wicked gleam in her eyes, or the way she said, "Do you think you will manage to get there?"

"Of course I will," Barry retorted indignantly. "I've got more stamina in my little finger than you two together. I've enjoy trekking through the mountains, but I'll be jolly pleased to get off this horse. It must be great to fly on a dragon." A whimsical look entered his eyes and Tansy answered sharply,

"You can forget ideas like that. What you saw way back was a one-off. We don't normally come into contact with those exotic creatures."

"But think how exhilarating it must be to glide through the air like Sue did," Barry protested. "Why couldn't they have taken all of us? If I don't get off this horse soon I shall not be able to sit down for weeks."

"In that case – get off now while we're alone. Before long we're bound to be seen. Someone will notice our approach and then there will be a welcoming committee at the Palace gates. It is absolutely essential that when you reach there you ride through. Not walk."

"Why? Is walking forbidden?"

"Barry!" Annalee exploded, "do you have to be so cantankerous? I'm really looking forward to knocking some sense into you. If you want to be a tracker like us, then you must do as we say."

Zeno moved silently behind them, and swinging down from his mount came alongside. He caught hold of Barry's bridle, saying gruffly, "Come on, I'll walk with you. I want to stretch my legs as well."

"They said…" began Barry

"Forget what they said," Zeno interrupted. "Women always exaggerate, or hadn't you noticed?"

"Well you're not a tracker." Annalee looked at him disparagingly. "Soldiers do as they please. People like Tansy and myself have a strict code of etiquette to which we adhere. That's why we're elite and Lex Ansell hates our guts."

She turned her back on him and resumed her conversation with Tansy. The four of them had taken three days to reach this far, three days of light-hearted banter and camaraderie. There had been no incidents and no renegades to cause trouble. The dragons had seen to that by flying low over the mountains. Their appearance frightened everyone off. With the exception of Zeno, who was really down in the dumps, they were all eagerly looking forward to the end of their journey. Zeno cast a dark cloud over everything by being withdrawn, and barely speaking; but Barry, pleased at his support, slid off his stallion and walked with the young soldier to the edge of a drop.

Therossa lay spread out beneath them, a place of magical buildings surrounded on two sides by a sparkling sea, which brought a gleam of excitement to Barry's eyes. He loved the sea. The dense forest of Redwoods could be seen to the east, and between where they stood and the walled city, there were many farms dotted about. Zeno pointed to one very near, at the foot of the mountains, where a few animals grazed, and a woman, looking little more than a dot, could be seen.

"That's my home," he said, his voice unemotional; "or what used to be my home."

"Would you like us to drop in and say hello?" asked Tansy.

They had not heard her come up behind them. At the sound of her voice, Zeno stiffened. "It would be a waste of time. I'm not welcome there anymore." His words were bitter, and he added. "In fact… I'm not welcome anywhere." Since no one said a word, he went on doggedly, "once we reach the city, the trackers and hunters will take one look at me and see a renegade – and if we happen to meet Lex Ansell he will…"

"He will have us to contend with," Tansy interrupted, her tone brooking no argument from him. "Snap out of it, Zeno. You've proved your worth and we shall all be behind you. I wondered what had been eating you up all morning. Now, Barry," she swung round to him making him jump, "anything you want to know before we set off, *riding*!" She emphasised the last word with a grin.

Barry did not answer. He was absorbed in the panorama unfolding before him. As the cool wind fanned his flushed cheeks, his eyes took in the towers and castle walls with their battlements, flimsy bridges that seemingly stretched to nowhere, and graceful spires surrounding colourful domes. "Do people actually live in those?" he asked, indicating the large buildings.

"Some do." Tansy loved this view of the city and appreciated how he felt. "They are mainly academies and other places of learning. The building with the golden dome is the Shaman's Palace and there are several others that have the facilities to train hunters and trackers. The army barracks are near the old castle, and," she paused because Barry's mouth opened, "before you say anything, the King's Palace is not visible from here. The trees in the distance hide it from view. It's not a huge building if that is what you are looking for. All state occasions are held in the old castle. That way, the whole city of Therossa can be held comfortably in its banqueting halls."

"And if you're still looking," Annalee added, "You can see a horse and rider heading our way. Someone has obviously been watching out for us."

Barry felt a surge of excitement. He screwed up his eyes, trying to locate where Annalee was pointing. "Would it be Sue?"

"I doubt that very much," replied Annalee. "She will not be allowed out on her own." She squinted at the moving dot. "It's a soldier – no, it's an old man with a wolf for protection."

"Then it is Thane," Barry blurted without thinking. He went even redder under Annalee's glare. "Idiot," she retorted. "Thane is not an old man and he no longer has a wolf. Anyway, he wouldn't leave your sister. I somehow think it's Amos. Tell you what, Tansy – let's stay here and wait for him, then..." She broke off because of a sudden movement near her and screamed, "Zeno! Come back."

He ignored her and leapt onto his horse. With tight lips he turned and headed back the way they had just travelled. Without any hesitation, Tansy lifted her bow and aimed an arrow at him; it missed his head by half an inch. Barry's blood ran cold that she could bring herself to do this, and Zeno was obviously shaken.

"If you don't stop," Tansy yelled out threateningly, "the next arrow will kill you."

Zeno jerked on the reins and swung the stallion round, his face white. "I'm not waiting for Amos," he shouted back defiantly, "that man hates me. I'll take my chances in the mountains."

"And that's no chance at all," retorted Tansy grimly. "He's got a wolf with him that will track you down and tear you to pieces. Take my advice, Zeno, and stay with us. I can guarantee Amos will not harm you."

This shooting was too much for Barry. He ran up to Zeno and caught hold of his horse. The young soldier looked down at him in surprise. "Let me get up in front of you," he panted. "Amos will never shoot if he's got to shoot me to get at you – at least, I hope he won't. He would never be able to face Thane and Sonja."

Zeno was amazed. He had such a low opinion of himself that it came as a surprise that someone would stick up for him. He swallowed an unexpected lump in his throat. "I'm not using you as a shield, Barry. I'm not that sort of a coward."

"Then in that case," cut in Tansy trotting up to him, "don't run away. Stay here and face him." Their eyes met and locked. His were fiercely determined and hers accusing. When he failed to speak, Tansy added nonchalantly, "Barry's friendships often lead him into some awkward situations, but his judgement of character has never let him down yet. He saved you in the cave, against us – think of that. Now you've got three of us to protect you against Amos. What's it to be, Zeno?"

Zeno bit his lip, unable to make a decision. "Well…" he stammered.

"Good," Annalee interposed, "then let's get the horses together and we'll sit over there and rest while we wait for the old man."

It was not what Zeno wanted to do, but he allowed them to have their way. They tethered the six horses loosely to a rock and made themselves comfortable sitting on a flat area. Annalee passed round a water bottle and they waited, their conversation desultory. Barry sat beside the young soldier in case he tried to do something stupid. Although Tansy gave the appearance of not bothering with him, he knew her sharp eyes never missed a movement. It was a desolate spot, with nothing to see except the cold rock face soaring high above their heads.

Nothing stirred in the late afternoon sun. They waited a long time before the sound of someone approaching reached their ears. Over the ridge came a white wolf, its eyes reflecting the glare of the sun. It walked slowly towards them, showing strong pointed teeth as its upper lip drew back in a snarl. Tansy and Annalee were motionless, their eyes locked with the wolf as it raised its head to take in their scent. They knew it would only harm them if they moved. Barry stood up and the wolf's head jerked in his direction. In disbelief and wonder he breathed, "White Hawk?"

Before Annalee could interrupt, the wolf's ears pricked up and he padded towards the boy with a whine.

"White Hawk, it is you," said Barry, flinging himself at the wolf and receiving a long wet tongue on his face. "You didn't die in the water."

The wolf moved from him to Zeno and snuffed round the young soldier's face to let him know he remembered him, then he acknowledge the two trackers. Annalee was ecstatic at seeing him still alive. In the midst of their delight at having him with them, no one noticed Amos approaching until he spoke.

"So you've all made it here safely, not that I expected anything different from you two" he greeted the girls, his face wreathed in smiles. His glance swivelled over Barry and barely acknowledged him, but when his eyes rested on Zeno, his face hardened. "Why isn't he under surveillance, at least with his hands tied?" he snapped testily.

"He's not a prisoner," Barry burst out furiously, ignoring the wince from Tansy at his outspoken answer. "We don't tie up friends."

"Friend! Him!" exclaimed Amos, and he nearly burst a blood vessel. His expression was like thunder and fixed on Barry. "You should think twice about whom you call a friend. You don't know who he is, do you, lad?"

"If you think you can shock me, think again," Barry growled, but he wondered at the same time what it was Zeno had failed to tell him. He happened to see the sardonic look on the old man's face, and stiffened. Bother Amos for his insidious way of sowing seeds of doubt. He would defend Zeno to the bitter end. "You ask the girls. They can vouch for him. If it had not been for Zeno, we should never have found Raithe."

"Don't make me laugh," the old man exploded. "I don't have to ask the girls anything. They know you're easily led, lad." He glared balefully at the young soldier. "Of course he knew where the Prince was. He put him there," he declared.

"That's a lie! "Barry flared, jumping to his feet and earning a growl from White Hawk.

"Is it?" Amos breathed heavily. "Have you asked him who he is? Or shall I spell it out."

Barry glanced uncertainly at Zeno who had maintained complete silence all through this repartee. "We all know he was a renegade, Amos," he started to say triumphantly, "but – "

"There are no buts about it," the old man snarled. "He's Lex Ansell's brother."

All eyes switched to Zeno, but for once in his life the young lad was not flustered. With a certain dignity he drew himself up proudly, saying, "I've never hidden that fact from anyone. I've just not thought it important enough to mention. Being Lex Ansell's brother is not a thing I'm proud of. Anyway, to get the facts straight, he's my stepbrother. The son of the bully my mother married. He knew perfectly well what he was doing when he dragged me into his organisation, and it's only thanks to Thane I had a chance to escape. Well, Amos, here are my wrists if you want to tie me up. I'm perfectly sure Sonja will vouch for me when we reach the city."

Zeno moved up to the old man and held out his hands. A flicker of surprise crossed Amos's face and a grudging respect leapt into his eyes. "Put them away, lad," he growled, "I'm only testing you. Right, the rest of you – let's head for the city."

* * *

Ruth gazed upon her sleeping daughter, still unable to believe she was really here. She was not going to risk anything happening that would whisk her away again. Reluctantly, she beckoned to the servant, and they both left. Even as the door closed behind them, Sue stirred. Something had woken her. She sat up with a start, momentarily confused at finding herself in unfamiliar surroundings. The sun streamed through tall open windows casting a soft rosy glow on the floor, indicating the day was further advanced than she thought. A cooling breeze billowed out the gossamer drapes and touched her cheeks. She rubbed sleep from her eyes and gazed around her expectantly. There was nothing in the room which could have awakened her. Looking out of the window, she saw it overlooked a parapet which separated her from the rest of the town, and now and again a Therossian soldier marched smartly by. Sue did not think the sound of his feet would have disturbed her.

The best thing was to get up and explore this new environment. It did not occur to her that maybe she ought to wait until someone came to show her where to go. On finding her clothes exactly where they had been dumped the night before, she quickly donned them, only to find they had been changed while she slept. She approved someone's choice. They were not exactly a tracker's outfit, but they were very acceptable, and there were soft suede boots, which laced up to her knees.

Although the room was lacking a mirror, Sue felt confident and ready for anything. Determinedly she moved towards the door when the sound that had previously awakened her was repeated. It was a voice, which called clearly, "Sonja."

Bewildered, Sue stared around. There was no one in the room. The sentry would never have called out, and anyway, he had long since passed by the window on his rounds. She walked back to that spot and cast her eyes in all directions, making sure no one was lurking outside. The uncanny silence started to get at her. It was so different from what she expected life to be. Without thinking she rubbed her hand because of the irritation there. It didn't help, only succeeded in making it hurt all the more. Glancing down, she realised the skin around the emerald ring was inflamed. As quickly as her trepidation had come, it faded. Raithe must be playing a joke on her, she thought. She lifted her hand and rubbed the stone, expecting to see his face. Astonishment rooted her to the spot as the ageless face of Deena stared enigmatically out of the facets. It was not possible. The snake woman had nothing to do with the ring.

"Well, at last? Can you hear me, Sonja?"

Sue tried to steady her nerves. "Yes I can. But I don't understand. I thought only Raithe could contact me on this ring. It's a bond between the two of us and no one else"

Deena's expression remained cynical. Her eyes bore into those of the startled girl. "You have a lot to learn about magic. None of you have my powers. They are great. Only King Sheeka's are greater. You have been initiated into the snake cult. You are now one of us and I can contact you whenever I want to."

"You forget I'm now..." Sue began, but the old lady cut her short impatiently. "I have not called you up for idle chit chat," she admonished. "I have something important to tell you and time is short. You are to carry out a delicate mission."

"I live in the Palace now. I can't go around doing jobs for you," Sue protested, but Deena pressed on relentlessly. "It is the fact that you live there that makes it ideal for you to carry out my mission. You have been chosen to unite the dragons with your people."

"Me!" The word squeaked out in her surprise. Sue quickly suppressed the quiver of excitement, which flowed through her, and asked, "How? I'm not in a position to do that."

Deena's face was unreadable. Her answer was equally ambiguous. "It is not for me to guide your footsteps, Princess, but when the time comes, you will know what to do. Two great nations should live together as friends." Sue felt duty bound to protest – but Deena cut her short. "Go now through the winter garden and into the open space beyond," she ordered. "Someone is waiting for you, someone whom you must keep with you at all times."

Startled, Sue demanded answers. Deena's face faded and she found herself looking into a dull green stone. Her finger no longer hurt. But tense excitement filled her. She moved to the door, eager to find this person waiting for her. She had forgotten her mother and father, forgotten she was under the rule of the King and Queen. She had to do Deena's bidding.

There were no servants around – the place could be deserted. Cautiously she moved down the staircase and through the arched doorway, which brought her out amongst the lacy ferns. Within minutes she came out at the other end and was in the Palace grounds. She breathed deeply, remembering the days spent trekking with her friends, sitting round campfires and talking beneath the stars. They were days of easy comradeship. She sincerely hoped that now she was installed at the Palace with Ruth, those days were not going to fade into obscurity. A winding path invited her to follow it. It was bordered on one side by low blooming shrubbery, and on the other, tall graceful trees were interspersed with lots of colourful flowers. Here and there was a stone bench which had arms and back for anyone who wanted to rest. No matter how much she searched, Sue could not find anyone waiting for her. Possibly Deena was playing some devious game. She was a fair distance from the Palace and could no longer be seen. Belatedly, she wondered if she had been unwise in coming this far. She sat down on one of the stone seats to relax, and jumped up immediately on hearing an eerie voice say,

"Thank goodness for that. I thought you were never going to stop. They should have chosen someone a lot younger than I am to do this job."

Sue counted to ten while she steadied her nerves and wiped perspiration from her forehead. Acting as normally as she could manage, she glanced casually around the deserted area, and said, "Well, now that I have, perhaps you would stop hiding and join me."

No one appeared. She wondered why she expected anyone to do so. Her courage was stretched to its limit and she had the uneasy feeling she should never have come here alone. Since no one appeared, a shiver of fear touched her, and trying to keep the tremor out of her voice, she exclaimed,

"I'm sorry, this might be your idea of a game – but it's not mine. I'm returning to the Palace," and as good as her word, she regained her feet, just as the voice panted,

"You're a hard taskmaster. You should have a bit more consideration. I don't move as quickly as you. I told you I was too old," and from beneath the shrubbery, a long black sinuous snake slithered to her feet. For one second only Sue was startled at seeing it. Then she swallowed hard and said in disbelief,

"I think I'm going mad. Was that you speaking?"

The snake reared its head almost like a cobra. "Of course it was. Why are you so surprised? We're not all alike, you know, so stop acting mindlessly. Now – are you going to pick me up or have I got to be undignified and slither up you?"

Hastily making sure no one was watching, Sue bent and grabbed the snake, which arched its body and muttered aggressively, "For goodness sake be careful. Let go… you're holding me like a sack of potatoes."

"Sorry." Sue apologised and released her grip, and the snake wound itself round her shoulders, its bright red eyes fixed unblinkingly on her face. "Well, that's better, you're learning. Now that we've met each other, let's get going."

"Excuse me. Get going where?"

"Why, to the Palace, of course. Goodness gracious, where did Deena pick you up from?" the snake snapped testily. "What place had you got in mind if not the royal apartments?"

Sue shook her head. She could just imagine Thane's face if she arrived back with a snake. "I can't take you there, the whole household would have a fit at seeing you," she protested, and the serpent sighed.

"Why do I get landed with people like you? What's the matter with everyone? I don't bite, you know. I'm not like my brothers and sisters in the mountains. I'm quite civilised. I talk."

Sue caught the snake just below its head and drew it in front of her. She scrutinised the squirming reptile. "Now let me get this straight," she said carefully. "You can't kill anyone."

"Guilty as charged," he muttered gloomily, then his voice sounded chuffed, "but I can scare the living daylights out of anyone."

"That, I can believe."

The snake wriggled from her grasp and said presumptuously, "Since I'm going to be living with you for a while, I don't mind being in your pocket until you need me."

"When am I…" Sue began, but her voice broke off because he slithered neatly into one of her deep pockets and disappeared from sight. Sue shook her head and wandered back towards the Palace, hoping no one could see the bulge in her jacket.

CHAPTER 21
THE DRAGON PACT

The little specks Sue watched from the Palace window became larger as they drew near. At last she could distinguish Barry and Zeno, but felt a tinge of uneasiness because they were walking apart from the others. Annalee and Tansy appeared to be in deep conversation, while Amos and the wolf preceded the small procession. She had been aware of their advance for some time, and found it frustrating to be kept within the Palace walls like a prisoner. Every nerve in her body wanted to ride up the track and meet them. She did not understand Thane's reluctance to let her go. Turning abruptly from the window, her eyes glared at Thane and Raithe who were both studying a map of the parkland beyond the battlements.

"Why can't we go and meet them?" Her voice sounded impatient. Thane shook his head without lifting his eyes from the map.

"It wouldn't be safe. There is something wrong out there."

"How can you possibly know that when you're in here? Even if there is trouble, shouldn't our friends be warned of the danger they're heading towards?"

"The danger is not up on the track," Thane replied. "It's down here."

Sue allowed her feelings to get the better of her and stamped her foot in frustration. "What could possibly be wrong?" she demanded, staring at the gates where a score or more soldiers were standing around. "I haven't seen Barry for days. So you two study that map. I'm going down on my own."

"You're not." Thane spun round, no longer preoccupied. He caught hold of her arm before she vanished through the door. "Be a little more aware of your surroundings, Sue," he admonished. "Take a look beyond the battlements. What do you see?"

Sue gave the scene a cursory glance just to please him. "A lot of people hanging around, but isn't that normal? If they can't get inside the gates then they've got to hang around somewhere else, so outside the gates seems to me to be the logical place."

"It's not normal," Thane growled. "Villagers do not turn out in these numbers unless something is about to happen. Since there is no function going on – it makes one wonder why they're all here. There's only Amos and a couple of trackers coming along and they can be seen any day, in any place. There is no need for this reception. I tell you, something is up."

"And I'm telling you that I'm going to find out," Sue retorted, refusing to see any danger, "So if you're not coming with me, I'll go on my own." She twisted nimbly from his grasp and vanished through the door. Thane muttered something uncomplimentary at her back and the pair of them had no option but to follow in her wake.

They caught up with her when she paused at the gates, where soldiers, seeing who was coming, stood to attention. The soldiers on the wall hadn't noticed them. All had quivers slung round their shoulders, and bows in their hands. Many carried a sheathed dagger tucked in the belt. Normally it was not necessary to be armed like this. They rarely met any trouble. Outside the gates today, people were milling around and looking threatening. A good percentage of them were well covered, unusual for such a nice day. The Captain in charge had his own suspicions and dismay swept over him when he saw Raithe and Sue approaching. One or two people gave a feeble cheer. Normally the villagers would have been lustier in their greeting. The young Captain's eyes were serious on meeting those of Thane.

"Begging your pardon, sir, But you shouldn't have brought the Princess here. I don't like the look of things. There is trouble brewing out there. My men are having difficulty in keeping the crowds under control. They keep surging forward."

Thane frowned, still inwardly annoyed at Sue's blatant disregard of his warning. "We don't normally have trouble from the villagers – do we?"

"That's the worry, sir," said the captain. "I don't believe they are villagers – and look over there to the sky. What are those dots that keep moving around? It's a bad omen." He glanced pointedly at Sue. "Under these circumstances, don't you think it would be safer for the Princess to watch from standing well back?"

"I quite agree," Raithe pompously cut in, "and make sure she stands well back with some soldiers in front of her."

The Captain nodded; relieved they had listened to him. He put out a hand to guide Sue, but she sprang back, her cheeks flaming and eyes furious as they swept over Raithe. "Don't you start telling me where to stand," she said angrily. "I'm staying here with Thane. I'm sorry,

Captain – you don't have to rearrange your men for me. Maybe Raithe needs escorting to a better position."

"It's the perfect place for you," Raithe snapped. His temper flared up at being contradicted by a woman in front of the palace guard, especially his own sister. But Sue glowered at him. "If it's that safe, what are you doing down here? I'm remaining where I am."

Raithe's jaw tightened. His fury increased. "You'll go where I…." But her temper equalled his own. She didn't give him the chance to continue but interrupted, "Since when have I gone only where it is safe? I'm as good as you are any day so stop trying…"

"That's enough," snapped Thane, "the pair of you are forgetting yourselves." He pushed his way between them, quelling a desire to shake some sense into both. He became uneasily aware of the many eyes focused on the Prince and Princess – not all of them belonging to soldiers. Many of the people beyond the protective line of guards had stopped and were listening with interest. "I understand how you feel, Sue," Thane added, but in softer tones. "If your father were here, he wouldn't want you in danger."

Sue swung round on him; her temper now directed his way. "I'm not in any danger," she insisted. "Nothing is going to harm me. I'm staying right where I am so that I can greet my brother and friends."

"He's not your brother," muttered Raithe unwisely because he was feeling rankled, and Sue nearly choked on her anger. From out of nowhere, a gruff voice said, "Oh boy! Oh boy! I wish I could show myself."

Only those in the vicinity heard the unexpected voice. One was the Captain who, with an annoyed expression on his face, looked sharply at his men. Raithe and Thane were nonplussed, peering around for the person who spoke. Feeling a movement in her pocket, Sue's face drained of colour. She had forgotten the snake, so now she tried to look as confused as the rest of them. When she met Thane's eyes, she shrugged her shoulders. The young Captain swallowed nervously and was saved from saying anything because just then White Hawk bounded through the gates and nearly flattened Thane where he stood. The crowd eased back a little, but no one noticed.

The wolf then went up to Sue and rubbed his massive head against her in his way of greeting. Suddenly, his ears pricked up and with a little whine, his keen nose gave special attention to her pocket where he worried the moving bulge with curiosity. Only Sue heard the muffled, terrified voice which came from there because of the noise going on around them.

"Get him away from me. This is not the way I anticipated my demise."

"Thane," Sue gasped weakly and immediately had his attention. His eyes roved over her and White Hawk, and he promptly issued a sharp order to bring the wolf to heel. When he spoke, his voice was accusing. "Sue, you haven't got a snake…" but he never finished the sentence. Amos and the others swept through the gates with a clatter, bringing the spare horses with them.

Barry leapt off his mount and was at Sue's side. She was enfolded in a bear hug. Then there were Tansy and Annalee to welcome. Grooms appeared like magic and the horses were led away. There was so much kerfuffle going on, Amos's voice was barely heard as he demanded to know what all the people were doing here.

Over the excited hum of conversation, no one was aware of the man who pushed his way to the front of the milling crowd, until he spoke. Then his sneering arrogant voice held everyone's attention. He made no attempt at all to disguise who he was and brazenly let the soldiers see his renegade uniform. "It seems to me that I've arrived at the opportune moment to collect what is rightfully mine. I didn't expect such a big turnout to greet me."

He stood before them, his thin face leering as it swivelled from person to person. Anger was simmering under the surface in all those who surveyed him. He was the type of man who had the knack of getting beneath everyone's skin. He was rakishly dressed, but this did not hide the fact he was fully armed. Amos gave a signal, which kept the guards from arresting him on the spot. His glare was full of contempt as it fell on his old enemy. "You've got a nerve coming here, Ansell. I should have thought you knew there is no welcome for you here. Take my advice and clear off now before I have you clapped in irons."

"Sorry, old fellow," replied Ansell, "but you've got my property. Return that and I'll consider it."

Amos narrowed his eyes and blocked Thane from coming any closer. "You're exhausting my patience. If you've got a liking for dark cells, you're going the right way to occupy one."

Lex's smile was supercilious. He stared down his long beaky nose back at him. He seemed very blasé in front of so much opposition – so much so the old man was wary and watchful for double-dealing. Lex said airily, "You can't arrest me, you silly old man. I haven't done anything wrong, yet. You put one step out of place and I'll make you look ridiculous. I'm asking for only what is mine to be returned to me. Of course," he added nonchalantly, inspecting his fingernails, "if you want to fight…" He left the rest unsaid.

Amos's face was suffused with fury, and this time Thane did step in front of him and asked Ansell in an icy voice, "Just what is this 'thing' of yours that we're supposed to have?"

"Thing." Ansell raised his eyebrows mockingly and he drew himself up haughtily. The people nearby withdrew slightly, giving him space to move. "Thing," he repeated the word, "I do love your phraseology, Thane." His eyes rested on someone in the crowd, then he added, "That is not what I would have called Zeno."

No one said a word following his stark announcement, but the silence was broken by Zeno himself, who pushed his way to the front and stood between the two bristling men. Instead of cowering as used to be his wont, he held himself erect and faced his stepbrother. His newly acquired assertiveness threw Lex off guard for a moment, but he soon had himself under control as he heard Zeno say,

"You've got no power over me. I don't belong to you, Lex."

"Oh yes you do, boy. You signed a paper," Lex snapped.

"Only in your dreams," replied Zeno, smiling sadly, "such a paper doesn't exist. You got rid of me weeks ago when you sent me on a spying mission, hoping I would never return. Well I'm not returning. I now work for Thane and the King."

Ansell drew himself up, hoping to intimidate the lad. His expression became crafty. "You can't do that," he snarled, playing his trump card, "you're a deserter – and as a deserter you're under arrest as from this moment. If you try to escape, my men will shoot you."

Zeno opened his mouth to protest but Amos pushed him aside and spat at the renegade, "Where's your army?"

"Show him," Ansell roared.

Then all became clear. From the trees in the distance galloped a flood of men on horseback, waving swords in the air. The cloaked villagers around the Palace gates suddenly revealed their true identity by dropping the cloaks covering them and showing a well turned-out army. The strategy was obviously well thought out. Their bows were ready for shooting. Ansell laughed almost like a maniac as he stared at the dumbfound Palace guards.

"Every one of you," he sneered imperiously, "soldiers included, are under threat of attack from my men. One word from me and you could all be wiped out. You are outnumbered six to one. If any one of you wants to shoot – go ahead, but you'll end up a dead man. Now, I appreciate we do not want to kill each other needlessly, so I've got a proposition for you. I will magnanimously give up my rights to Zeno – and in return, you will give me Sonja."

A babble of disbelief broke out in the air, which Thane quelled instantly by saying, "Over my dead body, Ansell. You think yourself clever, but you'll never get away with this."

"I already have," said Lex, his smile sinister. "There is absolutely nothing you can do. Your men will be dead directly they move."

"May I move?" asked Sue quietly, "or will you shoot me too?"

She heard Barry's cry of anguish and Raithe's hiss. Lex Ansell bowed to her like a gentleman and his tone was mocking as he said, "You are free to move, my lady."

She walked up to him and a warning glare from Thane stopped anyone from being foolish enough to intervene on her behalf. She deliberately avoided eye contact with her horrified friends, and stood before the renegade, saying clearly, "You have made a bargain. I have always been brought up to shake hands on a bargain. Will you shake my hand, Lex Ansell?"

Lex Ansell smirked at his men and held out his hand as he swaggered towards her. He was too conceited to suspect any subterfuge. Sue's hand whipped the black hissing snake from her pocket and grabbed the renegade firmly. The snake reared up at Ansell and he leapt back in terror – his eyes wide with fear.

"Get it off me, you shrew," he roared, as sweat poured down his thin features. The disturbance this caused was enough to make his men back away. At the same time an arrow from the palace guard pierced his arm and Ansell thought he had been bitten. Clutching his arm with one hand, he used the other to grab the snake and throw it at his stepbrother. If he was going to die, then so was Zeno. Sue caught sight of Zeno's terrified face. "Trust me," she yelled to him. "Catch it."

Zeno swallowed and nerved himself to take her at her word. He caught the snake in mid-air, and nearly dropped it as it said, “Thanks, son. I didn’t want to hit the ground. Put me in your pocket, please.”

Lex suddenly realised he was not dying. There was no snake. Maybe there never had been one. There was only the Princess, weaving evil magic spells to make him appear a fool. She still stood before him, a little apart from the others and she was still watching his reaction through hard eyes. She was not in the least impressed at the way he was acting.

Suddenly the renegade realised his army was not fully behind him. The men were breaking ranks, unnerved by what had just happened. Meecha’s story was widespread in the barrack room. This man knew her powers with a snake. Lex spun round and roared at his men.

“Keep under control, you dolts. We’re not beaten yet. We have still got the upper hand.”

“I don’t think you have, Ansell,” interrupted a grim voice, “you lost control of the situation a few moments ago.”

Lex Ansell’s mouth fell open in sheer surprise. He saw the King standing unexpectedly before him. Where had he come from? If Lex but knew, he was not the only one bemused at his sudden appearance. It was not possible for such a thing to happen. The feeling of magic vibrated in the air and surrounded everyone, except perhaps for Sue. She was used to her father’s sudden comings and goings.

With startling clarity she realised what the dots were which were circling in the air, and in a blinding flash it came to her what she had to do, to get rid of the renegades for ever. She raised her arms and called out clearly,

"Silver! Silver! Come to me."

Tam put his arm over her shoulder, giving her a reassuring squeeze, and his deep voice joined with hers as it boomed. "Sheeka! I summon you."

All the eyes of the watching people felt compelled to turn to the sky. The renegades tried to make use of the diversion for their own ends, and closed ranks – but they were too late. The sky became full of dragons. With roars and spurting fire they swept over the men, so low, some howled in pain as the flames singed them.

Tam turned back to the renegade. "Right, Ansell. Who's got the upper hand now? Remove yourself and your army from my kingdom; and never return. Otherwise you will not survive this day. I can't make myself any clearer than that."

Lex tried to bluster, but he was facing a barrage of arrows. The contempt on Zeno's face was like rubbing salt into a wound. There was no time to make threats to his stepbrother; the dragons were becoming more than a nuisance. He turned round and yelled out, "Get me a horse, someone."

But there were no horses. At the approach of the dragons they had bolted. His men had to flee on foot, chased by dragons that swooped low and passed over them with mouths gaping wide, and more than one was burnt. Screams filled the air. These monsters were invincible and chased them all away. Cheers filled the air from villagers and Palace guards alike, who stood on the wall, watching the panorama unfold before their eyes.

Barry dashed to his sister's side, and Raithe, determined not to be outdone by Barry, followed him. Sue was unaware of them because Silver spiralled down and landed in front of her, followed by Sheeka, whose green scales glistened as the sun caught them. The massive proportions of his body caused quite a stir amongst the watching people. He swung his huge tail round to acquire the best posture and show the gawking villagers how great he was. No one came close to him, but all the time his eyes were intimidating and watchful. Sue passed by him as though he didn't exist, and walked up to Silver, putting her arms round her scaly neck.

"You came, Silver," she whispered, and she could feel a tremor run through the dragon's thick skin, almost like a cat purring.

"You called," Silver answered politely. "Did you have a reason, other than for us to get rid of those men?"

"You better had," roared Sheeka aggressively, flames belching from his mouth, but he made sure they went in the air. "This summoning of us is becoming a habit."

Tam walked to his daughter's side, and eyed the white dragon warily. "I did not realise that you two knew each other. This is like the past rearing up its head again – yet I've got to say that it seems so right that it should happen."

Sheeka's tail thrashed and he flexed his wings, annoyed at being ignored by everyone. "Do not be taken in by his words, daughter," he thundered, addressing Silver, "his speech is too smooth to hold any substance. Remember, I know this man."

Smoke also issued from Silver as she roared, "Be silent, Father. I know this woman. Sonja and I are both daughters of a king, and we are friends."

Sheeka thrashed his tail again with more violence, this time just missing Tam. His voice thundered over the parkland and he noticed with satisfaction that several people covered their ears. "That is no reason to treat us like pack horses."

Silver's mouth opened wide and her head snaked towards her father. She blew hot smoke over him and he drew back in surprise. "It is common sense to be friends with these people. We share the same land." Her eyes fixed on him angrily. "If Sonja and I can be friends – why cannot the two kings follow our example? This warring is stupid. We should live in peace and help each other."

"Mutiny," was the only word Sheeka boomed out.

"No – not mutiny," Sue put in bravely. She moved away from Silver and stood close to the massive green dragon. She felt as though Deena was using her like a puppet. "Would you like me to tell you my thoughts?" But she didn't wait for him to answer, "I think all dragons should be allowed to land in the Palace parkland. It has been proven that they are wise creatures and full of knowledge. They could share their wisdom with us mortals, and in return, the people of Therossa would treat them for what they are – kings of the sky and friends. Some of us," and for the first time she looked daringly at Sheeka, who was watching her through half-closed eyes, "some of us could learn to fly on you if only you would condescend to teach us."

"You impudent woman!" Sheeka's roar filled the air and Sue tensed – but Silver raised her head haughtily and growled, "Remember the eggs, Father."

People watched with bated breath while the two dragons glared at each other. The situation could turn nasty, and might have done so had not a surprising voice near their feet, exclaim loudly, "If only you two would agree and act like Queen Deena said you would – I could get out of this place and go back to my nest."

The two dragons lowered their heads simultaneously to where a black serpent swayed back and forth with no thought of danger. His movement made it difficult for them to keep him in focus. Sue bit her lip. What on earth was the snake thinking of? If it were not careful, it would be barbecued.

"What is this thing?" Sheeka thundered, incensed. "This thing, who dares to blaspheme a queen. What does a worm like this know of such things?"

So saying, he lifted one huge taloned foot with the intention of bringing it down on the unprepared serpent. Zeno flung himself forward, and scooped it out of the way. Sheeka's foot hit the ground with such terrific force, the earth around him shuddered. Zeno's red embarrassed face turned a sickly colour when he realised how close he had come to being crushed. He turned to Sue with the snake writhing between his fingers and held it out to her.

"I'm sorry, Sonja," he gulped, "it got out of my pocket somehow."

Sue retrieved it with a smile. "Not to worry. At least you saved its life."

"I didn't want to be saved," hissed the snake, thrashing around angrily, "if Sheeka had killed me, I could have become a martyr. Now I've got to return and tell the Queen of the Mountains that I'm a failure. Do you know what that feels like to an old snake like me? I can't be trusted to do anything."

"Don't be stupid. You haven't failed," said Sue, but she was talking to thin air because the snake was trying to hide round her shoulders. Sue caught hold of it firmly and dragged it to the front. It eyed her balefully and said gloomily, "I was supposed to turn the tide between you and the dragons, but the way things are going – it's not going to happen."

Sue raised her eyes to her father, "Would there be any objection to my keeping this snake in the Palace? It's not all his fault. I'm as much to blame. I failed to carry out Deena's wishes. We can commiserate together. We are not very good ambassadors."

"Enough, Sonja," Sheeka boomed, his head snaking up to her, and Tam refrained from butting in, "you spoke words of wisdom, but it's not good to tell people like you because you get very big heads. I think it is a great idea for us all to work together – we should have done so long ago." Smoke came from his nostrils as he warmed to his theme. "We shall keep your land clear of unwanted people and in return, you can allow us to eat your cattle."

He paused because an angry murmur reached his ears and Tam's eyes were flashing. "Well, maybe not," he added, "but the dragon children and your children will grow up with each other and there shall be no fear." He turned to the King with a great flourish of his head and said, "Tomorrow we shall come and hold a council here," and with an almighty roar, he flexed his wings and took off. Silver nodded to Sue – and if dragons could smile, Silver did just that as she took off after her father.

Sue knew euphoria as she caught her father's eye and those of all her friends as they gathered round. Raithe was speechless, and full of pride that his sister could show such courage in front of the magical beasts that they all knew existed but did not dare to have anything to do with. Barry, however, had no such qualms. He pushed himself forward, and, disregarding all etiquette, went up to the King and said in his forthright voice,

"Do you think, sir, if you allow me to stay here, that I could work with the dragons? It would be such a fantastic life. Flying all over the land and being in command. I know it's my vocation. I knew directly I saw my first dragon." His young face was full of animation. It was doubtful that anyone was going to dampen his enthusiasm. Tam's lips twitched, recognising true desire when he saw it. He put his hand on Barry's shoulders and the boy instinctively stood tall.

"Someone told me you were keen to be a tracker – and what you have suggested has great possibilities, like tracking from high up," said Tam.

Barry could feel himself swelling up with pride. "Do you mean that, sir?"

"Yes," said Tam, "someone from the royal household must take up a position like that, and I do not think Raithe is all that enthusiastic to do it."

At his words, Sue felt a touch of alarm. She found it hard to keep a smile on her face. Was her father going to forbid her to fly?

Tam looked round at them all, his tanned face creased in smiles when he added, “I’ve just had a great idea. Sue, can you recall Silver without giving Sheeka a fit?”

Sue nodded, but her eyes were not shining, and she willed the white dragon to return. Silver was back amongst them in an instant – gracefully spiralling down and landing near her human friend. This time, quite a crowd of spectators grouped around them. She was not as big as her father. Although Sue walked up to her, it was Tam who spoke to the dragon. “I am the one who called you, Silver,” he said in a beguiling voice. “I wonder if I dare to ask a favour?”

Silver inclined her head, listening.

“Tonight I wish to give a special party for several of my friends,” said Tam, “but I want it to be held in the royal retreat. This means two days’ travelling by horse. May I prevail on you and some of your friends, to convey us into the forest? Some of us,” he said looking directly at Barry, “want to enjoy the experience of travelling on your back through the air.”

Silver’s tail twitched and her huge eyes switched from Sue onto Barry. “I shall make a point of carrying him myself – with Sonja. We shall be here at sunset. Please be ready,” she said, and once again she took off into the air.

CHAPTER 22
TAM'S STORY

The campfire was already burning fiercely when Silver shattered the tranquillity of the evening, by causing a miniature whirlwind. She landed a short distance from the Redwoods, alarming the tree people as she deposited her two passengers on the ground. They had been forewarned of the dragon's coming by the King, but were still unprepared for their majestic size and beauty. They didn't run, but stared in wonder from a distance. Although night was falling rapidly, enough light remained for the tree people to recognise the new arrivals. Then they stepped forward. Sonja and Barry were welcomed with open arms, although the people still eyed the dragon with trepidation. They made sure they kept a good distance from Silver.

With a roar Silver took off, threading her way back through the trees to the freedom of the sky. Barry watched her go, his eyes still not focusing properly after his magical journey through the air. He waited expectantly for the other dragons to arrive. Sheeka was not been involved in this venture, his body being too enormous to land in the space between the Redwoods.

While Sue explained to the tree dwellers that her mother and father were on their way to celebrate a very special occasion, bringing several friends, steps were taken immediately to sort out the Queen's retreat, that beautiful airy room high up in the branches of the

Redwood. White-clad servants swarmed up the massive sequoia, to make it ready for the celebration, while below on the ground, the other dwellers watched four more dragons swoop in, one after the other. They were an awesome sight – a mixture of red, green, gold and blue.

The people's fear of the beasts was obvious to Tam. With the Queen beside him, he quickly allayed their fears by telling them of the new constitution being formed between the magical beasts and themselves. It might take some time, but the people of Therossa trusted their King.

Sue was ecstatically happy. With the smell of wood-smoke tickling her nostrils, and Thane standing beside her, she felt free from the confines of the palace. This place filled her with nostalgia and she felt so much more relaxed than she had done the first time she was here.

After pleasantries with the people had been exchanged, they climbed to Ruth's retreat and took up positions on the scattered cushions. The servants departed leaving dishes of food and many lamps, which dispelled the gathering gloom and cast a rosy glow over everything. A myriad of translucent insects brushed against the gossamer drapes, trying to get into the light.

Tam looked around at his gathered friends – from where he was sitting on the couch, he could see every one of them. Ruth held his hand tightly. Only the Shaman had his own special seat, and if one thought deeply about it, no one remembered how he got there. He certainly did not fly on a dragon.

Annalee and Tansy sat with Barry and Zeno. Even now, Amos could not keep the disapproval from his face when his gaze fell on Zeno, who was there because Sue insisted. It was not much better when he looked at Barry

– but he had no say about that. Vance sat by Amos's side, near the entrance, almost as though they were on guard. Raithe, Thane and Sue formed their own little group. It was almost the same gathering of people who had been present the last time when Ruth told her story. This time, Annalee and Tansy were allowed to stay, by Tam's request. He gave a cough and immediately all eyes were fixed on him expectantly.

"I think it is time I explained to you all what has been going on," he said. "You are here because all of you have been touched in one way or another. You have been very circumspect by not asking questions and respecting my position as King. It is only fair that now I put you in the picture with regard to recent events. My story starts a long way back when I was a child, but bear with me because it is all very relevant. It was the time when everything in this land changed." Tam paused and looked around. He had no need to ask for silence – he had it.

"At the beginning there were four of us. We called ourselves Knights of Therossa and were full of great ideas as children often are. We were going to save the world and swore an oath always to help each other because we thought that sounded really important. Our elders did not take us seriously. We were only fourteen years old. They smiled benignly and said we would soon grow out of it. Well they were wrong.

"Oran came from a good military family but showed no inclination to follow its tradition. Even at that young age he had an eye for luxury and beautiful things. He wanted to own everything and we did not see the danger in that. Tyler's father was a devout priest who despaired of his son when he discovered he was only interested in following the stars and what position the moon held in the universe, instead of saving souls. Vance was the only sane one because he was studious. He was never carried away. His father was a great scholar and ambassador to the old King – my grandfather – but Vance, like the rest of us, had this insatiable desire to find out about magic."

Tam laughed softly as he reminisced. "We saw ourselves growing into great men and saving the world with great illustrious feats of wizardry.

"Everything changed the day we met an enigmatic old man who knew where dragons were still living, and he could tell us all about their secrets and magical habits. With those words he ensnared us. Dragons were something out of legends. From that moment on we were his slaves. We clamoured for more information, but he was canny. First we had to prove ourselves and pass a test, which he would set. Could we get away and follow him? Well that was easy. We told everyone we were going camping for about a week so that we could followed this mysterious man into the mountains.

"After many days of hardship and not seeing anything that resembled a dragon, we were feeling disinclined to continue. Then he beckoned us forward, and keeping well hidden, we saw a female dragon sitting on her two eggs. We were enthralled now. We couldn't take it all in. We were the first of our community to see a real live dragon close up.

"Then he told us what the test was. We were to steal the two eggs and bring them to him. It needed two people for each egg because they were so heavy. It sounded easy the way he said it, but we had heard dragons were ferocious creatures and would kill us as soon as look at us. We were only boys – while he was a grown man with a man's strength. Was this really a test? Or did he see us as gullible children able to do his dirty work? People he could dispose of easily when he no longer had use for us. Who would miss four boys when questions were asked?

"In spite of our bravado, we were frightened, but this man's eyes hypnotised us to do his will. When the female dragon left her eggs and went to hunt, we all crept down to the nest with the intention of stealing the precious eggs. Not one of us knew the male dragon was watching. We could not see him. He had the power to make himself invisible. The eggs were large and close up the shells had a lustrous sheen to them. I put my hand out and touched one. It was so warm and full of life. A life that would die directly it left the nest. I knew then I could not do it.

"Oran was furious. The avaricious look in his eyes shook me as he stared at the eggs. I was accused of jeopardising our chances to learn about magic. He taunted me for being a coward and said I should leave the Knights of Therossa at once because there was no place in the group for me. For some reason I was not offended by his words and turned away in disgust, I had no intention of defiling the dragon's nest, and after the briefest hesitation, Vance followed me. Tyler would not be drawn into the argument – so Oran was on his own.

"Knowing that by himself he could never move the eggs, he swallowed his ire and aimed a vicious kick at the nearest one before he retreated. The egg started to roll down the incline and there was nothing to stop it from crashing over the edge of the cliff. I dashed forward and flung myself down on the ground in its path, hopefully to stop it. It halted, but only momentarily, because it quivered, and would have rolled over me had not the male dragon descended with a mighty roar and clutched the egg in his talons. My friends ran for their lives, as did the strange man, leaving me at the dragon's mercy.

"Petrified, I picked myself up as the dragon placed the egg carefully back in the nest. Breathing fire and belching smoke, he looked awesome to my terrified eyes. The sunlight reflected off his green scales, blinding me. My way of escape was cut off. Only a fool would try and pass that massive body, whose legs were bigger than I was. He swung his large head round and looked at my puny form with fire smouldering deep down in his eyes. Trembling, I waited to be shrivelled up.

"You're a thief," he declared. His words roared like thunder through my head. Sheer amazement kept me standing there. I had no idea Dragons could speak and his next words only confirmed what I already expected. "I am going to kill you," he said. I stood stiffly before him willing myself not to let him see how afraid I was. He would never believe that I had tried to save his egg, because my intention at the beginning had been to steal it.

"That was my biggest mistake – not trying to defend myself. Dragons could read minds. Instead of blasting me off this world, he opened his mouth to show me his fearsome teeth, and picked me up with them. He was going to eat me. As the hot breath from his mouth fanned my body, my screams must have been heard for miles around before I passed out – no wonder word got back that I was dead.

"For six years I remained a captive of Sheeka – the king of dragons. They were six years of humility and being forced to perform menial tasks. Looking after and protecting eggs, especially the two we had tried to steal. I saw Silver hatch out and formed a special attachment to her. Her egg was the one I tried to save.

"Looking after and guarding very young dragons was a pain. They were worse than humans, being very free and easy with their fire. They took great delight in scorching me, especially if I yelped in agony. I got no sympathy from Sheeka. He thought this was hugely funny. In return for all this the dragons fed me and gave me the freedom of their lands. As I grew older, they drew me into the mysterious nucleus of dragon magic. They taught me how to transport myself through time, to become invisible and perform seemingly impossible tasks. With all this knowledge in my head, I could have escaped, but it never occurred to me to do so. I had become so enthralled I stayed to learn more.

"Maybe the dragons thought I had been there long enough, because one day Sheeka dropped his bombshell and told me that all those years ago, he knew I had tried to save his eggs and not steal them. Something exploded in my head. I was livid that six years of my life had been forcibly wasted. But that was a lie. The knowledge I had gained living with them was invaluable. I had achieved what we boys had set out to do. Now it was my turn to make Sheeka pay. Masking my thoughts as they had taught me, I issued my own ultimatum. I demanded that he would come to my aid should I ever summon him. Sheeka was on the verge of refusing, but then he saw Silver watching him. He agreed, and that night he flew me to a place very near my home.

"Before he left, he gave me two magical rings, explaining to me they had the power of telepathy. Who knows where dragons get their treasures from? The rings came with a warning. They must remain in my family. He suggested I gave them to my wife or children when I had any. That way they would work. He felt sure the day was coming when I would be in need of their power. He stressed that when that day came, if the rings were together and touching each other, any spell could be broken. It did not mean much to me then, but I thanked him and made my way home.

"Six years is a long time to be away. I was now a young man and I arrived back home to find everything had changed. In my absence, my grandfather had died and my father was King. Because I was thought to be dead, there was no heir. The elders insisted that Oran, a distant cousin, step into my shoes. I returned home and found them in the process of grooming him as the next heir apparent. My unexpected reappearance caused joy to my father and fury to Oran. He had no love for me since the egg episode. Now he hated me. The life of luxury which had been dangled before him, was whisked away.

"The society of Knights of Therossa was disbanded because we had all taken different pathways in life. In the six years I was missing, Tyler dedicated his life to being a spiritual healer locked away in an abbey. I never saw him until my coronation some years later. The meditation and fasting he was forced to endure had turned him into an old man, I hardly recognised him as my former playmate.

"I never saw Oran again. Rumour had it that he disappeared with the old magician into the mountains, and there the two of them were ruling the Drazuzi." A gasp from Sue made Tam pause and stare at her enquiringly.

"Was that the priest who kept me prisoner?" she asked in surprise.

"I should say so," Tam replied. "He's another man who became old before his time. The old magician would have been dead. Greed does funny things to a person. Only Vance remained by my side as a true and steadfast friend – but then he was married. This rather threw me into the company of Amos, my father's overseer, and also an older brother of Tyler. He made a thorough job of preparing me for kingship. I travelled the land with him, meeting trackers, hunters, soldiers and training wolves. I learnt each and every one of these crafts. It secretly amused me that he never included dragons."

"Amos developed a coughing fit and they waited while Vance thumped his back, then Tam continued. "They were carefree days. It was not all work. Inheriting the throne was a long way off. Two incidents stand clearly out in my mind. The first was when Amos got himself bitten by a deadly black snake. He would surely have died had not Deena been standing nearby with the correct antidote. She was not keen to part with it, so I pulled rank on her, compelling Deena to save his life. But she turned on me and in her hand held another snake, and insisted that I be initiated into the snake cult – otherwise the country would be without a Prince. Amos was left to recover in the care of her women, while I was dragged off to undergo the appropriate ceremony. After that, Deena became a good friend and I was a constant visitor to her caves when I had the need to get away from it all. No one ever went there because of the snakes.

"The second incident was when I travelled to the other world with Amos as my guide. I had no idea such a place existed. There was no real reason for being there other than that of curiosity. It was here I met and fell in love with my wife Ruth. Her sisters acted as a lookout to prevent me from being seen. I agonised for months as to how I could bring her back to Therossa because she loved her own home too much ever to leave it. Then Fate played its own hand. Her father disowned her and cast her off with her baby son. Amos and a nursemaid helped to bring her to Therossa. It was an unhappy occasion for Ruth because she was compelled to leave behind her baby daughter. I was the father of twins, and Amos and the nursemaid were the only two to know.

"My father lived long enough for me to return home and introduce Ruth and baby Raithe, to him. Then he died and I became the King. Vance's wife met with a fatal accident, and this marred my coronation. My friend was left with two children. Five-year-old Thane, a sturdy child, and baby Annalee whom Ruth took upon herself to bring up with Raithe until she was old enough to go back to her father.

"The years passed by and unrest flared up. Ruth began to worry because she was told the worlds were on the verge of breaking apart. She wanted to see her daughter before it was too late so Thane was sent to find her. At the same time I was called away on another mission, otherwise I would have gone. Ruth suspected treachery, and she was correct, but as King I could not ignore it.

"I walked into a well-laid ambush constructed by Oran. He had been plotting revenge ever since I returned home from the dragons. He never expected me to take the throne. He thought it belonged to him. He was now a man to be wary of. He had the power of a mighty magician and money to buy what he wanted. He bought an army of renegades, but didn't realise money did not always bring loyalty. My biggest sadness of this ambush was the loss of all my men, except for Vance. He was never going to be released and a spell was put on me. I was clothed in a black cloak. I could not remove it. People could not recognise me. It clouded my memory and most of my magic. I had little hope of it ever being broken.

"But dragon magic is hard to kill. I found I could transport myself and leave the cave. This way I discovered the nursemaid had told Oran that I had a daughter in the other world. He immediately made plans to have her removed. He wanted no contenders to the throne left alive. Raithe, whom he thought was on his side, let him down when he began to champion Sue. He had to be imprisoned. Once Oran had Sue in his clutches, he was set to march on the throne. Sue fell into his hands easily when the Drazuzi captured her. She would never escape from there. He ruled the place.

"Oran then turned his attention to me, so drunk with power he had become blasé. He saw no point in killing me – he put a spell on me that was worse than death. A spell no one could ever take away. For the rest of my life I should always be clothed in a black cloak and no one would ever recognise me as being the King. I was unable to speak the words that would tell of my true identity. I had no intention of languishing in captivity forever so I said goodbye to Vance and promised to come back for him one day; then I transported myself away.

"There were things to do if I ever wanted to get this spell broken. I then remembered Sheeka's words. Oran received a shock when he found I had gone, and an even greater one when he heard Sue had escaped from the Drazuzi. Several people met me in my black cloak. Deena recognised me, Barry thought I was some saviour and Thane knew who I was by what Sue told him. To White Hawk I was still the King; Oran could not camouflage my scent. You cannot fool a wolf."

Tam cleared his throat and asked for a drink. He looked apologetically at the others and said, "I'll answer questions in a minute."

* * *

No one wanted to question Tam, except for Barry. Amos noticed this and thought how typical it was of him. But Barry had caught a glimpse of Amos's dour expression and changed his mind. Tansy was not so easily cowed by the old overseer. She remembered the Drazuzi well from her time with them, and asked what was going to happen about the way Oran treated them. Her question made Sue's ears prick up. She had thought a lot of those skeletal people who worked as slaves. Tam obviously had given a lot of thought to his answer, because he frowned.

"Oran is an unknown threat while he lives underground. If he comes out into the open, we are ready for him. I think you worry unduly about the Drazuzi. Have you ever heard the expression of the worm turning? They are well able to look after themselves. I like to think that even Oran doesn't know the extent of their magic. It's the same with the Gypsies. They do not have any magic, but with dragons abroad in our skies, they will have to find a different lifestyle. That applies to some of you sitting before me."

Sue felt her father's eye on her and her blood ran cold. Surely he wasn't going to ban her association with Silver? That would be the end of the world for her. She couldn't stay here if they made a captive spirit of her. Much as she loved her mother, she would leave and find her own way back to Tamworth Forest where she had freedom. Thane was standing beside her and squeezed her hand. Annalee grinned reassuringly, but Sue was not comforted. She knew she couldn't stay in the palace day after day.

A white-clad servant moved effortlessly amongst them and stopped before the King and Queen, bowing deeply. Whatever was said, only they heard. Tam immediately raised his hand to get their attention. "The village chief has invited us all down to join in with the people's celebration around the campfire. There will be dancing and plenty of food, but the celebration may go on for many hours. You will have to spend the night here."

No one raised any objections to that. They all hustled to get out. The Shaman just vanished. But Sue was one of those who were at the end and one of the last to go. Tam asked her to stay behind and she couldn't keep the dismay from her face. He was going to lay down a few rules. Barry hovered around with her, but the King waved him away.

"Not you," he said firmly. "Your future is secure, son. If you want to ride dragons, you have my blessing. Raithe's future is already laid down for him, but Sue." He paused and she swallowed nervously. "She cannot be allowed to drift around."

Her stomach turned over. She didn't want to hear this. She saw Barry pause and the sympathy on his face. Then

Thane gently pushed him out and he put his arm round Sue, giving her a squeeze, warning her to be silent.

"Sue will not be drifting around." He eyed both elders impassively and she sincerely hoped they were not going to teach her the rules of etiquette, but Thane's fingers digging hard into her arm made her remain silent. "With your permission, sir, I should like to take her to the home I've made near the forest. Here, I shall train her thoroughly in the arts of self-defence. Then, once she's learnt to track, by her own request she would like to ride Silver and join Barry in the skies."

Ruth objected at once, her face alarmed. "That is not the life for a Princess, especially Sue," she began, but Tam cut her short, retorting, "It's exactly the life for a Princess. We are going to build up a fleet of dragon defenders, my dear. "We need some royal blood amongst them. Mind you," he stroked his chin and went on thoughtfully, studying Thane, "we also need someone reliable to be in charge." As Thane met his eyes, his smile broadened, and he clasped the King's hand in agreement. "I knew you would see it my way."

"What are you going to do about White Hawk?" Tam asked.

"If he won't learn to sit on a dragon, he'll have to follow by land," retorted Thane, "but White Hawk will know which way is best for him."

Sue's eyes were shining with excitement, even though they were wet with tears. Her face radiant, she hugged first her mother and Tam, then turned and hugged Thane. "Thank you all," she said. "You knew I could never sit in the Palace all day. I will make one promise though. I shall come home regularly – and on one of those occasions, Mother, I shall teach you to sit on a dragon."

Ruth waved her away, but she was mollified by Sue's words. "Not at the beginning you won't," she said, "I can't think what has got into the female population. Already Annalee and Tansy wish to join the dragon squad."

Before Sue could comment any further, Tam waved her and Thane away. "We shall join you later," he answered with a smile. "You two have got a lot to celebrate; but just one thing more, Sue."

Sue looked at him expectantly.

"Welcome home, daughter," he said happily. "It's good to have a complete family at last."

THE END

If you enjoyed
Book 2:
THEROSSA
Have you already read the first in the
MAGICAL WORLD OF THEROSSA series

Book 1:
The SECRET OF TAMSWORTH FOREST
In which Sue meets Thane, is introduced to the magical world of Therossa and meets the family she never knew she had lost.

Also look out for
Book 3:
THE CRYSTAL HORSE
Priscilla is united with Sue and Barry – but not in the way she expected.

To find out more about these books and their publication dates vist the Brighton NightWriters' website at:
www.nightwriters.org.uk

Made in the USA
Columbia, SC
14 October 2017